D0585474

The Mexican Tree Duck

Also by James Crumley in Picador

THE JAMES CRUMLEY COLLECTION

The Wrong Case
The Last Good Kiss
Dancing Bear

One to Count Cadence

The Mexican Tree Duck

JAMES CRUMLEY

PICADOR

First published 1993 as a Mysterious Press book by Warner Books, Inc., New York

First published in Great Britain 1994 by Picador
a division of Pan Macmillan Publishers Limited
Cavaye Place London SW10 9PG
and Basingstoke

Associated companies throughout the world

ISBN 0 330 32451 9

1 3 5 7 9 8 6 4 2

A CIP catalogue record for this book is available from
the British Library

Printed by Mackays of Chatham PLC, Kent

for
Martha Elizabeth

ACKNOWLEDGMENTS

I want to thank my agent of many years, Owen Laster, for sticking by me, and Otto Penzler for taking a chance on me. And thanks to the guys with the stories and the attitude: Kent Anderson, Mike Koepf, Andy Fishback, Mike "Megamind" Norton, Robert Applegate, and Louis Davis.

"Nobody called, nobody came in, nothing happened, nobody cared if I died or went to El Paso."

Philip Marlowe
The High Window
by
Raymond Chandler

PART ONE

When the 3:12 through freight to Spokane hit the East Meriwether crossing, the engineer touched his horn and released a long, mournful wail into the wet, snowy air of our second early fall storm in western Montana. It sounded a hell of a lot like the first note of a Hank Snow ballad. I slipped the dolly from under the jukebox and plugged it into the extension cord. When I dropped a quarter into the slot, the large machine burped, the bubbling neon tubes glowed softly in the night, and the machine seemed to settle more solidly onto the railroad tracks.

"You sure you know what you're doing, Sughrue?" Lawyer Rainbolt asked, squatting beside the roadbed.

"Hey, man, I don't know who this supposed rock-and-roll guy is and I don't even much care if he sings like a girl," I maintained, "but I've shaken hands with Hank Snow, by god . . ." I waved the damaged Herradura tequila bottle across the white space of the parking lot toward the back of the Hell Roaring Liquor Store and Lounge. ". . . right over there, and they ain't got no right to take him off the jukebox."

Solly took the tequila from me, had a hit, then handed it back, and dumped a small but dangerous pile of crystal meth into the palm of his scarred hand. He glanced up, smiling, huge snowflakes melting in his shaggy blond hair. "Which one is *he*?" Solly asked. "All those country and western singers sound like girls to me."

"Asshole."

Solly was very amused, grinning like the cat that fucked the canary before he ate it. Fucking amused lawyers.

"Let's do it before it blows away," he suggested.

I make it a policy never to argue with drug lawyers: they have decent arguments and the best drugs.

So we knelt together as the engine came around the long curve at the base of the Devil's Hump, its brilliant headlamp whipping through the snow-cursed night, knelt and snorted the speed off the circular cicatrix in Solly's palm. I stood up, shakily, stepped onto the tracks, and punched P-17. Solly limped across the parking lot toward the shadowed rear of the bar as the engineer hit his heavy note one more time.

The first time I saw Solomon Rainbolt, he was dead. Or we thought he was. The base camp CP bunker had taken at least three direct RPG hits, and after forty-eight hours under the monsoon rain, we couldn't tell the bodies from the sandbags. When one of the muddy lumps opened a pair of red-rimmed eyes and grinned, white-toothy and wild, one of my FNGs shit his pants and touched off an M-16 clip into the clotted Vietnamese sky before Willie Williams could grab him. Then the lump became a head, raised itself, grinning.

"Hey, Sarge," it said in a deep southern accent, "where the fuck you guys been?"

"Sorry, sir," I said, "but the rain held us up . . ." I had the lead squad of a company patrol at the end of a four-day hump into the dark heart of the Central Highlands. Our choppers had been grounded by the monsoon, and the regiment had pushed us hard to get to the overrun ARVN position, not to garner survivors but to dig the code safe out of the CP. Solly was the bonus upon which no one had counted. ". . . and nobody knew you were waiting."

Solly shook his head as if coming back from death hadn't been all that pleasant, then he struggled out of the sucking mud, shifting aside the dead Rhade mercenary who lay across his legs, pulling his lanky frame upright. Then he held up his left hand and clenched his fist. Even in the rain, I could hear the bones grind against each other. A ribbony snake of blood drifted out of his tight, muddy fingers and down his thick wrist.

"Captain Solomon Rainbolt," he said as he looked at us, "bound for the free world." Then he stared at the remains of his advisory command. Only he had survived. By playing dead, perfectly. Suddenly, Solly laughed, thunderous in the hammering rain, squeezed his fist again, and shouted, "Pin my Purple fucking Heart to my ass, boys, and send me home!"

They pinned it to his chest, though. And some other chicken-shit baubles, too. But he left most of his lower left leg there floating in a rice paddy and he didn't find his way back to the free world for a long time. He did one more tour for the green weenie, then another long one as one of those spooky hard-assed dudes dressed in tiger-striped tailored fatigues, Swedish assault rifles, and eyes from hell.

But finally, he came home. Not to Athens, Georgia, though, where his mother taught chemistry and his father law, but to California and law school at Boalt in Berkeley, where he kicked ass and took names, just as he had in the war, a joy he continued as a federal prosecutor and then in private practice in San Francisco once he had tacked his sheepskin like another military bauble to his wall.

By then, I was back on the mean streets of home my own damn self, busy with my own troubles, so our paths didn't cross for a long time. At one point I had tracked a runaway wife from Wichita to San Francisco, where I found her among the remains of the flower children. I stayed for the end of the era of peace and love, stayed until Tricky Dick Nixon gave up his political ghost and left the sixties without purpose.

Solly's name appeared in the paper, so I went to court to watch him work one afternoon. He was defending a rather famous biker against a murder-one charge. Solly was something to see—a half-Jewish, half-peckerwood, half-crippled war hero. One of the courthouse buffs whispered to me that Solly could make a jury eat his shorts and convince them it was fettuccine Alfredo. He never lost a murder case that went to trial, and his plea bargains were taught in law schools all over the country.

I stopped by the defense table to say hello after the jury acquitted his client, and he seemed glad to see me. It looked as if it might be easy to renew the friendship we had begun during the four-day two-ambush hump out of the bush. So we exchanged numbers, promised to call. But I went to Vegas on a skip-trace and when I got back, Solly had dropped suddenly out of the public view. There were rumors of an acrimonious divorce, a dead child, a missing ex-wife.

Solly eventually reappeared in Denver, where he specialized in defending heavy drug dealers, guys who moved serious weight. He seemed to have a real hard-on for the DEA, and he kicked the government's ass with disturbing regularity. When he had taken whatever revenge he intended—I don't know because we never talked about it—he cooled his jets and moved his practice to Meriwether, Montana, a town I had called home for a while now, and we picked up that friendship we had left in the bush. Friends, true, maybe even running buddies, so I made it a practice never to work either for him or against him. He seemed to agree. However brief our time in the bush, we both clung to the notion that it was better to have a buddy to watch your back when the hump got tough.

And things got tough for me that year. The PI business died with a blizzard the third week of September that dumped sixteen inches of cold wet snow on Meriwether. People seemed to be able to divorce quite nicely without my help during the cold snap and icy drizzle that followed the blizzard. Those local merchants who might have had repossession on their minds chose to be nasty to deadbeats up close and personal.

I wouldn't have had time, anyway. The part-time bartending job at the Hell Roaring Liquor Store and Lounge that kept me fairly solvent had degenerated into a full-time chore as the customers lurched madly toward the stone-cold heart of winter. The owner of the Hell Roaring, Leonard the Sly, a man whose heart usually only sang with the music of the cash register, suddenly fell in love with Betty Boobs, our prettiest cocktail waitress. They fled to Mexico before the first snowflake hit the ground. God knows what Leonard thought. Perhaps he thought his wife, Betty Books, who kept them, might not notice their absence. No such luck. A week later, she picked up the week-end cash deposit bag and climbed on an airplane bound eventually for Fiji, muttering something about "revenge fucking in the third world." But she said quite plainly to me, "It's yours, C.W. Drink it up or burn it down—I just don't give a shit anymore."

I didn't have time to do either. The help, surly in the best of times, rankled quickly under my guidance. When Big Linda's check was short the second week in a row, she responded by drop-kicking a tray of drinks across a five o'clock throng. One poor woman protested the death of her silk blouse, and Big Linda hit her so hard half of her houseplants died. Big Linda quit on the spot, moved to Tucson the next day to follow a career as a professional mud wrestler. All the mud in Meriwether was frozen. Little Linda followed quickly, packing her three kids and two broken television sets from four marriages into her old Falcon station wagon, with a large sign that said SNOW painted on the back window. She planned to drive south until somebody asked her what *that* was, that snow thing. Then the cruelest blow of all: my best, most experienced, most dependable bartender, the Original Linda, fell back in love with her second husband when he got out of Deer Lodge Prison. They got married, joined AA, and Linda quit her job.

Bars can be nice places, comfortable, homes away from the loneliness or confusion of home, but nobody, not even the most confirmed degenerate drunk, can spend eighty or ninety hours a week in one. I went through so much help that I actually hired a woman so drunk she had forgotten that I had fired her the week before. I don't know what my excuse was. Something to do with my nose, I suspect. As far as I was concerned, the sun was something that happened in another country. I didn't care if it came out. Then it did just to prove me wrong.

The first day, the snow melted like sugar in a golden shower. On the second afternoon it was all gone, and I had hammered my few customers with free drinks until they mostly sat still and silent, stunned in the flat rays of the lowering sun that flooded the front door of the Hell Roaring, an autumn light alive and full of hope and glory. I played every Hank Snow song on the jukebox ten times. Two of my semi-mobile customers—an inde-pendant gypo-logger with a broken leg and a real estate sales-woman with a broken arm—had fallen under the spell of the gravelly romantic voice; they danced with clumsy grace around the pool table. I could have danced myself.

A thousand years ago when I first came to Meriwether, the first time I set foot in the Hell Roaring as the sixties drifted, late as usual and dying, into the seventies, I found that soft autumn light filling the magic afternoon easiness of the bar. I eased myself onto the stool next to the poor schmuck I had been chasing for six months. He looked so pitiful I nearly walked away, but drink in hand, I swiveled around and stopped in that light, that sun-filled silence.

I don't even remember his name. Just some wretch from Redwood City, California, a pale, wrinkled man, a pharmacist once, an unhappy man wedded to a woman hard with unhappy fat and a gut bucket for a mouth. The pharmacist read the wrong books, maybe, or watched the wrong television shows, whatever, he became convinced that the sexual revolution had taken place without him. So he faked a robbery, fled with the money and the drugs and a hippie chick with flowers in her hair, fled toward the peace and freedom of the Mountain West, Montana, the word like a benison on his trembling lips.

By the time I caught up with him, though, he had had enough of his dream. He should have been glad to go home. I bought him a drink and explained the hard way and the easy way back to California. He wept like a child, a man leaking everywhere, everything. He had a junkie's sniffles, oozing tracks inside his elbows, behind his knees, and between his toes. A revolutionary strain of gonorrhea had started a commune in his urinary tract and none of the miracles of modern pharmacy could dislodge it.

But it hadn't all leaked out. When I tried to console him with the information that his wife still loved him, wouldn't press charges, and wanted him back in the family home, he shook his head, murmured something about his additional curse of a weak bladder, then raised a flaky eyebrow and nodded toward the john.

Maybe if I hadn't turned my stool back to face that blessed light, I might have heard the muffled thumps from the bathroom. Five minutes later when I decided that not even the most painful piss should take that long, I went to check. He really wanted to die. I found him on his knees in front of the urinal, hanging from his belt, leaning into the leather strap. This time everything had finally leaked out.

Almost twenty years later, I poured myself a healthy tot of Herradura tequila as Hank Snow, the Singing Ranger, chorded into "It Don't Hurt Anymore." I raised my glass to the autumnal light. "It don't hurt any less, either," I said to nobody in particular. Then I raised my glass again to the Leaking Man.

Actually, it was his fault I was here. His wife had hounded me with lawsuits until I had to give up California. Naturally, I came here. The tequila tasted as smooth as the smoky sunlight.

When I put my glass back on the bar and surveyed my domain, I noticed that Kathleen and Bill had managed to sprawl on the pool table. They writhed as if they could escape their casts. Kathleen had a history on the pool table.

"Goddammit," I said, feeling some obligation to civilized behavior, "can't you two wait until dark?"

"Fuck you, C.W.," Kathleen said smugly as she touched her nose. Then she grabbed Bill by his cast and towed him toward the men's room. I didn't care anymore. I thought about following them into the can, but just the thought of cocaine made my knees weak and my kidneys ache. I had another tequila and forgot about them.

Forgot about them until they sidled out of the john toward the back door without bothering to dump their drinks into go-cups. When I checked the can, I found the toilet reduced to a heap of porcelain shards standing in frothy water. I shut off the valve, dashed outside with blood in my eyes, ready to do battle over a busted toilet. My patience seemed to be growing thinner with each passing day. Maybe the straight life didn't exactly agree with me.

The crippled lovers were giggling on the front seat of Kathleen's Buick. When she saw my face, Kathleen sobered enough to try a drunken grin, then gave up when it wasn't returned.

"Goddammit, C.W., I'm outa cash," she whined.

"I'll take a check," I said.

"You'll take shit," Bill growled as he leaned over Kathleen, "you rotten bastard." Bill didn't like me, sometimes, and sometimes I returned the favor. "Son of a bitch . . ."

"Smile when you say that, motherfucker," I said, then reached over and popped him on the nose with the heel of my hand. It opened up like the Red Sea.

"Jesus Christ," Kathleen said as Bill scrambled around trying to staunch the flood and get out at the same time.

"Moses," I said. "Gimme your fucking keys."

Kathleen reached into her purse, then smiled. For an instant I thought she was going to bring out a piece. But her hand came out clutching a white bindle of cocaine. "Take this instead," she said. "It's almost an eighth."

Then she started the Buick, dropped it into reverse, placating Bill with one hand and steering with the other. "Next time just chop up the fucking toilet!" I shouted as the star-cast lovers sped away, plaster of paris scraps drifting out of the Buick's windows while I considered the bindle in my hand.

A better man, which I plan to become someday, would have thrown the blow away. Or at least sold it to pay for the broken plumbing. Or even saved it for a rainy day. I sensed clouds on the near horizon. So I just did a little.

Back in the bar, I found the mindless goons from Mountain States Vending servicing the jukebox and the gambling machines. One had been a ranked light-heavy once, the other a defensive tackle in the CFL. "New format," the ex-pug explained, changing records. "Ain't some of these Hank Snow records yours, C.W.?" the former tackle asked, then chuckled as he tossed them into his toolbox. I started to protest, but I would have had to kill them to stop them. I thought about it.

"New format," I echoed, a coward in the face of necessity as they went about their business.

The sunshine didn't even last until dark; it fell under the weight of another snowstorm. The new format and the cocaine lasted exactly ten hours. After Solly and I had a few post-closing drinks, I gave him some of the cocaine as a retainer. When that ran out, he gave me some of his crystal—somebody else's retainer—and I got the dolly and the extension cords out of the basement.

When the cowcatcher on the engine pulling the 3:12 fast freight to Spokane hit the jukebox, the high thin voice sang one last empty screaming wail that died quickly beneath the thundering steel wheels. The collision filled the snowy night with an explosive rainbow shower of plastic and pot-metal, worthless quarters and inflated dollar bills that covered the pale parking lot like a hard post-apocalyptic rain falling.

"Absolutely fucking perfect," I said to Solly. "Hank Snow would be ecstatic."

"What the hell, man, I suspect Michael Jackson might have liked it, too."

"I don't care," I said.

"I can tell you're happy, Sughrue," Solly said, "and I'm happy, too."

"Yeah?"

"You're happy playing the music critic from hell, Sonny, but I'm glad I don't have to play your lawyer."

"What are you gonna do, counselor? Sneeze my retainer all over the parking lot?"

Solly grabbed his nose as if he might consider just that, but he laughed as we climbed into my pickup, headed for the happy confusion of darkness and laughter.

We spent several days arranging various alibis, all of which involved acting as if nothing had happened. We spent some time in Butte, a perfect Montana place to hide—nobody would ever look for you in Butte—then even more time at Chico Hot Springs, where Solly bathed his old wounds while I sought liver damage in the bar. Eventually, though, Thanksgiving was upon us, and we, or Solly to be more exact, decided that we, meaning me, had to return to Meriwether to face, as it were, the music.

They were playing our song, and this was my dance: civil suits had surrounded me like a tribe of Hollywood Indians. They had all filed: Leonard the Sly's slick business lawyer, Betty Books from Hong Kong, the railroad, and Mountain States Vending wanted damages for their property. Even the engineer driving the train asked for psychic damages, claiming the collision with the jukebox had caused him to hear strange voices and to see lights in the darkness.

Criminal charges were forthcoming, the Meriwether County attorney said, just as soon as he stopped laughing.

That was too much for Solly. He deigned to accept all my cases; on his advice, I became as liquid as dirty dishwater. And about as useful. All my portable goods except my weapons were converted to cash, which somehow all landed in Solly's pocket. I gave up the apartment where I had lived forever and moved into the basement of Solly's law firm offices, a building that had served until recently as a mortuary. It wasn't too bad. I had an embalming table covered with a foam pad for a bed, a tiny hot plate on a baby refrigerator on a coffin stand, and a chance to spend the next ten or fifteen years listening to Solly's chuckles as I chipped away at my legal fees interviewing witnesses, transcribing depositions, and sweeping up, while we waited, as he said, for some *real work*, a job worthy of my talents, whatever odd sort they might be.

Survival came to mind first. Laughter, too, an ability to laugh through whatever vicissitudes life rolled my way, and certainly a willingness to be amazed. For instance, the wonders of Montana weather never cease to amaze me. The winter broke again, and Indian summer visited the scene into deep October. Another long-predicted snowstorm finally arrived two days late and seemed more like the fulfillment of a weather forecast than a prophecy of icy doom. I even learned to sleep among the ghosts of the lately dead, knowing they rested warmly under a cold white mantle. But most amazing of all, Solly actually found me a *real job*.

I was doing something disgusting involving scrambled eggs and canned chili—I don't seem to be especially sensitive to women's domestic needs out of the bedroom nor do I cook worth a damn, which may explain why I've never married—over my hot plate that morning when Solly creaked down the concrete stairs, his step light and jolly for a crippled man, his chuckle absolutely amused.

"Sughrue, my old friend, you're going to just love this one," he said, handing me a business card, "just absolutely love it." He laughed all the way back up the stairs.

I glanced at the card. *Dahlgren's Tropical Fish and Pet Paradise*, it said. I liked it already.

* * *

Dahlgren's version of Paradise sat on the edge of a section of Meriwether that in other towns would be called "across the tracks." But since Meriwether, like most western towns, had been developed with an eye to utility rather than aesthetics, everything was just across the tracks or beyond some mystic river or over some other arbitrary line just around the corner from space and time. So we just called it Felony Flats, as a friend of mine had named it back in his days as a deputy sheriff. Cheap rents mean cheap locks, and felons don't make the best of neighbors. Often it seemed that the entire neighborhood traded material goods and/or spouses every six or eight months, whether they wanted or needed to or not.

From the look of Dahlgren's parking lot, littered with new foreign cars, though, I suspected he did most of his business in richer climes. I pulled the Japanese pickup Solly had loaned me in beside the store's van, a three-quarter-ton Ford decked out in tropical seascapes. It looked a bit odd covered with six inches of fresh snow.

When I opened the front door and stepped into the soft, bubbling light of the tropical fish section, a slight young woman with a large mouth and a small moustache darted swiftly through the sparklingly clean tanks. She stopped in front of me, her slim body still trembling, and whispered, "Yes-s-s-s," breathlessly, her pale eyes bulging with the effort. I handed her my last card, a tattered bit, and asked to see Mr. Dahlgren.

"Which one?" she murmured wetly. I lifted a shoulder as if I might break out in an Australian crawl or a butterfly. She understood, nodding. "I'll get them," she said, glancing at my card. "Mr. Soo-goo?" she ventured.

" 'Shoog' as in sugar, honey," I said, slipping my card out of her slick fingers and resisting a sudden urge to chuckle her behind the gills, "and 'rue' as in rue the goddamned day."

She smiled coldly, exposing an enormous number of very large white teeth, then turned, smoothing her shimmery blue skirt over her tiny hips, and wriggled toward the dark, watery recesses at the rear of the store.

As I waited, I watched some brightly designed fish wander

from one end of a tank to another, a miniature school mindlessly following the lead of the alpha fish. They were nice to watch, but I couldn't pronounce their name or afford their price. One of the last times my mad father came back to South Texas to visit, he showed up in front of my mother's shotgun house in a rattletrap pickup. A dark woman with sharp features and quick hands sat in front, a bundle of snot-nosed kids beside her. Occasionally her hands darted at the kids, sometimes cleaning their noses with a dirty thumb, sometimes delivering a sharp crack on the noggin. My father looked slightly embarrassed as he came around the truck, a plastic bag of goldfish in one hand, a bowl in the other.

"Better than a bunny rabbit," he explained after he hugged me, "and more likely to survive than colored chicks." He handed me the gifts. I gathered he thought it was somewhere near Easter-time, which it wasn't, and I began to understand why my mother called him "a cheap-trick, white-trash mystic."

After he left in a cloud of slow dust, heading west one more time, seeking visions again, my mother came out of the house and collected my father's gifts. The fishbowl became her favorite ashtray, the grave of millions of Viceroy butts, and she dumped the goldfish into the algae-clotted horse trough behind the salt cedar windbreak where they grew large and ugly on a diet of mosquito larvae and dragonflies, where they might still be living now for all I knew, though my mother had long been buried by the Viceroy butts.

As I peered at the sweeping motions of the tiny fish, I suspected they survived on a more expensive, less useful diet. Before I had time to consider it, the sounds of soft confusion and muttered "excuse me's" came from the back of the store. I peeked around the corner. Two very large, fat men were stuck in the office doorway with the tiny woman lodged between them. Her eyes seemed ready to pop out of her head, but she slipped one slim hand out, then slithered from between them with an audible *plop* and rushed toward a nearby tank the size of a deep-freeze. I expected her to dive in, safe at last, but at the last moment she veered into an empty aisle.

The two men lumbered toward me, their steps raising tiny

waves in the tanks, dressed in matching polyester sport tents. They were a pair of giant twins, at least six-six and three hundred pounds apiece, hugely fat but somehow willowy, too, as if their massive flesh rode on green sticks instead of bones.

"I'm Joe," one said. "Frank," the other chimed. "Dahlgren," they sang, then giggled and offered me oddly delicate hands. Although the boys looked a great deal alike—so much alike, in fact, I could never tell them apart—they had difficulty doing things together. Like shaking hands. I think I shook Joe's hand twice and Frank's not at all, but I was never sure.

"I understand you gentlemen have a problem," I said, and restrained myself from shouting *weight* at the top of my lungs, "but Lawyer Rainbolt didn't fill me in on the particulars."

"Particulars," they said in a jumble, then glanced at each other. After several moments of hesitation on both their parts, both reached into their plaid sport coats and withdrew folded sheets of paper. I took both just to be fair. They were copies of invoices, a long list of names I assumed to be various fish, tanks, and other equipment. The total price came to $5,354.76.

"Somebody's mighty serious about their fish," I said, trying to smile. The Dahlgrens didn't return it. In fact, they frowned so deeply I thought fat, greasy tears might slide down their downy cheeks. Then one of them handed me a yellow personal check covered with NSF and DO NOT REDEPOSIT stamps. "So what am I supposed to do," I asked, "repossess a bunch of fish?"

"Please," Joe said. "Without violence," Frank added.

Rue the day, I thought, *giant pacifist twins*. Then I looked at the check, as if I knew what I was doing. It had been drawn on a small state-chartered bank one county west of Meriwether. The bank had been fleeced by a California resort developer, forced into receivership, absorbed by a midwestern holding company, then closed. The account in the dead bank was in the name of one Norman Hazelbrook, a vaguely familiar name. Then the comment about *no violence* made sense.

"You guys took a check from Abnormal Norman? Are you batshit crazy?" I asked. The boys attempted to look at their feet as they blushed.

Abnormal Norman Hazelbrook was president and chief executive officer of a biker gang known as the Snowdrifters, a gang made up of misfits and rejects from gangs all over the country. If you couldn't cut it with the Angels, or were just too disgusting for the Banditos, Norman would take you into his gang. Their headquarters sat at the head of Clatterbuck Creek on the old Moondog mining claim. Norman had purchased the property after he got out of the Oregon state pen, where he was doing time for aggravated assault. The story was that Norman got in a scuffle with an Oregon state patrolman and somehow managed to bite his nose off. Then the fool added grievous insult to massive injury when he chewed it up and swallowed it in front of the horrified officer.

"Didn't his rather odd attire give you some idea that Norman might not be exactly an outstanding citizen?" I asked.

"You know Mr. Hazelbrook, I take it?"

"I hate to admit it but I know Norman," I said. Fun is where you find it, right, even if you have to follow your nose. "But I wouldn't take a check from him."

"He was very persuasive," one offered shyly. "Very," the other added, glancing over his shoulder as if Norman might be lurking behind the gerbils. "Ah, he ate our entire supply of African leaf fish," the one I decided to call Joe said. "Then he ate Li Po," Frank whispered, "swallowed the old gentleman without a gulp. I hesitate to think about his last moments, the horror of drowning in that, that monster's stomach acids."

"I can understand," I said, "even sympathize. But who's this Lee Poe guy? Edgar's little brother?" I know I shouldn't have laughed, but I thought I hid it quite nicely behind a coughing fit. The fat boys frowned anyway.

"One of our rarest and finest Siamese fighting fish," Joe said. "We took the check before his, ah, friends joined in."

"Norman never goes anywhere without his friends," I said, "not even to sushi bars." The boys frowned again. "But seriously, now, boys. Stop me if I'm wrong, okay? You want the fish back, is my guess, not the money." They nodded ponderously, jowls trembling. "I might be able to get the money—with a Sherman tank—but I can't repossess five thousand dollars' worth of tropical fish from one of the worst motorcycle gangs in America."

"Actually, we have a tank," Frank said softly.

"Right," I said, smiling at his little joke, "lots of them. But we need more than that. I take it you took this to the sheriff over there?"

"He suggested that it was our fault for doing business with people of that ilk."

"I wouldn't know where to begin with these guys," I admitted.

"You know him," Joe said, "you could at least talk to him. We would pay you five hundred dollars just to talk to him."

"Cash?"

"Of course," Frank said. "Just give us a moment, please, to get the money." With that, they heaved about, ships spinning in the night, under way for their office, their large buttocks rocking slowly like a gelatinous surf.

I strolled over to a turtle tank to wait. For the sake of old times, Norman might talk to me, and if I came out of it alive, the five hundred would make walking around Meriwether a lot more fun. Solly had deep pockets but he was reluctant to put his hands into them for my good times. I stared down at the little captive turtles, took a deep breath, thinking perhaps to sigh over my weary plight. Forget it. Never take a deep breath over a turtle tank. Live on fish heads and rice, suck on a wino's sock, make pancakes with rotten eggs, but never take a deep breath over a turtle tank. By the time I had stopped gagging, the Dahlgren boys had returned with the cash.

"I want to borrow your van this afternoon," I said as I counted the bills, "and I want you to write a letter to Solly explaining that all I have to do is talk to Norman and that you promise to cover all my medical expenses as a result of this interview. Fair?"

"Fair," they agreed as we shook hands, tiny tears of hope glimmering in their eyes.

The living quarters of the Snowdrifters had grown organically, in the same way fungus grows in a bachelor's refrigerator. They had started with a couple of converted school bus campers backed up to the old mine shacks. Then Norman got middle-class pretensions. He had a log house built into the hillside in front of the old Moondog shaft. Then bit by furry bit everything became connected, and whatever members of the gang were in residence at any one time seemed to live wherever it suited them. One big happy family. Some of them, more than you would think, had jobs. Some even had families and had built houses away from the main complex for their old ladies and children. The sixties seemed alive and well up Clatterbuck Creek, if a little gray and dull and semi-communal, but I knew that however much fun and polite these guys could play, they could also play rough given the slightest reason.

I wouldn't want to burn them on a drug deal, or try to enforce the county zoning laws, that's for sure. The county sheriff, who had been repeatedly reelected since the early sixties, occasionally made noises about cleaning up the mess up there, if only the county attorney would give him the papers, but it was just noise. I knew some DEA types and some state narco boys who were convinced that the Snowdrifters ran an amphetamine factory in the old mine shaft, but they were part of the same group of law enforcement turkeys who promised to rid the county of drugs by . . . well, by sometime . . . and who lied to the press about the value of the few drug busts they made. Besides, Norman might look funny, but he could count on his fingers and toes, and he hadn't taken anything but misdemeanor busts for fights and traffic violations since his release from Salem. And if the truth be known, I had worked for Norman a few times riding shotgun on deals and runs. I remembered him as half-good company, the times almost fun. Except perhaps for the last time, when we went off the top of Rogers Pass in a stolen green Saab with a trunkload of AK-47s. That's another story, though.

Norman also had the best illegal satellite video system in western Montana, which I had occasion to watch, but Norman's main fault seemed to be the ease with which he got bored. After the satellite dish came video games, which irritated me a little, and after the video games came the white rats. They didn't bother me— they were oddly affectionate—but Norman took to getting stoned and taking potshots at them with a Ruger Blackhawk .44 magnum, and rumor had it that he occasionally bit their heads off for effect. I didn't believe that. If I had, I might have been nervous.

When I telephoned, Norman's longtime old lady, Midget,

shouted for him. I heard him shout back, "Tell the old fart to come on out. We'll twist one, have some fun like the old days." Then I heard wild laughter, the ringing crash of gunfire, nameless squeals.

By the time I wrestled the Paradise van up to Norman's gate, I thought about being nervous, even thought about giving the money back. Some clients think private eyes have a code, something like *never quit* or *seek justice whatever the cost* or *punish the guilty whoever they might be*, but the code is probably more like *never give the money back*. So I leaned on the horn, the chain-link gate rolled back, and I drove toward the end of the canyon over the rough, snowy track. As I came around the last corner, I could see Norman sitting in the school bus that served as one of his front entrances. He had started without me. A cloud of smoke shrouded his head, he cradled an AK-47 in his arms, and his smile glowed in the snowy light.

When I trudged up to the bus door, Norman levered it open. "You got them fat boys stashed in that fish van, Sughrue?"

"They wouldn't fit," I said, stepping into the moldering funk of the bus.

Norman leaned the rifle against the far window and asked, "So what the fuck you doin' here?"

"Just trying to make a living, Norman."

"Bullshit, man," he growled, then stretched and yawned, his wild eye roving in its socket. He took a hit off the remains of the doobie, then ate it, fire and all. His grimy hand rubbed at his bearded chin. The hand came back dirtier, if that was possible, without dislodging the pieces of what looked like last week's anchovy and jalapeño pizza. "You can't hardly make enough livin' to pay for your fun." He laughed. "What was playing?"

"Some nutless cretin."

"Figures," he said, hugely amused with himself, "homophobic bastard." Norman watched too many television talk shows on his dish, which might prove that the method of the education is more important than the actual information. "Goddammit, Sughrue, not even in my wildest days, not even in my worst moments, did I ever consider somethin' like that, somethin' that—what can I say?—that fuckin' *abnormal*," he said with what seemed to be great admiration. "Wish to fuck I'd thought of it," he added, then laughed so hard he seemed about to come apart.

Aside from looking even crazier than he was, Norman seemed to be the only survivor of a genetic disaster, a man of parts, and all the parts from totally unrelated people. His lank greasy hair draped thick and black around a long pale face with light gray eyes and a wispy, almost oriental moustache. His long skinny arms ended in tiny hands; his short legs tried to carry the torso of a large man on feet so tiny a Chinese prince might love them. Then of course there was the eye, always staring with deep interest just over your shoulder into some demented fourth dimension. And the smell, a mixture of stale urine, bad teeth, marijuana, and probably acid rain and crotch rot, that followed him like bad karma.

Norman's laughter ended in a terrific fit of dope coughing. He dragged something living from the gravel pit of his throat, then hawked it onto a side window where it quickly froze among others of its kind, then thumbed toward the back of the bus where it connected through a cabin to his log house. "Let's go twist one, man."

I had an attack of fastidious hesitation, but moved quickly along when he raised his arm to throw it affectionately around my shoulders. "Goddammit, Sughrue, it's a fuckin' kick in the ass to see you again, my man, remember that fuckin' time I stuffed that fuckin' Saab through that snowbank and we flew off Rogers Pass . . ."

As he told the story that I remembered all too well, I worked my way through the debris of a particularly untidy life, managed to dodge the double sleeping bag on the bus floor where Norman's second-in-command, Beater Bob, reclined calm and supine. Bob was as large as both the Dahlgren twins, so heavy he hadn't straddled a hog in years but rode with the gang on a specially sprung trike with a bench seat and powered by a Volkswagen engine. Bob didn't seem to be in the bag alone. Someone or something bobbed at his crotch, low grunts slipping forth from the center of the bag.

"C.W.," Bob said pleasantly.

"Bob," I answered as I stepped aside and tried to hold my breath. Bob had his arms propped behind his head, and I could tell he hadn't been to the car wash since the cows came home at the beginning of winter.

The clutter faltered in the cabin behind the bus and died completely, thanks to Midget, in the large living room of Norman's house. Except for the rats. And the rat turds. The former either coursing about the room in great cinematic stampedes rife with the pitter-patter of tiny feet on the oak flooring, or just hanging out in quivering bunches. The latter crunching under my boots. A large naked woman I didn't recognize snored in a hammock stretched in front of the stone fireplace across the room. At the far end, Norman's video equipment sat about like a showroom display, silent and gray. But the near wall, covered with the fish tanks in question, shimmered with movement and light. Midget, a small, hard woman dressed in a baby-doll nightie, sat on a ladder, a fish book in one hand and a box of something dried and disgusting in the other. She seemed to know what she was doing, though. The water in the tanks was as limpid and lively as that in Dahlgren's Paradise.

"Hey, C.W.," she said without looking up, then shook her head and glanced at Norman. "This fish shit is complex, man."

"Ain't that something," Norman said proudly. "Mary's my full-time fishbitch."

"Norman," Midget scolded.

"Sorry," Norman said. Their relationship must have taken a turn. I'd never known Midget's given name and never known Norman to apologize for anything. "The royal keeper of the fish," he amended as he swept a cluster of sleeping rats off a tattered recliner. I perched on the front of an old couch, trying to take a seat that wasn't moving. Norman drew a packet of smoke out of his overalls pocket and quickly twisted a number the size of a mouse. "So what's up, Sughrue?" he asked after he lit it. "You come for the money?"

"The fish," I said as he handed me the joint. Norman looked as if I had hurt his feelings. "Hey, man, it's just a day's work for me, and I've already earned it. After me, though, comes the county sheriff and his minions."

"Fuck the sheriff and his fuckin' onions," Norman said calmly as he took the number from me. "That pustle-gutted pissant bastard shows up on my property, I'll have Bob squeeze shit-for-brains 'til his head pops like a pimple, then Mary can feed him to the fish."

"Now, Norman, you know that's not right," Mary said, shaking her head fondly.

"You get the picture," he said. Norman offered me the smoke, but I waved it away. "I'm keepin' the fuckin' fish, man. I like 'em. A lot. I picked 'em up on orders . . ."

"Orders?"

"From my doc, man," he explained. "He told me to get them, but I'm attached to the little fuckers now, Sughrue, you wouldn't believe it . . ."

"Don't believe it," Mary interrupted. "Norman don't even know their names, man, I'm the one's attached. He's just barely involved."

I felt as if I had missed something very important, so I took the number back from Norman and had a healthy hit. I wanted to fit in with the weird. "Your doctor told you to get the fish?" Norman nodded. "What the fuck for?"

"Ah, shit, man," he sighed. "I got this ah, you know, this fuckin' blood pressure problem. Hypertension, you know. Stress-related, they think."

"Certainly lots of stress in your business, Norman."

"Damn straight. You oughta try runnin' a business, not a big business but a business, with the kinda creeps I got hangin' around me. It ain't easy, man. Somebody's gotta be responsible, right? So I guess it's gotta be me. I can't depend on these other fuckin' jerks . . ."

"Thanks, Norman," Mary said.

"Except for Mary, of course," he continued, "and I'm sorry, man, we been friends a long time, but I'm keepin' the fish. I guess that's the bottom line, dude."

I kept thinking that there must be some easy way out of this, but since I didn't know what it might be I said, "I know I shouldn't ask, man, but what the hell do the fish have to do with your blood pressure?"

"I always liked that about you, Sughrue. Even when you're stoned senseless, man, you always ask the right question. You can go back to work for me anytime. Just ask . . . Where was I?"

"Fish tanks and blood pressure," I said.

"Thanks, man. See, I had these headaches, and the doc said it was my blood pressure so he gave me these tiny little pills but they made my pretty little pecker absolutely fuckin' useless . . ."

"Never was all that useful, anyway," Mary giggled from the ladder, then she took a hit off a roach, blew smoke across the water, and laughed again.

Instead of dragging one of the pistols off the end table and killing her, Norman joined her laughter fondly. I took another hit. Quickly. Norman took the number from me, then picked up a rat off the arm of the couch and set it on his chest, where he stroked it gently and blew dope smoke softly into its tiny gaping nostrils.

"So he told me to try fish. I watch 'em two hours ever' day. Works like a voodoo charm," he said, then patted his crotch. "Watchin' them little fucks eats up that stress, man, makes me mellow."

As if the idea of *mellow* worked on him, Norman wriggled his ass, settled his bulk into the recliner, and tilted it back. A loud, painful squeal ripped from the recess of the Lazy Boy. "Oh, shit, man," Norman groaned. He handed me the roach and the rat, which I took as calmly as if I had been just waiting for the chance to hold them, then he stood up, carefully turned over the chair, and gently dug a damaged rodent from the springs. "Poor baby," he crooned as he held it in his hand. The rat thrashed around on its broken back, then sunk its teeth into Norman's thumb. Norman let it. After a moment, he quickly snapped its neck, stroked it with his thumb once more, then tossed it toward the fireplace. It bounced off the fat lady's hip and into the fire. She neither woke nor sang, but then it wasn't time yet. "I fuckin' hate that, man," Norman said as he righted the recliner.

"You don't use them for target practice anymore?" I asked as I handed him his pretties. The rat had been sweetly affectionate as I held it, and I swear it gazed at me with longing as I gave it back.

"No way, man," he said. "I'm a changed man, Sughrue, massively mellow."

"I'm glad to hear that," I said.

Norman stopped petting the rat on his chest and gave me a hard look. Not that mellow, I guess.

"So maybe we can work something out."

"Don't fuck with me, man."

"Maybe if you'd just pay the Dahlgrens, Norman, and maybe let them see what a good job Mary is doing with the fish, maybe visitation rights," I suggested, "maybe they could help Mary."

"Mary don't need any help, and I don't want those fat fucks in my house. Can you dig it?" Norman said, his good eye hard and his bad one nearly focused, his voice bottomed out on the line. Then his mood shifted again, quickly, and he mused, "You know what, man? If those fat fucks hadn't been so scared of me, I might have given them a good check."

"Norman, you ate their entire supply of African leap fish," I said.

"Leaf fish," he corrected.

"And somebody who sounded like their grandfather."

"Li Po," he said. "A Siamese fighting fish. Shit, it was strange having those fish swimming around in my tummy, man."

"Norman!" Mary screeched from the tanks, but we ignored her.

"So the boys were a little scared," I suggested.

"They shit their baggy pants."

"Well, what would you do if I came in here and bit the heads off your favorite rats?"

"I wouldn't be surprised. You always were crazier than me, Sughrue. And never scared of me or treated me like I was a freak," he said. "That's why I always liked you . . . And goddammit I hate it when some fuck treats me like I'm a freak. Hey, man, I'm a human being, you know, and I got fuckin' feelings like anybody else, so when people are afraid of me, unless I mean for them to be, it makes me weird. Okay?"

"Well, it's okay with me, but I think the boys will go to the law."

"What do you think I got lawyers for, man? Traffic tickets?

It'll take 'em a year just to get through the gate. Maybe by then my blood pressure will be down . . ."

"Fuck your blood pressure, Norman," I said. We were both sort of stunned, but I carried on in my foolishness. "You fucking criminals are the most self-centered assholes in the world. All you think about is yourself. Think about somebody else for a change. Just give the Dahlgrens their money and let them see that the fish are all right, and all this will go away."

"Maybe you should go away, asshole." Norman had feelings, and I had damaged them. "Out of my house." He stood up slowly.

"Norman," Mary said softly from the fish tanks.

"I'll be back," I said, standing too.

"Like I said, asshole, you always were crazy."

"Keep that in mind."

"Don't get crossways with me and the brothers," Norman said.

"Fuck you and the brothers," I said as I walked toward the door, the skin crawling like rats across my exposed back. But Norman snorted, bitter and tough, and I knew I had walked out this time. Next time, well, who knows about next time.

As I drove away in the van, I found my hands trembling on the steering wheel. It didn't feel like fear, though, but some sort of anger, maybe even rage. Norman was just Norman, and I didn't think I was mad at him. I was just me, on the back side of forty, bedded down on a slab. Not even my own slab.

The snow-slick roads back to Meriwether gave me plenty of time to consider my life, but sometimes I simply wasn't interested in my life. So I'd never married, hadn't had a date in a year, hadn't slept with a woman in so long I couldn't remember it, I mean really slept with a woman, but I didn't seem to care. I might think that the Dahlgrens were ridiculous, but they really cared about their fish. I couldn't fix my life, maybe I could get their fish back. Maybe that was my life, helping those who could still care, even if I couldn't. At the moment it didn't sound like such a bad life.

When I got back to the store, I found Frank and Joe at a workbench beside the office door, leaning over a panting fish spread-eagled on a scrap of white cotton gauze. Frank held the clown-colored fish as Joe trimmed its dorsal fin with a single-edged razor blade, their gloved hands as carefully delicate as brain surgeons'. I told them what had happened up Clatterbuck Creek. Joe paused to look up at me.

"Since he seems to care for the fish," he said, "perhaps we could appeal to his kinder, gentler instincts." I snorted. "Doesn't have any, eh?" Frank said.

"I don't want to say anything bad about Norman," I said, "but he is determined to keep the fish, and equally determined not to pay you."

"I don't understand. Why?"

"Norman's not to understand, okay? He likes being an outlaw. Hell, so do I, for that matter," I said. "But he's not without feelings. I take it that he felt as if you, or somebody here, had treated him as if he were a freak. As Norman said, that makes him weird."

The boys exchanged a knowing glance, then Frank said, "Mona," and Joe blushed. I didn't want to know. Joe gave his attention back to the fish, sliced cleanly through the fin, then Frank picked up the fish in a gauze net and placed him in a small tank at the back of the bench. Joe held up the bluesteel blade, which glistened greasy as blood in the soft light. "Sometimes I wish we were more like the General," he said sadly.

"The General?"

"Our father," Frank said. "A man possessed of a violent nature," Joe added.

"I believe that's what people pay me for," I said.

"Can you get our fish back?" they asked.

"I can't guarantee their safety," I admitted, "but with enough money and firepower, I can get them back."

The twins stood together. Today they wore matching psychedelic sweaters the size of my last bad trip. "We have plenty of both," Frank said. "If you get our fish back," Joe said, "we'll give you five thousand dollars."

I nodded. We remembered how badly we shook hands, so we didn't bother. Frank and Joe grinned at each other.

"God love the General," Joe said. "Walk this way, Mr. Sughrue," Frank said.

I followed them instead, through the office, where they stripped off their gloves and grabbed violently orange down parkas, and out the back door, where they stared at their matching white Cadillacs for a moment before Joe said, "You can ride over with Frank, then back with me. All right?" The inmates had been in charge all day, so I quickly agreed. Frank and I climbed aboard his ride and we followed Joe down the alley and across Felony Flats.

As we headed toward the southern fringe of Meriwether, Frank sang along with a Beach Boys tape. He had a high, sweet voice, but when he noticed me listening, he turned down the volume.

"I suppose you think it's odd that Joe and I don't ride in the same car?"

"Oh, no," I lied.

"Twins are supposed to be psychically connected," Frank said, "but Joe and I were never like that. Even at birth, you know, we both tried to come out at the same time. Killed our poor mother. I don't think the General ever forgave us."

"Your father was in the Army?"

"And grandfather, and great-grandfather, ad nauseam. When it became clear during our freshman year at VMI that we were not, so to speak, military material, it nearly killed the old gentleman," he said. "Wouldn't that be irony of ironies? Killing our poor mother with our confusion and size, then doing the same to the General." Frank giggled as if this were an old joke well considered.

After he finished laughing, we rode in silence out the highway to a storage rental place. It had their name on it, too.

"We have several business interests here," Frank explained as we pulled through the yard to a large building set some distance beyond the rest of the storage units.

"The fish business must be okay."

"The fish, they're merely one of our hobbies," he said as we parked beside Joe's Caddy, "our favorite, of course, but only one of many financial interests."

We dismounted, the auto sighed with relief, then we waited at the door. Frank held the doorknob as Joe punched a code into the alarm system. The door unlocked with a loud, metallic click. Frank pushed the door open slightly, then paused.

"You may remember, Mr. Sughrue," he said, "that we told you we actually had a tank."

"No," I said, "no-no."

"Yes-yes," the boys sang, and opened the door, flicked on the lights, and waved me inside.

As the ranks of fluorescent tubes in the ceiling twinkled into light they revealed my father's war, good old WWII, racks of M-1s, walls of grease guns, Thompsons, and M-1A carbines, several water-jacketed Browning .30-caliber machine guns, a bevy of BARs, a trio of air-cooled .50s, a half-track shining with fresh OD paint, and by god a fucking Sherman tank.

"Jesus fucking Christ" was all I could say.

"Largest collection in private hands in North America," somebody said.

"No shit," I said. It seemed to be the response the boys wanted. They grinned like Tweedledum and Tweedledee. "You inherit this from the General?"

"Some of it," Joe answered smugly. "The Sherman was our latest addition. Isn't it lovely," Frank said.

"Lovely," I whispered as I wandered into the arms of that past when America still believed in itself, when my father went to war, the war my mother blamed for his madness. I hope her memory forgives me, but I always blamed her. As far as I knew from my father's war stories, nothing had happened in the South Pacific that would convince a fifth-generation Scotch-Irish Texan that he had been suddenly transformed into a member of a lost band of the Kwahadi Comanche. My guess was that he was loony before he left my mother's house the first time, and that his later vision quests into the Far West were just excuses to keep moving. Mysticism as motion, a life I understood, I thought as I stopped beside a canvas-shrouded .50-caliber mounted on a tripod.

"You boys have any ammo for this baby?"

"Only about a thousand rounds," Joe said.

"And a class-three license?"

"As legal as your car."

"I don't have a car," I said, "but I'll take this. Nostalgic target practice, you know."

"We'll give you a hand," Frank said as he opened an ammo locker and lifted out a long skein of belted .50-caliber rounds.

"What ever happened to the idea of nonviolence?" I asked the boys.

"It only works against the guilty and the liberal," one said, then the other led the way out the door, laughing.

As a downy snow drifted in the gray dawn, Frank pulled the Paradise van up to Norman's fortified gate. I scrambled out the rear doors, picked the lock with my most delicate burglar tool—a bolt cutter with three-foot handles—kicked the gate open, and leapt into the back of the van as it trundled past. Frank pushed it hard up the canyon road, as I had told him to do because the alarms were already clanging throughout the Snowdrifter complex. I held on to the .50-caliber, which I had anchored with seventy dollars' worth of nylon straps and bungee cords, but Frank and Joe, too large to fit into their seat belts, tumbled about the cab of the van like large balloons that had lost their tethers. But they stuck it out, held on until we made the last corner, and Frank spun the van in a tight circle, skidding until the rear doors faced the school bus that protected the entrance. Then we waited.

After a moment the alarms ceased their clangor and the Snow-drifters tumbled outside, armed and sort of alert. I suspected that Norman's merry band might not be at their peak at dawn during the best of times, but this morning as they scrambled out of their holes and gathered in front of the bus as surly as a pack of rabid coyotes, they looked particularly bad. Coyotes might have arrived better dressed. Beater Bob was massively naked but for a shotgun and his socks, which seemed to have merged with the skin of his feet. Everybody else looked as cold and confused as the Donner Party just before their first catered lunch.

The Dahlgren Boys, though, were as spiffy and organized as the VFW on parade, garbed in the height and breadth of military fashion in tailored camouflage fatigues, spit-shined jump boots, and varnished steel helmets perched like teacups on their giant heads. Frank and Joe dismounted as quickly as they could, the van rocking wildly on its springs, and I could hear the snow creak under their soles as they strode to the back of the van, crossed their arms, and faced Norman's motley crew. The confrontation had all the weighty elegance of a sumo match, until a very grouchy Norman pushed through the crowd.

"What the fuck do you fat boys want?" Norman screamed.

"Our fish," my boys answered calmly, "our fucking fish."

Norman considered that, clutching the assault rifle in his hands, then shouted, "You got ten seconds to get the fuck out of here!"

"And you've got five seconds to get our fish out here," Joe said. "One, two," counted Frank, "threefourfive." Then the boys grabbed the handles of the rear doors and slammed them open.

When the Snowdrifters saw me behind the giant grasshopper shape of the .50-caliber, they simply stared, unable to move, as if faced with the ghost of John Wayne. Bad drug experiences do come true. I stuffed wax in my ears and settled the protective muffs as tightly as I could. When I hit the butterfly triggers, the gang paused for a nanosecond before seeking refuge in the six inches of snow on the frozen ground, their weapons flying out of their hands.

The .50-caliber fires a 500-grain projectile at 2,900 feet per second. It's like being shot at with fishing sinkers. The six-round burst shredded the roof of the school bus and knocked half of the cedar-shake shingles off Norman's front roof. It felt so good bucking against my hands I didn't want to stop. Of course, I'd been up most of the night waiting for the excitement, and even the single line of crystal I'd done couldn't account for the second six-round burst. That was just pure fun, pure rock-and-roll automatic fire.

"Get the fucking picture, Norman?" I shouted into the sudden stillness after the echoes of the second burst tumbled out of the narrow canyon.

After a long moment, Norman stood up slowly, brushed the snow off his overalls, shook his head like a defeated general, then almost grinned. "Let's talk *fish*, you crazy fucker," he said. I couldn't even hear my own shout earlier, but I read his lips.

* * *

A few minutes later, I leaned on the mantel of the fireplace as Norman laid a fire. The fat lady, still naked and unrecognized, now slept on the couch beneath a Hudson's Bay blanket decorated by several sleeping rats. The rest of them clustered in a corner by the kitchen eating something I couldn't imagine, but which I swear looked a lot like rat turds. Efficient little beasts, I thought as Norman lit the fire. He stood up to lean against the rock mantel, raised his coffee cup to toast mine. At the far end of the room Mary, less than modest in another baby-doll nightie, and the twins engaged in serious conversation in front of the fish tanks.

"I guess it's your action, man," he said quietly. "I haven't heard anything like that since Tet."

"I didn't know you were a vet," I said.

"I didn't know you were," Norman said seriously.

"Sort of," I said. "I guess we were too busy doing drugs and having fun to talk about it. First Cav. Central Highlands. Sixty-seven."

"Fuckin' graves registration," Norman said. "Two Corps, sixty-eight. Fuck it, man. That's how I got started in the business."

"Shit, I heard about you guys but I didn't believe it."

"What the fuck, everybody else was making a bundle. Fuckin' civilian contractors, Red Cross cunts, even the fuckin' CIA runnin' the poppy trade out of the Golden Triangle. Fuck it. The stiffs didn't care what they carried back. They were already fucked." Norman sipped his coffee. "Seemed like the thing to do at the time."

"Didn't John Wayne say that?"

"He said lots of shit," Norman said, "but what are we going to do now? With the fish shit?"

"I don't fucking know. All you had to do was play straight with me yesterday, Norman," I said. "But you pissed me off."

"Yeah, well you pissed me off, too."

"Sorry."

"Yeah, well, fuck it. I'm sorry, too. I meant what I said about you going to work for me again, C.W."

"Let's work this out first, okay?"

Norman nodded seriously, as if we would talk about working for him later.

"If you'll pay the boys, I'll talk them into leaving the fish."

"What the fuck," Norman said, shrugged, then lifted a vial of coke out of his pocket. "One blast for old times' sake."

I'd done more blow for old times' sake in the last six months than I'd done on my own for the last six years, but it seemed impolite to refuse. So I nodded, and Norman laid out two wormy lines on the mantel, which we promptly did. I sniffled, then turned to the other end of the room.

"How the fish look, boys?" I shouted.

Frank and Joe turned, confused, as if they had forgotten why we had come, then they gathered themselves and answered. "Beautiful," Joe said. "Perfect," Frank said, patting Mary's arm, "she's a wizard with fish."

"Fat fuck," Norman muttered.

"If he pays you, will you leave them here?"

The boys looked at each other for a moment in mock seriousness, then at Mary, who grinned, then shouted back at me, "Only if we get visitation rights."

"Deal?" I asked Norman.

"Fat fucks," he answered, resigned.

"Cash money," I said, and he almost smiled before he headed toward the rear of the house.

By the time Norman came back, Mary and the Dahlgrens had joined me. I fed the fire while they discussed various filtration systems. I kept an eye on the teeming rat pack still cluttered around their bowls by the kitchen door. Norman strolled into the room, handed me a bundle of bank-banded hundred-dollar bills. "Six K," he grumbled, "paid in full with interest." Then he stalked toward his Lazy Boy.

The money made me jolly. "What do you feed those rats, Norman?" I said.

"Friends," he said, stopping long enough to glare at me. "Fuckin' friends." Then he flopped into the chair and picked up his forty-function remote.

When I handed the bundle of bills to Frank, I noticed that Mary was shaking her head sadly at me.

"What?" I said.

"I think you hurt his feelings, C.W.," she said.

I took a deep breath, but it didn't help. "Well, excuse the fuck out of me. There ain't nothing worse than a fucking sensitive biker to ruin an old boy's morning."

Frank handed the money back to me. "It's yours," Joe said.

I kept one bundle, handed the others back to Frank. "This is plenty," I said. "Let's call it even."

Then Mary suggested, "Maybe you should apologize."

I slapped the bills against my palm as if I might be thinking of how to apologize. "Since everything worked out so well, Mr. Sughrue," Frank said, making points with Mary, "maybe you should take the young lady's advice."

I took another bundle from Frank's hand. "That's my price," I said shortly, "for apologies. I'm sorry, I'm so fucking sorry I almost can't stand it, you silly fucking assholes."

Nobody argued with me. In fact, nobody even looked at me. I stuffed the bread into the pockets of my down vest, then gave the crowd one more chance to say something before I stomped into the kitchen to grab two beers out of the reefer. I opened them both and carried them back out to the video area, where I flopped on the couch next to Norman's chair. I didn't care if I sat on a rat or two. Norman was relentlessly searching the channels with his remote when I offered him one of the beers.

"It's amazin', man, how much shit there is out there wandering the cosmos," he said, then shook his head at the offered beer. "Too early for me, man."

"Too fucking early for technological philosophy," I said. "I'll drink the motherfucker."

"Jesus, man, you're on a short fuse."

"Old age," I said. "Everything's hairier and closer to the ground, man, and either less or more serious."

"Right," Norman said, looking very nervous. "You ever fire one of those fifties before?"

"Not in this life or that one."

"You didn't fire any practice rounds?"

"Norman, they must cost five dollars apiece."

"Jesus," he sighed, "that makes me nervous."

"That was the whole point, asshole," I said.

"Damn it, Sughrue, you shouldn't a-done it that way." Norman sounded wounded and serious. "You shouldn't oughta."

"You should've paid attention the first time," I said. I had money in my pockets, blow in my nose, and Norman by the nuts with Mary flirting wildly with the twins.

"You sure *got* my attention," he brayed, then laughed wildly. "Got all my attention, dude, but you fucked up Bob's sex life forever."

"Forever?"

"Claims he lost his little prick in the snow."

"Sucked it right up inside him," I suggested.

"Bob's the horniest fat person I ever met," Norman said, glancing over his shoulder at Mary and the Dahlgrens. "I don't like the way those fat boys are looking at Mary."

"They're harmless," I said without conviction. "They only care about fish and firepower." Norman raised a small chuckle. "They got a goddamned Sherman tank," I said, "a working Sherman tank."

"Jesus," Norman said, then paused to consider that. "That's hard to call, even for me. Shit. How much did they pay you for all this?"

"Five bills for talking to you yesterday," I said, and Norman smiled proudly. "A grand for shooting over your head, and a grand for apologizing to you."

"I don't remember any apology."

"Don't hold your fucking breath."

Norman liked that one better, a great deal, in fact. "Not bad wages," he said when he stopped laughing.

"Almost legal, too," I said, "but I'm usually cheaper."

"And almost worth it, too." This time I laughed with him, but when we quit, Norman looked at me seriously again. "Hey, man, how much you charge me to find somebody?"

"Who?" I said, hitting my beer.

"A woman."

"You already got a woman, Norman."

"This is different, Sughrue."

"Fuck, you're serious," I said, sitting up and brushing the rats off my legs. Norman nodded slowly. "Somebody local?"

"Nope. Long-distance," he said.

"I don't know, man," I said, trying to change the subject. "I'm out of practice. Sometime in the late seventies people stopped running away. Or people quit looking for them. I haven't chased anybody in years but bail jumpers, and I hate that shit."

"Bad guys, huh?"

"Their families. Boy, you see their families, you understand where they all come from," I said. Norman looked uneasy but I ignored it. "Last time I got shot at, man, some dude's mother laid down on me with a twelve-gauge through her apartment door. Missed me by a cunt hair. I heard the safety click. Killed the old boy across the hall, though. Now she's doing hard time and her ratfuck son's still running."

"This won't be like that. How much do you charge?"

"I don't know, Norman."

"You don't need the bread?"

"Sure, I need the money."

"So give me a figure," Norman said.

I dragged something out of the air. "Three bills a day, expenses, a bonus if I find this woman."

"Okay," Norman said.

Clearly, I hadn't made a living in the private investigation business because I had never asked for enough money. I considered strolling back over to the Dahlgrens and taking the rest of the six thousand. But I didn't.

"I don't even have a ride anymore, Norman."

"I'll loan you one of mine."

"Fall won't last, Norman, and I don't do scooters in the wintertime."

"I wouldn't let you on my hog, asshole," he said, smiling, "but I got a ride for you."

"And I'd have to have a written contract." I knew that would stop him.

Norman paused in his cosmic channel search, leaving us with something that looked like Olympic-class boredom, Greek music videos. "I don't like that much, man. Don't you trust me? Let's just do cash and a handshake."

"Cash is fine, man, but I need a contract," I explained. "I trust you, but if anybody asks, I need the paper."

"Shit."

Then I had a bright idea, dumbfuck me. "You know what we can do, man. Come in tomorrow, hire Solly, let him hire me, and you're covered."

Norman shifted in the chair. I noticed that several rats scurried from under the recliner. Who said they never learned?

"I know he's your asshole buddy, man, but I haven't trusted that son of a bitch since I lost all that meth on the Canadian deal," he finally said.

"What Canadian deal?" I asked.

"I lost a bunch of shit and two brothers when I was dealing with one of Solly's draft-dodger clients," he explained. "He wasn't involved," Norman said quickly, "but I just don't trust him."

"He's a lawyer; you're not supposed to," I said. "You trust your lawyer?"

"Right fuckin' on."

"Then let him do it," I said.

"I don't want him in this, man."

"Sometimes I don't know which is more complicated," I said. "Lawyers, guns, or money."

"Warren Zevon," Norman said. "Okay, Solly can do the papers."

"Great. Who you want me to look for?" I said.

"My mother," Norman said quietly. I have to admit that it never occurred to me that Norman might have a mother. "Mary and I are going to get married, man, and she wants my mother there. I guess I do, too." Norman stared at me a long time, then dumped a small pile of cocaine on the web of his thumb. I hit it, then he did himself the same favor. "Are you up for it?"

"Sure," I said, "why the fuck not? Where do I start?"

Norman ducked his head. "I got these newspaper clippings, man, and all the shit from the orphanage in Texas. A buncha shit."

"Bring it tomorrow," I said, suddenly tired as I finished the beer. "Okay?"

"Thanks, man," Norman said, and I shook his oddly tiny

hand. "Thanks." Then he stood up. "Mary, let's have some grub."

Mary paused, nodded, then glanced at the twins.

Norman interrupted her thought. "We can't afford to feed those fat fucks."

Mary apologized to the boys, who looked as if they wanted me to take my apology back, and they made their farewells full of promises to visit the fish in both places soon, then we eased out through the ruined bus.

Enough fresh snow had drifted through the shredded roof to cover the debris of the wandering life of a biker gang with a soft cold blanket. It looked like a New York alley after the next war. Beater Bob himself huddled under a blanket in the driver's seat, his eyes sad and distant when he watched us leave.

"I don't know how people live like that," Joe said as we stepped out of the bus door, brushing the snowflakes off his fatigues as if they were ashes.

"You've always been such a prissy bastard, Joe," Frank said.

"You're just saying that because you fell for that dirty little girl," Joe responded.

"I'm not the only one who likes little girls."

"At least Mona's clean," Joe claimed.

"She smells like the turtle tank," Frank said.

"Boys, boys," I interrupted. "Either shut up or give me another thousand dollars."

By god, they thought about it, but finally gave up their tiff, even though I could hear them fussing under their breaths as they heaved themselves into the front of the van. I climbed into the back, anchored the machine gun before I closed the doors. Norman stepped out of the bus door, followed by Bob, who looked like a major religious figure draped in his blanket.

"Hey, Sughrue, ask those fat fucks if they want to sell their tank!" Norman shouted, then laughed.

"Tell him that if he calls us fat fucks again," Frank said, his voice full of love, lust, and rage, "we'll deliver it personally."

"Damn fucking right," Joe said, and he sounded as if he meant it.

Out the back windows of the van, the cloud cover began to

divide, blue sky glittering through the cracks. It looked like another wave of weather confusion for Meriwether: snow showers for breakfast, sunshine for nooning. I couldn't keep from smiling.

When the boys dropped me off at Sollv's office, we waved goodbye as if we were old friends. The souna of aimed gunfire, however quickly over, sometimes does that to men. I took two steps toward the basement entrance, where the dead people once arrived, glanced at the courthouse clock, which said 9:45. Fuck it, a full day of Native American sunshine. The cash shifted in my vest pocket as I paused, then I dug into my shirt where I knew a small pile of crystal lay twisted into the end of a bit of plastic. Here I was way beyond the age of consent, looking fifty in the eye and still sleeping on somebody else's floor, or embalming slab to be absolutely correct, so I jammed a tiny pinch of speed up my nose and hoofed it toward the Slumgullion for a bait of fried mush and fresh side pork. If I'd had a Corvette, I'd have driven it there.

Even though I knew it wasn't on the menu anymore, I walked in the back door and ordered it anyway. In a very loud voice. The early morning drinkers paused with their whiskey in the air and the poker chips gave up their rattle. The last time I'd stopped in the Slumgullion for breakfast, I'd gotten western with a couple of Canadian Bloods, but we made friends in jail. The short-order cook concentrated on a pair of eggs and the waitress wouldn't look me in the eye. She kept her eyes down like an ex-con, which she was, seven-and-change for popping a cap on her father-in-law.

"We ain't got none a that," she whispered, drifting away.

"Ain't your fault, honey," I said, "but where's the asshole who owns this place now? You, cookie! Who owns this shithole now?"

"I don't know," he said to a pile of smoldering hash browns.

"Some fucking yuppie from California, right, who doesn't know shit from brains and eggs, fried mush from fresh side pork, and the next fucking thing you know, man, this will be a bread and break-the-fucking-fast haven for wino yups addicted to a good really interesting Chablis."

Then the bartender, an old friend and running partner in the detective business, strolled down the end of the bar. "Jesus, Sonny," he said softly, "leave the fucking cook alone. You shout at him again and he'll shit his pants and ruin everybody's breakfast. Come over here. I'll buy you a drink. We'll talk about the old days when we were young and foolish, and able to afford it, instead of just foolish."

"Sounds like a deal," I said. My old partner always had that effect on me; talking to him worked better than a handful of Valium. He poured us both shots of unblended Scotch and cracked me a bottle of Canadian beer for a chaser as I bellied up to the bar.

He held up the shot glass, stared at it fondly, then dumped it down the drain. I sipped my shot. "How long's it been now?" I asked.

"Nearly two years," he said, running his hand through his coal-black curls.

"No, really," I said.

"Fuck you, Sughrue," he said, then smiled. "I don't count the days. I didn't quit. I'm just resting. Sounds like you might give it a rest, too."

"Bad dreams," I said, which was more than half-true, "but I've been sober since, since the musical incident. Nothing like sleeping in a morgue to give an old boy bad dreams and sobriety."

The bartender sniffed the air, then grinned and touched his nose lightly.

"Had a beer and a bump with one of our old friends this morning," I said, "but strictly in the line of duty."

He raised an eyebrow over a sulky Slavic eye, and I told him all about it. As you get older, old friends are a tonic, a blessing beyond counting. When I finished my story, he reminded me of the time we had gone to Japan to retrieve a champion Labrador retriever from a Japanese automobile executive who didn't understand free enterprise until we held his head in his carp pond. But that's another story. After I drank my second setup, I hooked a cab down to the Riverside Inn, checked in, ordered breakfast from room service, and fell into a lovely dreamless sleep before I finished it.

Sometimes fun can be tiresome.

* * *

Shortly after noon the next day, I found myself in Solly's office yelling at Norman again. Never a good sign for me.

"This is fucking crazy!" I shouted.

Solly sat behind his oak desk, trying to look avuncular as he shook his head as if to suggest "abnormal" at the very least.

"As far as I can tell, the police forces of three states, the FBI, the Secret Service, and probably the fucking CIA are looking for this woman, who you think might be your mother, and they can't find her, so what makes you think I can?" I waved Norman's collection of newspaper and magazine clippings in his face, then stalked across the office to stare at the shiny neighborhood. I had had a good night's sleep, a nice breakfast, and even a good hike over to the office. I didn't have any reason to be mad at Norman. Except that he was fucking crazy. "What makes you think I can find her?" I repeated.

"I don't know, C.W.," he said quietly, "I just do." Norman had left his colors at home; dressed in a flannel shirt and tweed jacket, he looked almost normal. Mary looked absolutely splendid in a sleek wool dress, panty hose, and green suede pumps that matched her dress exactly. The long sleeves of the dress even covered her tattoos, as the new makeup nearly did the hard lines of her pretty face. "I just do."

"Can you believe this?" I asked Solly, but he just played dumb. I consulted the clippings and turned to Norman again. "You don't even really know if this Sarita Cisneros Pines is really your mother. I mean what the hell, man, she's just the missing wife of the President's special envoy to Mexico, and he's not your father, but you think she's your mother, right?"

"I don't think it, man, I know it."

"Sarita Pines," I said to Solly, "sounds like a housing development, right?"

"Goddammit," Mary explained hotly, "Norman was six when she gave him away and he fucking remembers his mother."

"He doesn't even fucking look Mexican," I said.

"She was half Irish," Norman said.

"Oh, that explains everything," I said, "half fucking Irish.

That's makes it perfect, man. I'm used to clients lying to me, but usually the stories make a little sense. This is bullshit."

"What the hell you so mad about, man?" Norman asked, leaning forward on the creaking leather couch. "Too much blow, or not enough? I got some right here, man, you need some." Norman reached into the pocket of his sport coat.

"Not in my office," Solly said, "please."

Norman gave him a long, hard stare. "Sure, counselor, whatever you say," he said finally. Mary put a hand on his arm as if to restrain him. "So what the fuck's with you, Sughrue?"

Solly shifted in his chair, his plastic foot clanking against the side of the desk, and raised his hands, the scarred palm shiny in the diffuse light. "Norman, I would like to suggest that C.W. has plenty of reasons to be on edge about this case without you implying that he has a drug problem, which sounds a bit shitty coming from you, man, so why don't you consider apologizing . . ."

"Fuck that shit, Solly," I said. I didn't know who to be mad at. "Norman and I have been friends long enough so that we can do business without apologizing every fucking five minutes, okay? Right, Norman?"

"Damn fucking straight, counselor." Norman didn't know who to be mad at, either.

"Okay, fine," Solly said, dropping his hands back to his lap. "Then let me see if I can't cut through some of the crap . . ."

Norman and I snorted like warthogs from hell. As if any lawyer ever cut through the shit when the clock was ticking.

"Point well taken, gentlemen," Solly said, grinning, then glancing at his Rolex. "So let me put it this way. I'm not on the clock. I've got a lunch in a few minutes, if that's all right with you gentlemen. So let's get down to the nut-cutting, boys." Either Norman or I nodded. "Hazelbrook, how much money do you have to put into this project?"

"Midget," Norman said, and Mary stood up, rocking sexily on her unfamiliar heels, opened her purse, took out a pile of money, and tossed it on Solly's desk. It landed with a wonderfully solid thump. "Forty K," Norman said, "plus whatever the fuck you need."

Solly asked the right question. "Clean?"

"Pris-fucking-tine," Mary said, her lip curled. "You could eat off it, Mr. Rainbolt. Which is more than I can say about your desk." Mary drew her finger across the front of Solly's desk as if she were on a white-glove inspection. I didn't see any dust, but Mary blew something off her delicate fingertip.

"All right, C.W.," Solly said, not even glancing at the money as he dropped it in his desk drawer, "I'd suggest that you accept Mr. Hazelbrook's word that he is convinced that this woman is his mother, whom he hasn't seen since he was six years old, and join the government in its search for her. If you have any objections, personal or ethical, please let us know. Now, please. So I can get to lunch."

"Goddammit," I said, then turned back to the cold window. My breath clouded on the glass. Beyond the window a half-moon glowed in the blue-white sky. I hadn't worked in a long time, and I really wanted to work again. No more bartending, no more sleeping on a slab, no more Solomon Rainbolt in charge of my life. Not that Solly had been a pain in the ass; he'd been a prince; but I didn't want to work for a prince or a pain in the ass; I didn't even want to work for Abnormal Norman Hazelbrook; but it might be like working for myself again.

"Fuck it," I said as I turned around. "Contract city."

And Solly drew them out of his desk.

Twenty minutes later, I had cash money in hand for expenses, the keys to Norman's extra VW van, which looked as if it had spent the last twenty years in storage but which he promised was as sound as a Swiss franc, a handful of clippings, an invitation from Solly to stop by his house on my way out of town, and a sweet kiss warm on my cheek from Mary, which excited me more than I could understand. The weather stayed warm while I packed my gear. Or maybe it was just my old heart pumping again.

PART TWO

PART TWO

At three that afternoon I finished packing for the mad road trip. Norman's supposed sainted mother was married to a world-class Republican, so the weapons went on top of the load: the old dependable Browning High-Power, the new S&Ws, a .38 Airweight and a double-action 10mm semiautomatic, a Mossberg Bullpup 12-gauge, and my favorite spring-loaded sap. Then I sat down on the footlocker to run through the clippings one more time.

While I shook my head, one of Solly's endless series of leggy blond legal secretaries clicked down the cement stairs in wonderfully high heels. They all wore them, as if Solly had convinced them that women as lovely as they were deserved to suffer. But I never heard one of them complain. I also never found out if Solly ever bedded one. I knew I hadn't. Quite frankly, they intimidated me. All the way down to my scuffed boots.

This one, particularly. She was always nice to me. Nothing more frightening than a beautiful woman when she's nice to you.

"Mr. Sughrue," she trilled politely. "Mr. Rainbolt just called. His lunch plans have changed slightly, but he really wants you to stop at the house before you leave town. He said you knew where to find both the house key and the Scotch whisky."

"Gee, I don't have any idea . . . You wouldn't know, would you?"

"Of course not," she said. Then the perfect trace of a smile flirted with her perfectly painted lips.

I knew it was impolite to watch her hips stretching the warm folds of her skirt. By the time she reached the top of the stairs, I wanted to ask her along for the ride. Lord only knew when a working PI might need a legal secretary who looked like a swimsuit model. Then she stopped at the door and gave me a smile that made me feel like a tomato worm. And a teenager again.

"Good luck, Sonny."

Norman's extra VW van was one of those camper models, a deep shiny blue, but with a ton of cash in my pocket I knew that my idea of camping out was going to be staying at a motel without room service. My duffel, footlocker, and random gear didn't even cover the kitchen-carpeted floor. It wasn't bad. Even had a tiny televison. Everything was spotless, which I attributed to Mary, who, I noticed as I adjusted the rearview mirror, had left a lip-print on my cheek.

I wiped it off as I cranked over the engine and found first. Then I popped the clutch. If I had been paying attention, I might have noticed the oddly smooth sound of the engine, the crisp linkage of the transmission, and the small radar detector on the dash. Instead, I gunned the engine and popped the clutch, which lifted the front wheels off the pavement, ran two stop signs, and nearly threw myself into the back of the van where my gear had tumbled.

First chance I had, I parked and opened the engine cover in the rear. The transverse-mounted V-6 lurking behind the cover had never been anyplace near a Volkswagen factory. How perfectly Norman. He couldn't do anything normal if he tried. I wondered if the bastard might be hiding behind an elm laughing up his rat-infested sleeve as he watched my hog-on-ice driving style.

When I had asked Norman why he had an *extra* VW van, he had responded, "Nostalgia, my man, pure nostalgia."

For what? I wondered as I climbed back in the driver's seat and fastened the seat belt tightly.

A brand-new Toyota 4Runner pulled up behind me, and Norman climbed out, shouting, "Hey, Sonny, you best watch *La Gloria Azul* or she'll eat your lunch for breakfast."

"You wouldn't want to trade rides, would you?" I said.

"You're already sittin' in my favorite ride, man. Once you get used to her, you'll love her like I do."

"Thanks."

"You need anything, Sonny, or find any fun you can't handle, check the bottom of the glove box and give me a call, you hear?"

"Right," I shouted, then tried to run over his foot as I tore out of the parking place, roaring down the road, his laughter ringing behind me.

Solomon Rainbolt lived up the Hardrock Valley in a log mansion built by a Swedish architect for a Hollywood actor whose career hadn't survived his first rush as a Brat Pack second banana. After the actor became pudding, Solly picked up the house for a song; the actor sang until he was blue on a Washington state cocaine distribution bust; Solly kept him out of the walls at Walla Walla and kept the house.

The drive wasn't a long one, just long enough for me to ease into the scenery, an old Montana addiction. Under all that baby-blue sky it could have been July, the early snows simply bad dreams. But the cottonwoods and creek willows were seared with borders of yellow, and the western larch on the mountain slopes yearned to shed their needles one more time.

Young men find spring the time of renewal, but those of us with a few beers under our belts and even more miles on our butts find spring to be simply a false promise of greenery destined to wither, a flowered, frenzied promise never meant to be kept.

In the clear, hot sunshine of autumn, the promise of winter waits just inside the shade of the pines, a vow always honored. Whatever winter brings—aching bones, starving elk, frozen children—we've got this moment of blue clarity. Western Montana at its best.

The tourist horde had departed, the streams ran low around the sun-bleached rocks and driftwood, the pools sparkling with the soft drift of your fly, the lurking mouths of trout. Things worth the dying. In Montana, too, you're even free after death.

Sort of. If you don't want it, the professional vultures can't
embalm your husk or saddle your kith and kin with fancy satin-
bedded coffins. Your people can just wrap you in a wagon sheet
and drop you in a hand-hewn hole in the backyard. Then retire
to the nearest bar to remember you in stories, and remember you
until the stories become the children you never bothered to have.

Somebody once said, *Hell is other people*. Of course, they neglected to point out which other people, and seemed to forget that
the obverse is true. Maybe Heaven is our people, and Montana our
place.

A few miles up the Hardrock, a string of slow traffic clotted
the highway. I spotted a small opening, downshifted, blasted
past the traffic like a blue windowpane acid flashback, then throt-
tled back to lead the pack, slow and easy, happy with the road.

The whole situation, however, left me a bit concerned. Clients
always lie to you, one way or another, omission or commission,
and you have to take that into account, try to work around it,
try to figure it out. Even though Norman was what the authorities
called a career criminal, as if some of them were just doing it for
a hobby, I had never known him to lie to anybody but the cops.
Until I knew better, I had to assume that Norman was convinced
that this woman, Sarita Cisneros Pines, was his mother and that
he wanted her at his wedding.

The wedding, that could have bothered me, too, but I'd seen
too many biker betrothals lately to think much about it anymore.
It's always frightening when the worst sort of people decide to
join the best.

Norman's having a rich and lovely mother, that bothered me,
as did the disappearance of said Mrs. Pines from a fancy lodge
over in Snowy Lake, Montana, where her husband was addressing
a convention of natural gas producers. That was a problem,
too. According to the papers, her husband, Joe Don Pines, had
returned from an afternoon speech to find their room empty, her
purse and room key on the coffee table.

Mrs. Pines sometimes jogged in the afternoon, so the alarm
wasn't raised until dark-thirty when she still hadn't appeared.
For ordinary people, the hue and cry would have waited the usual
twenty-four hours, and the FBI not called in for weeks, but Joe

Don was a personal friend of the President and his special envoy
to the Mexican government for oil and gas imports, a position
he had obtained by running unsuccessfully for a dozen state
offices, on his own nickel, and by large and frequent donations
to the Republican cause. Perhaps that was the same way he had
risen from Army Reserve captain to bird colonel during the
Vietnam War Games. Whatever, Joe Don waited at one of his
ventures, a resort cum fat farm cum golf course—El Rancho
Encantada—just over the New Mexican border west of El Paso,
Texas, while the feds left no stone unturned.

I also wasn't crazy about stumbling over feds at every step along
the way. Some of them were just plain semi-ordinary assholes who
believed in getting the job done the best and easiest ways, while
perhaps even having an occasional bit of fun along the way. Some
of them were simply bureaucratic assholes with guns. Others
were driven, dedicated assholes who would pop their grannies for
a single lungful of pot when they were trying to hold down their
last meal against the nausea of chemotherapy. But whatever they
were personally or professionally, they were the fucking feds.
And I wasn't. But if I played it right, I could at least make more
money in a couple of weeks than they did in a month. Money
counts with bureaucrats. When Dan Rather makes more money
than the President, who the fuck's really in charge?

About twenty miles south of Meriwether, I turned left across
the Hardrock River to pick up the Eastside Highway, then followed it on south to the Burnt Fork Road, which led a twisted
trail to Solly's cattle guard.

Solly didn't keep any cattle, just two crazy goats, a string of
riding and pack mules, and one old gander named Millard Fillmore. When the goats weren't trying to play king of the mountain on his guests' automobiles or chew up their seat covers, they
kept the scrub brush and short grass down inside the house fence.
The mules allowed Solly to tackle the wilderness behind his house
in some ease and luxury. I wasn't sure what Millard Fillmore,
the goose, did. As far as I could tell he thought he was an Alsatian
watchdog with an attitude.

Solly's driveway was only a couple of miles long and lined with
about five hundred poplars, which weren't breaking any wind,

but their long, thin shadows held strips of the most recent snow across the hard-surfaced driveway. His house sat on the lip of a bench that commanded a view of the Burnt Fork, the Hardrock Valley, and the rocky peaks of the mountain range that gave the river its name. It had been constructed of huge red cedar logs stacked on a granite rock foundation, and enough glass walls to make Montana Power simper with joy. It shimmered like a diamond in the lowering sun, the A-frame front flanked by two sweeping glass-walled wings.

As I parked by the steps up to the deck and the front door, Millard Fillmore came rushing out of his goose door in the garage, his wings spread wide, his neck arched like a snake about to strike, screaming as loudly as his huge lungs and pissant-sized brain would let him. You couldn't scare Millard, you had to confuse him, so I let his beak nearly touch my pants leg before I leaned over, grabbed his neck, and threw him into a snowbank in the shade of the front steps, which exploded like a down pillow. Millard came out, as always, a changed goose. Ignoring me, he waddled over to inspect my new ride as the two goats, Frick and Frack, loped around the corner of the house and came to a sudden halt when they found a vehicle they couldn't leap on or in.

I laughed all the way to the front door, which opened as always without a key, then stepped into the huge, silent emptiness. Solly lay on one of the leather couches, his prosthesis loose on the floor, lying, dead or wounded, a man of scattered parts. I had a flash from the old days in the bush. Then he lifted his arm from his face, stared at me as if I were a stranger, and he a stranger to himself. Then he slowly sat up.

"Six thousand square feet of living space," I said, once again marveling at the spotless house filled with modern art and expensive furniture, "all dressed up and nowhere to go. Hell, this place needs a woman's touch—cocktail franks and clam dip, martinis, green onions wrapped in cream cheese and thin pastrami slices— yeah, you need a serious woman and a really serious party before the snow sticks."

"All the serious women are working too hard," Solly said, "and all the parties are the same, so fuck it." Then he hopped over to the raked glass walls that flanked the front door, waving out at the fine afternoon in our view. "Someday, my son, this will all be yours." Then he paused, staring at the van. "What the fuck is that?"

"Norman's idea of a joke," I said.

"Jesus, C.W., I ran away from San Francisco in one of those in seventy-eight, took off with a bunch of freaks, traveling light. Sixty thousand dollars, twenty pounds of meth crystal, and a Colt Commander in a backpack. Those kids would have shit if they knew . . . I finally bought the van from them down in Taos. By god those were the days . . ." Solly drove nothing these days but 7 series BMWs sporting handicapped stickers. "What the hell is it like?"

"Interesting," I said, walking over to join him. "As far as I can tell, the fucker will do a wheel-stand in first, second, and third gear."

"What about fourth?"

"I haven't been in fourth yet."

"That fucking Norman," he said. "How the hell did you ever get mixed up with him? You've got some strange friends, Sonny."

"Thanks, counselor," I said. "And I got involved with him some years ago in a drug deal, then some time later in some hassle about fish."

"Oh," Solly said as if this were news to him. He was watching Millard stroke his beak on the chrome bumper of the van.

"What the hell's he doing?" I asked. "Sharpening his beak?"

"Falling in love with his own reflection," Solly said quietly, touching his aging image on the glass wall. "What's that writing across the front?"

"*La Gloria Azul,*" I said, and Solly nodded.

"The Blue Glory. Shit." Then he turned to me suddenly as if he had something really important to say. "Geese don't sharpen their beaks, you turkey," he said solemnly. "Let's have a drink." Then hopped over to his lower leg and strapped it back on and led me into the kitchen wing, which covered the whole first floor above the three-car garage.

"How'd you beat me out here?" I asked.

"Fucker canceled lunch on me," he answered, "and this

weather is playing hell with my stump. Phantom aches and pains."

"Too bad."

"For him. I charge double for missed appointments," he said, reaching for the really good Scotch. He poured two neat tots into crystal shot glasses.

"Your clients put up with that sort of shit?"

"They beg for it," Solly said, grinning. "Makes them think I can move mountains."

"Or juries," I said, sipping the Scotch, which tasted like pure gold.

"That, too, and makes federal prosecutors eat out of my shorts."

"Can't you?"

"Given the proper motivation . . . You like the Scotch?" I nodded as coolly as I could. "They only make a hundred cases a year," he said. "One hundred sixty-five dollars a bottle."

"Not even an hour's work for a big-shot lawyer like you."

Solly laughed like a man whose whole life had been one big joke on the world as he picked up the bottle and a .300 Weatherby custom-built rifle leaning against the sink and carried them toward the front door and the deck, where he did his serious business, as serious as he could stand behind the laughter.

"So what the hell am I doing here, Solly?" I asked as he poured the second Scotch.

"Just wanted to see you before you took off, man. We don't see each other enough these days."

"Hell, I'm just another one of the trolls down in your fucking legal morgue," I said. "Move me into your house and I'll really keep you company. Me and a couple of those lovelies from the office. You could wax nostalgic while I wax their thighs so their cunt hair doesn't show in a string bikini . . ."

But Solly was someplace else, couldn't even come back long enough to complain about my sexist crudity, something he was usually careful to do. He picked up the Weatherby, adjusted the variable scope, then jacked a round into the chamber. Quick as a flash, Solly fired an offhand round at his favorite target: a five-gallon can of water at five hundred yards. He was a marvel. I never saw him miss; I never saw him hunt; just shoot like an angel with god's eye.

"Remember when we were coming out of the bush that time?" Solly asked suddenly.

"There was only one time, man."

"Remember that kid in your squad, skinny black kid with glasses, the one that got caught on the trip wire?"

"Willie Williams," I said.

"Never saw anything like that. He nearly turned white when he felt it catch, but he stood still while you dug out the mine. Never will forget that, Sonny, never saw that kind of trust . . ."

"He was just stoned," I said, "smoking hash right through the number."

Solly reached down to scratch his calf, where I knew he had a piece of jungle rot that wouldn't go away. "What ever happened to him?"

"Did his time and went home," I lied. "Why?"

"No reason. Just thinking about it the other day." Then Solly paused. "You know, I knew this Pines asshole in Vietnam . . ."

"What?"

"Oh, nothing, I just ran across him once in the bush. Some sort of REMF brass . . . He's probably still got connections in D.C., but you know I've still got some favors owed back there, too. If you need any help, give me a call. The FBI is not going to like you nibbling around the fringe of their case."

"They never liked me in the first place," I said.

"They must know what they're doing." Solly grinned suddenly, his teeth flashing in the sunlight, then slapped me on the shoulder. "You watch your ass out there, old buddy. I'm not crazy about this case. Are you?"

"Luckily, I'm just crazy."

"And getting worse every year," Solly said, not laughing. "So you stay in touch, okay? Try to check in every other day."

"Yes, Captain Rainbolt, sir," I said, but didn't bother to salute.

"What's first?"

"Snowy Lake," I said.

Snowy Lake lay north of Meriwether toward the Canadian border, one of those small Montana towns that seem to live on snow four months of the year and cocaine the rest. Meriwether wasn't exactly a Methodist summer camp, but Snowy Lake played in the big leagues. I didn't know a soul in town these days and given the preponderance of DEA agents and informants, I didn't want to.

So I stopped at the local K mart, bought a cheap suit and some short-sleeve white shirts and thin ties, then dropped the van at the Snowy Lake airport, rented an anonymous gray sedan with Solly's corporate gold card, and drove to Snowy Lake to check into the Powderhorn Lodge, looking as bureaucratic and mysterious as I could.

Except for brief forays into the bar, where I drank cheap vodka like a cop but overtipped wildly, I stayed in my room for the first couple of days, neither shaving nor using deodorant after my frequent showers. Then I cleaned up my act, put a smile on my face, and went to work late one evening just as the bartender, a pleasant youngish woman named Mel, a professional ski bum, was about to close the bar. Given the way I had tipped, her bartender's conscience wouldn't let her close me out.

I had two quick ones while she cleaned up as I watched her until she became convinced that my next move was to either hit on her or ask where to buy cocaine.

Just as she walked over to lay down *last call*, I said, "You know, it's a real pleasure to watch a pro break down a bar and get everything ready for the day shift. That used to be one of my favorite things."

"Thanks," she said, then asked, "You a bartender?"

"Wish to hell I'd never stopped."

"You got time for one more . . ."

"How's your martini?" I asked.

"World-class," she said proudly. Then added, "When I want it to be."

"Have one with me?" I asked, and she looked at me for a long time. "Mel, you know what I do for a living, right?" I said, tearing off the cheap tie. "But I haven't always been a cop. I used to be a fair-to-middling bartender and I'm off the clock tonight then outa here tomorrow. This undercover junk is the shits."

"Okay," she said, trusting her bartender's instinct, long honed in ski lodges around the West. Or so I learned after the second martini. Copper Mountain, Vail, Angelfire, Red River, and half a dozen others. She'd come north from Telluride in her late thirties, looking for easier slopes and more polite customers. But the Canadians were about to drive her insane, and she was considering marriage, again, perhaps children, maybe college down in Missoula, looking like a woman facing forty with no place to go, a woman who had chosen the fantasy of powdered fun over the middle-class fantasy of security. It's all an illusion, though. The bear of real life is waiting for everybody. She'd had her time in the sun, on the slopes, around the bars, and now she'd probably make some decent man a terrific partner, a man who could see past the frivolity to the hard, lovely core of her character.

I wasn't that man, though.

At some point later she closed the lounge door, placated the bar manager, then pried my recipe for the Dead Solid Perfect Martini, which I had perfected years ago with friends down in Austin, from my reluctant fingers. A frozen glass, a swish of vermouth, a smidgen of olive juice, a smudge of jalapeño, a cocktail onion, and good gin washed over ice until it smokes in the humid air.

Well, we weren't in Texas, so the humidity wasn't right and we couldn't make smoke, but we had a couple anyway. Then made a pitcherful and retired to my room.

If you've never done this, you don't know what it's like. It's not about sex, it's about stories. She tells you the one about the drunk who wandered into her bar with the end of a ski pole stuck in his thigh and demanded a dozen schnapps before he'd go to the hospital to have it cut out. Then you tell the one about skiing through the lift line at Eldora, over the snowbanks around the parking lot, and into the side of a pickup truck. Moving. Hit it so hard I knocked the driver out. And so it goes on. Making friends.

Then about three o'clock, slightly drunk with a wonderfully surprising clarity, Mel looked up and asked the right question.

"So what do you want?" she said, her round face glowing with intelligence around her smile. "Obviously not my no longer nubile body, though you might be welcome to it another time, more than welcome in fact, but for tonight, Mr. Sughrue, what do you really want?"

"You remember the woman who disappeared from here last month?"

"Sarita, little Sarah," she mused. "Sure. She was a beauty. Not just for her age. She said she was fifty-one, and I believed her. I'm sure you know how unusual it is for women of different social and economic classes to tell the truth about their ages . . ." She paused. "Okay, man, I went to college, too. Lots . . . Lots of times." Then she laughed and poured us another martini. "She wasn't beautiful for fifty-one. She was just flat fucking beautiful. Great cheekbones. Terrific skin. And wrinkles in all the right places . . ." I must have raised an eyebrow because Mel shook her head at me as if I were a stupid child. "Laugh lines, asshole. Smile crinkles. A sad, thoughtful little crease between her eyes. And unlike her rat turd of a husband and all the other rich turds around him, she was unfailingly polite to the help. Even when she wasn't in public. She was a true aristocrat. Wynona told me . . ."

"Wynona?"

"Wynona Jones. With a 'y.' She was the maid for their condo. Secretly," Mel said, leaning over the coffee table, "I think maybe she knew something about the . . . you know, Sarita taking off . . ."

"Why do you say 'taking off'?"

"Anybody with a lick of sense would know that her husband wouldn't pay a dime to get her back, and nobody that stupid could get next to her."

"Did this Wynona Jones say anything?"

"No, but she took off the same day, you know, and I knew

she and Sarita had gotten to be pals or something, you know, but it wasn't like she disappeared or anything. She gave notice a month or so before, said she had a gig down in Aspen, hopping tables at a fake British pub called the Quirky Arms, said her baby would be closer to his dad down there," she said, then paused again and reached to touch my cheek, her breasts swinging heavily under the thin fabric of her uniform shirt. "Why the fuck am I telling you this?"

"An honest face?" I suggested.

"Not that honest," she whispered, then leaned over to kiss me. Her lips moved against my mouth. "I'll bet you were trouble when you were young," she whispered, then moved away. "Oh, stop that," she said to herself.

"Well, not that much trouble," I said, and Mel laughed without rancor. "What did the FBI have to say about this?"

"The fucking FBI, man. You must be kidding," she said, then picked up her martini, nuzzled it happily. "Shit, you may have something here. Can you copyright a drink?"

"I don't think so."

"Fucking government. They get everything assbackward."

I draped my arm around her shoulder. She cuddled into the curve. "So what about the FBI?"

"Lemme tell you something, Mr. Sughrue . . ."

"I wish you'd stop calling me 'Mr. Sughrue.' "

"Fuck you."

"Please."

"Oh, quit it," she said, giggling. "Just quit it. How come one minute you're this cool, regular middle-aged guy, then the next minute you come on like Joe College?"

"Women make me stupid."

"Well, that's a beginning," she said, then kissed me again quickly, softly. "So let me tell you how it is here. Some of the help, they're locals, but most of us have been around ski slopes since we were kids. Everybody either knows everybody else, or knows somebody everybody else knows. And there are always lots of drugs. And rich people. As you know, Mr. Sughrue, that kind of shit draws cops like tumblebugs to cow shit. Most of the help here, they gave up drugs years ago. We get high on downhill shit and beer. So nobody even gave a weather report to the dumbfuck FBI. Never did, never will. What the fuck do you care for, anyway? You're off the clock, right?"

"Right. But this Wynona with a 'y' left about the same time?"

"Just a fucking coincidence, Mr. Sughrue," Mel said, then stood up to stretch. "If I ask you for a hug, can you promise not to attack me?"

"If you'll stop calling me 'Mr. Sughrue.' "

"Ain't worth it," she said without hesitation, then grabbed my hands and jerked me to my feet and hugged me until my backbone crackled like corn popping. "You're leaving tomorrow?"

"Have to go."

"Right. Off to Aspen looking for Wynona Jones, right?"

"Nope. Just back to the desk."

"Tell her I said hi when you find her. And come looking for me sometime, all right?" she whispered, then kissed me again, hard and hopeless and wonderful, released me and headed for the door, where she paused for her exit line. "Wynona drives an old tan VW Beetle with Idaho plates, Blaine County plates."

"Blaine County?"

"Sun Valley, my friend. I think maybe she even grew up there. And Mr. Pines strikes me as the kind of asshole who would have a house there . . ." Then Mel smiled, tired, happy, half-drunk, and said, "You really going to come looking for me?"

"First chance I get."

"Mr. Sughrue, it ain't polite to lie to your friends, new or old," she said, "but thanks for at least taking the trouble to lie."

"No trouble," I said.

But she was gone, leaving me with the warm taste of her mouth, a lipstick-smudged martini glass, and half a pitcher of oblivion. As I drank it, I rode the cable channels looking for something I couldn't quite find.

If you've got enough money, say five million dollars, I suppose Aspen can seem like an ordinary mountain town, but I didn't. It pains me to have to even talk about a town where the help can't afford to live. During the season, buses hauled bartenders, cooks, dishwashers, and maids from as far away as Glenwood Springs. Not my kind of town at all.

But I got there as quickly as the laws of physics, biology, and pharmacology would let me. I only stopped for calls of nature, gas tank refills, then once to dig around in Norman's glove box. Treasure time. A bindle of crank and the same weight of cocaine. Also detailed directions about how to open the false bottom of the propane bottle that fed the stove and kept the refrigerator cooling and concealed an ounce each of both magical motion powders. So I made good time. Couldn't have beaten a private jet but I gave the commercial flights a run for their money.

I also must admit that I had a little fun, running hard through the night, playing all of Norman's old tapes—the Stones, the Buffalo Springfield, the Doors; music I hadn't bothered with in years, memories I'd forgotten to remember—and searching the skips for mad prophets of doom.

I especially loved the guy who tried to convince me that aliens had landed on earth and were fucking our good Christian women. It was an opinion shared by some of my former customers at the Hell Roaring, but on other nights most of them thought women were aliens, even the women.

One of the history profs from the college across the river, though, usually maintained that we were historically and politically incorrect. Women, he claimed, *were* from Mars, granted, but men came from Juárez, and children from Hell. But what the hell did he know? His children were truly monsters, sure, but he couldn't find Mars in an empty sky, had only been to Juárez on a weekend pass after basic at Bliss, where, he told as truth, he had been humping a whore who wore white high heels and a bra, and when he offered her fifty cents to take off her bra, she considered the offer, then wanted to know if he had the change. He said he laughed so hard that his erection went back across the border without him. I suspect the facts are slightly different.

In fact, he had stolen the phrase from me, and I had lifted it whole cloth from Corporal Franklin Ignacio Vega, my M-60 gunner, one night when we were smoking Thai stick in the hooch. When he finished his riff, I asked the Super Nacho where he called home.

"I'm just an asshole from El Paso," he whispered, chuckling deep in his giant chest, then filled it with smoke.

But that's another story.

My early take on Aspen: getting there is not just half the fun, it's the only fun there is there.

Or so I told Solly when I called from the road. I *had* promised to stay in touch.

"What the hell are you going to do in Aspen?"

I told him.

"What makes you think this kid's got anything to do with Sarita Pines?" he asked in his lawyer's voice. "I mean all you've got is the drunken ramblings of some bartender. What are you thinking about?"

"Now I know something they don't, Solly, and don't fucking ask me what I'm thinking about. You know better than that. That's not how I work. Questions and answers don't mean shit to me. Just another chance for people to lie. And lies don't help. If I could just get half the people I talk to to tell the truth, I'd be a rich and famous private eye, instead of an unemployed bartender sweeping up your leavings . . .

"And what the hell do you care? I'm not working for you, man. You're just a funnel for the money and a place to lay the fucking blame . . ." I paused for breath.

"Norman left you a bunch of crank in that van, didn't he?"

"Some Colombian boogie dust, too, man."

"Where the hell are you, Sughrue?"

"Somewhere in the middle of Wyoming. I don't know and don't much give a damn," I said, lying for no good reason.

Actually, I was standing at the only pay telephone in Jeffrey City, Wyoming, staring at Split Rock and the geologic roil of the Rattlesnake Mountains on the eastern horizon while the wind tried to blow the remains of my hair through the back of my head.

"What's the name of that place in Aspen?"

I told him that, too.

"I'll check into it."

"Gee, thanks."

"You fucking call me, Sughrue, when you get there, and before you start asking questions."

"I'll try to remember that, sir."

"And maybe you should get some sleep, Sonny."

"Maybe you should kiss my enlisted ass, sir," I shouted at him, and slammed the telephone back into its cradle. Of course I missed the cradle and heard his last words, faint and far away as the receiver dangled in the stiff wind:

"You need a keeper, Sughrue."

Some guys never got over being officers, but I wasn't sure that gave me the right to shout at and hang up on my second best friend in the world, however misplaced his worry might be. I almost called back to apologize, but when I looked around, the knife edge of the wind had scraped the sky to a pale autumn blue. Not a cloud in the sky. I cracked a beer, drove to the Split Rock roadside turnout, then tried to nap on the backseat of the van.

When I woke out of the nameless terrors of a dream I couldn't remember, some dream that recently decided to occupy the rest of my life like an invading army, a slick, dangerous sweat covered my shoulders, neck, and back, and dead Turks had camped for months in my mouth. Only fifteen minutes had ticked off the clock but I woke up with the strange sensation that I wanted to kill somebody. Or perhaps already had. No details from the dream remained, though, just the miasma lurking.

I never had much cared for other people's advice, but I tried not to be too crazy all the time so I stopped in Rawlins, checked into a motel room just to brush my teeth and take a shower, then had a steak and a drink, and one thing led to another.

When I carried my hangover to the van the next morning, at least I smelled like good whiskey instead of bad dreams.

Thus I came to Aspen, Colorado, where just getting there is all the fun there is.

The Quirky Arms reeked of big, bad money, old cherry wood and black walnut sparkling with silver filigree, a lot of money wasted to ape some West End London club here in the Rocky Mountain West. The place suited the town, rich with fake gentility, phony fortunes, and serious foolishness. It also suited my bad mood perfectly. I leaned my foot on the gleaming brass rail of the bar and ordered a can of Pabst just to watch the jacketed bartender curl his lip, then took a pint of piss-warm Bass ale to keep from being thrown out on the seat of my faded Levi's.

Once my eyes adjusted to all the dark wood and shadows, the first thing I saw was an alarm system designed for a bank, a Constable and a Turner hanging at either end of the bar, and the rest of my day-drinking pals. I hadn't missed the dress code by much.

Except for me and a mumbling drunk in an outfit by Orvis at the end of the bar, the place was empty. The other customers sat around a table at the back. The five guys might as well have worn signs. They affected expensive cowboy hats ringed by bands of exotic feathers or good Navaho or Hopi silver. Silver, turquoise, and coral bracelets cradled their Rolexes. Their boots probably cost more than a good used pickup truck, and the trims on the five identical drooping, black moustaches probably cost more than a year's supply of haircuts for me.

Of course, these weren't the kind of people who actually paid for a haircut or a trim with anything as mundane as money. I suspected that Aspen possessed a number of hairdressers with very happy noses.

Who was I to judge, though? I still checked my nose for the white rim in the rearview mirror before climbing out of whatever ride I was driving. Of course, that was more habit than regular usage. In fact, until Kathleen tossed her bindle on the parking lot to cover the broken toilet, I hadn't seen much coke in years. My old partner used to have a steady supply, but it usually disappeared before I made it to his house. So who was I to complain that these guys dealt in tons and bought and sold government officials as if they were Monopoly properties across three or four countries? Any other time, I might have tried to be their friend. They looked and sounded like an interesting group.

Three of the guys, the two great big ones and a flea-sized one, spoke Tex-Mex, the Border Spanish I remembered from my South Texas youth. The other two, average-sized, looked more Arab than Spanish, and spoke with accents perfectly suited to the decor. As for me, I seemed to be racing along on a wave of crank and coke and hunches. So instead of trying to be their friend, I stepped over to the table and said:

"Any of you *cholos* know my friend, Sarita Cisneros Pines, from El Paso?"

That got their attention and stopped the conversation dead.

Fiddles murmured discreetly and another day drinker limped into the bar, his cane thumping on the hardwood. But nobody spoke. The little guy glanced behind me but I didn't turn around. Didn't need to. The customer's reflection stood clear in the glass over a shooting print. A three-piece suit leaning on his cane, he carefully lit a huge cigar. He didn't look like trouble. Unless he was a lawyer.

"No? Maybe my information was fucked," I said.

The Chicano with the gut said, "Maybe *you're* fucked, my friend."

The little guy touched the big guy's arm, then said, "I've met Mrs. Pines several times. But why do you ask?"

"I'm looking for her, *pulguita*."

"Little Flea," he said with an ugly smile. "That's funny, man, but you don't look like a Mexican to me."

"*Tejano*," I confessed.

The little guy nodded as if that explained many things he had been wondering about for a long time. "I hear a lot of people are looking for her," he added, tenting his ringed fingers in front of his face.

"I'm the only one who isn't a cop," I said.

One of the Middle Eastern types laughed with a quick snort. A tiny white rock shot out of his nose and bounced across the polished walnut of the table. The little guy casually crushed it with a crystal ashtray.

"Then why are you looking for her?" he asked, sudden interest in his dark eyes.

"Actually, I'm looking for an old friend of ours," I said. "Wynona Jones. Mrs. Pines is a friend of hers."

Behind me the bartender filled a glass with the tinkle of ice, the splash of whiskey.

"Sorry, my friend, but that is a name with which I am not familiar."

"She's supposed to be working here," I said.

"The help, man, they come and go," he said. "I'll have to check the files." He turned to the Chicano on his left, the one with the flat belly and even flatter nose. "Chato, why don't you let Mr. . . . I missed your name, sir?"

"Sonny Sughrue," I said for no good reason.

"A good Texas name," he said, reaching out his hand. "I'm Dagoberto Reyna." I shook it. Unlike most people lately, the little guy was familiar with my family name and pronounced it correctly.

"Chato will take you back to the office and let you look at our employment files and recent applications. That's the best I can do."

"Thanks," I said, thinking, *Oh, boy, the private investigator's favorite moment on a complex case: a trap*. I could barely restrain my joy. Whatever happened, I was bound to learn something back in the office. "I really appreciate your help."

"No trouble," the little guy said, then leaned back in his chair.

Chato stood up. It took a long time. He jerked his chin toward the back of the bar. It was a chin you wouldn't want to hit with anything smaller than a two-by-four. And his nose was so flat you hardly needed bother hitting it at all. The Airweight began to feel good nestled at the small of my back under my vest.

As we pushed through the swinging doors into the kitchen, I heard Reyna making his apologies and goodbyes to the two swarthy dudes with Eton accents. Chato led me through the great kitchen, the kind of kitchen coke dealers always seem to buy when they go into the restaurant business, then down a long dim hallway to a steel door. He even held it open for me, polite devil.

Fresh produce had been stacked against the far wall of the large room and a bank of file cabinets stood behind the door. Chato stepped over, opened the top file drawer, and lifted out a 10mm

Glock, the automatic pistol of choice among the fast crowd these days.

"Shit, Chato, this is not the office," I said. "What is this? And what's that? A gun? Hell, you're big enough to hunt bear with a willow switch. Kiss my ass, I'm really disappointed in you with this chicken-shit gun crap."

"You put your hands up, *puta*, then you can kiss my ass," he said.

"I'm very sorry for you, Chato," I said sincerely, and he looked properly confused. "I guess you're one of those big slow guys who couldn't lick your lips in a real fight."

"Fuck you, man, I went six rounds with Tex Cobb once," he said.

"That what happened to your nose? Couldn't fall down quick enough?"

Chato smiled happily. This was what he wanted in the first place. He set the Glock down, doubled up his fists, and shuffled toward me. When he got far enough from the automatic, I stuck the Airweight in his face.

"I'm sure you know the drill, Chato."

"*Chingadero*," he said, "I knew you were a fucking cop."

"Just assume the position, asshole, or they'll be serving romaine and pepper-belly brains tonight."

"What the fuck," he said, resigned but relaxed, a man who knew he had a legion of expensive lawyers standing behind him.

Once he got settled, leaning hard into the wall, his back to me and his legs spread as far as his designer jeans allowed, he released a bored sigh and said, "Let's get this shit over, *pendejo*."

I took a step and tried to drop-kick his nuts into the back of his throat. From the sounds he made, it almost worked. Chato hit the floor on his nose in a puddle of pain and puke. He made so much noise that I missed the sound of the door.

The other big Chicano reached around and took the Airweight out of my hand as if I were a child, then spun me around, covering me with my own pistol. True humiliation. Maybe Solly was right, maybe I needed a keeper. Certainly I felt that way. I knew what waited down the dark barrel: wadcutter slugs reverse-loaded in front of a Plus P amount of power waited to knock chunks of my flesh, blood, bone, and nerve endings all over the strawberries. I also didn't think the hunting knife held loosely in Sr. Reyna's right hand was there for decoration.

"You fucking Texans," he said, tightening his hand on the handle and waving the blade like a snake at my face, "you're always so tough with your guns, so *macho*. This is a man's weapon," he continued, spinning the knife, "*el cuchillo*, a man's weapon. You can kill a man with a gun and never see his eyes. What was it they supposedly said at Bunker Hill? 'Don't shoot until you see the whites of their eyes'? Fuck that, man, I'm one of those Mexican *corbardias* with a blade and we're going to see what sort of *cojones* a native-born Texican carries between his legs."

"Actually, Dagoberto, I minored in Cultural Anthropology over in Boulder, so I already knew all that shit about knives and guns . . ."

"What was your major, man?"

"Literature."

"Figures."

"Beside, I was born in Deming, New Mexico."

"Deming?" he said. "What a fucking hole." He paused for a moment. "Shit, man, I don't think I ever killed anybody from Deming." He turned to the guy with my pistol. "Can you think of anybody, David?"

"There was that guy with the airplane, *hermano*," he answered, "but you just fucked his wife and cut him up a little bit. In the pool hall down in Columbus. I don't think he died. If he did, it wasn't in the papers, so it don't count."

Dagoberto actually scratched his head. "What was that fucker's name?"

"Johnny Carson," David said.

Dagoberto looked at me. "You know how it is, man. Somebody, he's got the same name as somebody else you know and you never can remember it."

"Sure," I said. "But a lot of people remember my name and they all know that I'm here."

"We'll make it look like an accident. No problem," he said, smiling happily, "a really bad car wreck, *gringo*."

I always knew I'd be killed by a cliché.

Then somebody rapped sharply on the door.

"Who the fuck is that?" Dagoberto asked David.

He shook his head and opened the door. Somebody asked if this was the men's room, then David grunted as if he had been shot, staggered across the room, turning as he fell into a stack of strawberry flats. I didn't bother with my piece but darted for the Glock. But it was over before I picked it up.

Out of the corner of my eye I saw Solly sweep into the room, twirling his knobby cane like a mad kendo master. Dagoberto had a cracked collarbone, a broken wrist, and a knot the size and color of a rotten plum in the center of his forehead before I picked up the automatic.

Solly looked at me, puffed on his cigar, then took it out of his mouth and held it up for inspection. Not a tooth mark, not a single flake of ash lost.

"Next time, Sughrue, remember to call me," he said, grinning. "I'm not just your friend, I'm also your lawyer."

I don't know exactly how Solly did it, but his Lawyer Rainbolt act worked like a snake charmer's flute. First, he plucked Dagoberto's fangs with laughter by pointing out that he had been taken by a one-footed old man. Which was of course true, but as Solly kindly pointed out, his many years had given him much time to practice kendo. And Solly was really sorry to have hurt Dagoberto, but age had slowed him so that he couldn't take a chance on the reflexes of a younger, quicker man. Perhaps a tequila and a toot would lift everybody's spirits, he suggested, a motion to which even a groaning Chato agreed.

So the *patrones* disappeared into the real office like *hermanos* while the hired hands headed for the employees' john to tend their wounds.

A few minutes later, I had filled a sink with ice where Chato sat in his shorts while David cleaned up his face and I flushed strawberry seeds out of the Airweight with hot water.

"Not much of a piece, man," David said. "You might not have stopped my *cunado* with that peashooter. I seen Chato take a thirty-eight round in the chest, then break this fucking cop's

nose, cheekbone, and jaw. Shit, then he drove both of them to
the emergency room."

I dumped the hand-loaded rounds into my hand. "The cop
didn't shoot him with one of these," I said, "that was his first
mistake."

"The second?"

"He only shot him once," I said.

"You were in Vietnam," he said. It wasn't a question. "My
father used to tell me that same thing. He was a *veterano*. Not
like you, though, man, like the dude in the suit with the hard
eyes and the bullshit smile."

"I only did six months," I said. "Solly was there forever . . ."

"*Es verdad*, man," he said. "Now let's see about that drink."

Chato shifted his weight, rattling the ice, but decided he'd
had all the fun he could stand.

It didn't take too long for Dagoberto to come to the same
conclusion, so we made dinner plans before David took him to
the hospital, then Solly and I looked for another place to drink.

The streets were fairly empty on this late afternoon in the
shoulder season—the summer had gone and the snow hadn't
arrived yet—and by the time we walked to Norman's ride, we
had decided to catch the last of the sunlight shimmering among
the aspen up toward Independence Pass, so we grabbed a six-
pack of Coors and headed south, Solly behind the wheel, looking
for whatever nostalgia Norman had cached therein.

"That was pretty dumb," Solly said a few miles up the road
as he eased the van around the curves over the white rush of the
Roaring Fork.

"If you're looking for 'Thanks,' Lawyer Rainbolt, I'll be happy
to say it." I let him sit on that, then added, "Of course, then I'd
have to point out that I didn't ask for your fucking help." Then
I paused, laughed, and said, "Next thing you know, we'll be out
of the car, trying to kick each other's ass."

"I'd be sorry about that, Sonny," he said without turning to
look at me.

"You won't have the advantage of sympathy," I said, "or surprise. This time."

Solly drove silently for a few minutes, then slammed on the brakes, shouting something at me. But he had his own troubles almost immediately. The van slid into a turnout over the river, shuddering on hard springs across the stony dirt until the right front tire dropped over the unprotected edge. On my side.

Solly and I sat there for a moment, silent, then I rolled my window open and stared down the cliff to the rocky avalanche of water ninety feet below.

"Can I get out on your side?" I said.

Then we laughed so hard we nearly rocked the van over the precipice into the cold river below.

After we got out of the car and stopped howling, Solly cracked two cans of beer and brushed the tears out of his eyes.

"Sughrue, Sughrue, what the fuck is wrong with you?"

"My life lacks reason," I said, "and rhyme, too, said C. W. Sughrue."

That set us off again. They say laughter makes you live longer. I twisted a doobie and we added years to our lives. And some scenery to the neurons firing.

We were just a few miles from a town I found particularly offensive, a chancre on my notion of home, but that few miles was enough in the Mountain West. We watched the shadow of the western ridges slice through the fluttering aspen, sat on gray-green rocks giving back the sun's heat, all under a high-altitude blue wash of a sky. But we couldn't be old hippie tourists forever.

"Thanks," I finally said after we had stopped laughing again, laughing about some jibe that short-term memory was bound to lose, "for pulling me out of the scrape. But it's insulting for you to dog my tracks like that, Solly."

"What would you have done?"

"Doesn't matter, man. I'd rather be dead than suffer that kind of insult."

"That's dumb."

"Of course," I said, "but let's get down to the really smart

part, okay? What if I had been looking at the employment
files? What if I could've found this Wynona Jones and she knew
something? Remember, man, you've got major law enforcement
hordes out there searching for Mrs. Pines. They've got manpower,
computer wizardry, and access to shit I can't even imagine . . ."

"I can get that for you."

"Fuck that. If they could find her that way, she would be
found by now. So I'll make a deal with you," I said.

Solly thought about that, then shook his gray-blond hair in
the shadowed light. "What deal?"

"I'll stay in touch better and you stop dogging me."

"Fuck, Sonny, you won't stay in touch and you'll just keep
stepping in shit. How's that a deal?"

"It's the only one you're going to get."

He didn't take it well, but he took it. He also let me back the
van off the cliffside. As we headed back down the highway, I
asked:

"What were you shouting about just before you tried to kill
us?"

"Don't be such a hard-ass."

"It's a shitty job, but somebody's got to do it," I said.

"Proves my point," he managed to say before we started laughing again.

Solly went home to his telephone, computer, and Washington,
D.C., contacts. I went to Sun Valley in search of Wynona Jones.
We both hoped we were both right.

During his brief social moment with Dagoberto Reyna, Solly
discovered that Dagoberto didn't really know Sarita Pines, but
he did know her husband, in that social way that rich people
along the border all know each other. Dagoberto also knew Joe
Don Pines politically. He said he had contributed to Joe Don's
unsuccessful runs for state offices—governor, state senator, railroad commissioner, and most recently for the Texas Board of
Agriculture—so he had supped expensively with Joe Don. Dagoberto also let Solly examine the employee files, where he found
no record of Wynona Jones.

"They weren't really going to hurt you," Solly said as I dropped him at the Aspen airport so he could grab his borrowed private Learjet ride back to Meriwether.

"I may be crazy, Solly, but I'm not stupid, and this is not the first time I've played this game," I said.

"Maybe you're out of practice," he said. "Anyway, I believed him."

"That's your problem," I said, "not mine."

Then I drove west all night into the broken-back Jack Morman heart of Idaho, then turned north toward the smell of money.

It didn't take me long to find out that whatever kin or friends Wynona Jones might have once had in or around Sun Valley or Ketchum, nobody knew her name now. Except the driver's license bureau, but the people at the address the bureau had in Hailey had never heard of her. I spoke on the telephone to a lot of Joneses who all said "Wynona who?," then hung up.

I tried combing the bars for somebody who might remember her but I was out of my territory now. Except for one drunken, stoned trip to the Hemingway grave in Ketchum back in the early seventies just after I finished my thesis at Colorado—I had to graduate to get loose of the Defense Intelligence Agency and get on with my life—I had never been there before and hadn't paid much attention to where I was. This time I did, so I dredged up the right real estate broker and went to work.

If it sometimes seems that Aspen was home to half of the mediocre actors in the world, then Sun Valley looked like the home of ten thousand crooked brokers, bankers, greenmail goons, and assorted gangsters. But maybe that wasn't the right explanation. Maybe only a Republican tax expert could explain that. I just couldn't understand what sort of people could afford a three-million-dollar vacation home to use two months out of the year.

When I finally found the right real estate broker, one Rose Rosenbloom, a not too badly parched widow, she said that was what the Pines vacation house had cost. Three million dollars' worth of smoked glass, stonework, redwood, and formed concrete. It sat on five acres above the Elkhorn golf course, and it just barely fit. Rose, who claimed to be in the business just for gossip and fun, was happy to point it out with a diamond-studded hand fifteen years older than her face. We were drifting from one

$150,000 condo to another on the basis of a telephone call to check up on me with Solly's office. Maybe she *was* just in the business for fun. She didn't care that I was a "lookie-loo" or respond to my hints that my money might be in cash. Until late that afternoon.

Over mediocre martinis at The Lodge, where I'd taken a room, she gave me the real skinny on the marriage of convenience between Sarita Cisneros and Joe Don Pines: he was just the face; Sarita had the real money, Mexican money from her relatives on the other side of the border, money that had fled the devaluation of the peso in the early eighties.

Sipping the third martini, Rose lifted her watery but still sharp blue eyes to stare at me and propped her chin among her diamonds. It was a good act. Holding her chin in the air knocked ten years off her face and her hand blocked my view of the fine network of scars along her neck.

"Who are you, Mr. Sughrue? I mean really," she said with the sort of sincerity one only finds in gin.

"Retired military," I lied.

"You weren't an officer," she murmured. "I've fucked enough retired brass out here to start my own military establishment."

"Senior master sergeant," I said. "Did my thirty."

"What kind of outfit?"

"I did it all when I was a kid," I said, which was sort of true. I'd served three different hitches between various stints playing football at junior colleges that didn't really care what my name was or what sort of eligibility I had worn out or where. Then Vietnam changed all that. "But mostly I ran NCO clubs."

"Ah-ha, so you do have a nest egg, in cash, right? You know, my husband left me a place up Warm Springs; it's not near the golf course and it's not too big, but for cash, we could perhaps work something out. You understand?" Maybe I didn't answer quickly enough. Rose's face didn't fall, but she shook her head. "You're pretty good, Mr. Sughrue, but I've spent my adult life around phony assholes," she said sadly. "You're not exactly a phony but you're not telling me the truth."

"Jesus, I must be losing my touch," I said.

"You're just out of your league," she said. "My husband owned a piece of every book between Cleveland and Rochester. Every snooty bitch in town looks down on me, even the ones whose husbands either did federal time for white-collar crime or rolled over like piss-soaked puppies. My Jacob never saw the inside of a cell, never even had to hire a criminal lawyer. So don't be so hard on yourself. You're still young. Still pretty good, too. But out of your league."

"Thanks," I said, trying to get used to the sound of the word in my mouth.

"So what do you really want?"

"You know, Rose, in my business I'm not used to dealing with people who tell the truth. Maybe I've become cynical. Or maybe I got cynical and quit working the job. I don't know. But whatever," I said, "here goes."

When I finished, she stared at me. "I can't help you with the kid, but maybe I can get you in the Pines place. If you'll take me to dinner."

Once again I hesitated too long.

"Hey, soldier, if I wanted to get fucked, we wouldn't be here. We'd either be in bed or going our separate ways. I just want to go to dinner with an acceptable gentleman who isn't young enough to be one of my children, god love them." After the brief speech, she sighed and sipped her martini.

"It's a date," I said quickly. "Water your vases, Rosie, I'll bring flowers."

"Wonderful," she said, grinning. "Wear a tie, too, if you've got one."

I went out and bought one.

If our approach on the Pineses' three-million-dollar vacation hideaway had gone as well as our dinner, Rose and I would have found Sarita sitting in the cavernous living room just waiting to hear from her long-lost abnormal abandoned son, Norman. As it was, the Mexican housekeeper refused to let us inside for love or money, both of which we offered her; and the FBI swarmed all over us like butterflies on wet cow shit before we got to the end of the driveway.

I don't know how Rose got out of their custody, but she did, and I never saw her again. I got out by referring all questions to my lawyer and keeping my mouth shut. They really hated that. Special Agent in Charge Nicholas Cromwellington, one of those guys who looked like a hairy butthead who had tried to razor a part through his wiry curls, told me to get the fuck out of the state and never cross his sphere of influence again.

"Nickie," I said, leaning close enough to his ear to kiss it, which I did, "I love you, man, but until I break the law and you can charge me, I'm going to go or stay as it suits me, and you can't do a thing about it."

SAC Cromwellington's mouth tried to stop looking like his asshole but it didn't work.

"And if you bother me, remember that I've got liver cancer and I'm HIV positive from the last operation, and nothing to lose but a few years of really interesting pain and dying, so if you fuck with me, fella, I'll kill your family, your friends, and everybody you ever knew. Then I'll show you what revenge really means. So stay out of my hair, Nickie."

"Ah, ah, ah," he sputtered.

"If you even open your mouth to me, you homophobic turd, I'll spit in it." I hawked up a wad of phlegm worthy of Norman, puckered up like a redneck with a bad chew, but the Fibbie shut his mouth so tight he had to breathe through his colon.

God knows it was a cruel lie, but it wasn't exactly against the law, unless they could prove it. As I drove away from the county jail, Nickie looked like a SAC whose tie had finally strangled him. I laughed all the way to the next pay telephone, where I called Solly. I could tell he wanted to complain about how I stayed in touch, but he couldn't stop laughing. However, he finally promised to keep covering my ass.

I called Norman, thinking he might enjoy the story, at least get a laugh for his money. I was right. I could hear him shouting at Mary over the telephone. Then he got serious.

"You gonna find my mom?" he asked.

"You better believe it," I said. "It's personal now."

"That's good news," Norman said, then added, "You know,

Sughrue, you ain't just somebody works for me. You're my buddy. You need anything, call me. I ain't no fucking rich-shit lawyer, but I got some clout here and there."

"Thanks, Norman," I said. And meant it.

Well, hell, this private eye business isn't all sex and glory. Sometimes it's just pissant paperwork and bad hunches. Or good ones. Good or bad, they both take about the same long boring time.

Now that I had pissed off the FBI, worrying about what the local police and sheriff's departments thought about me seemed a terrific waste of time. In every state in the Union, law enforcement blotters are matters of public record. Of course, and with some reason, the cops hate that; but they particularly hate showing the reports to smart-ass private eyes. I didn't blame them, but I didn't let them off the legal hook, either.

It took three days' wading through three jurisdictions before I found it. Wynona's VW Beetle abandoned just beyond the confluence of the East Fork and the Wood River. Then another day at the Blaine County Courthouse to find out what it meant.

Joe Don Pines didn't actually own his vacation home; he just owned a major portion of the corporation that owned it, Overthrust Drilling and Production, Inc. Overthrust sounded more like a porno film company than an independent oil company that drilled holes and pumped oil. After a moment's thought, though, my first notion sounded closer to the bone of truth. But a telephone call to El Paso told me that OD&P was only a wholly owned subsidiary of something called Franklin Mountain Funds, which became particularly interesting when I discovered that FMF owned a property between Ketchum and Hailey up the East Fork of the Wood River. According to a Blaine County deputy's report, Wynona Jones's beige Volkswagen bug had been found abandoned, still running, just south of the East Fork Road.

Somehow I had to dump my FBI tail before I took a look at the house. They must have felt the budget crunch, too, because they only had one car to assign to my care and keeping. Anybody can dump a single car, but I felt like being fancy, plus I wanted to lose his car radio and his portable unit, too. I drove over to the Ketchum ranger station.

Several hours and many miles later—thanks to a bit of basic woodcraft and a Forest Service map, about the only service they provide that doesn't kiss the subsidized ass of the logging industry—the Fucking Bureaucratic Idiot was afoot, hopelessly lost, five miles up Uncle John's Gulch with four flat tires, to hell and gone out of radio range. Nothing I had done since kissing SAC Cromwellington on the ear had made me feel that fine. I laughed all the way back to town.

After my brief close-up view of Joe Don's ten-thousand-squarefoot vacation home, I couldn't imagine why he had bothered with another property so close to his mansion. The tax rolls listed its value at seven hundred fifty thousand, but who knew what that much money might buy fifteen miles out of town.

An unimproved dirt track led north off the East Fork Road up Hardy's Gulch through stunted cottonwoods and dwarf aspen into the sagebrush desert mountains. A locked gate blocked the access to Joe Don's place, but I worked the van back and forth across the old mining roads until I found a place to look down on the house.

When I glassed it from the ridgeline above, I saw that it caught three acres behind an adobe fence with good old-fashioned broken glass running along the top like sharp lace. The house was adobe, too, real adobe, not cheap stucco over cinder blocks, a real *adobe hacienda*, complete with a foliage-clotted patio and a dusty fountain, nestled in a narrow sagebrush canyon in Idaho. Actually, it looked pretty good from where I stood, white walls shining among the dusty shades of gray. Nothing moved down at the house. It looked so perfectly deserted I went back to town to get ready to move into the neighborhood.

When the van was filled with water, beer, bad food, and good books, including the joy of a new Stephen Greenleaf novel, I bought a roll of camouflage netting and drove back to settle in for the duration, the van backed into a dry gulch filled with bushy sage and sunshine. Unless you've spent a lot of time looking for people in the bush, you wouldn't believe how easy it is to hide in plain sight.

Although this kind of surveillance had never been my strong suit, I convinced myself that I had earned a few days out of the FBI's mind, a respite for my nose, and a vacation for my liver.

I lasted a full twenty-four hours before I began talking to myself, telling myself that I was operating on a hunch so slim that it verged on the edge of madness. I wondered if Hank Snow would understand or appreciate just how much trouble he had caused me. Or even care. The PI Driving Train Early Winter Blues.

During the first forty-eight hours nothing happened. Which was pure torture. At least the feds didn't find me. Or if they had, they were watching me from a satellite. That was okay with me. But late in the afternoon of the third day just as the sun fired the peaks of the Pioneer Mountains, I glassed the ridges around me and caught the flash of a large lens on the ridge on the south side of the East Fork. When I raised my spotting scope, I discovered that I wasn't the only one watching the adobe house.

Three men in desert camouflage had made camp at the head of a heavily timbered draw. It didn't look like the sort of place the feds would make camp. They would have had better equipment, too. And food. These guys had a ratty brown tent that had so many patched holes it didn't need to be camouflaged. And they seemed to be living on beans and tortillas. Also, I was almost certain that the FBI hadn't started carrying AK-47s or hired Chato to work for them.

Then I looked back at the adobe. The dusty fountain sputtered on like a hot garden hose, and a young woman had opened the French doors on the east side of the tiled patio. She sat in a leather director's chair, her face tilted to catch the last hour of the sun before it dropped behind the ridge above me. She had opened her blouse to nurse the small child in her arms. Occasionally, she touched the unoccupied breast as if it were tender. Her hair looked like golden wire in the sunlight, her skin as smoothly and lightly tanned as thick cream.

Wynona Jones.

Even if I hadn't found her with what almost seemed magic, I

still would have fallen simply in love with the sight of her, sunning herself like an ancient sybarite maiden, the lovely child happily snuggled against her timeless beauty.

When I glanced back at the Mexican camp, they were breaking it down as quickly as possible. I had to get to her before they could, to save her before moonrise. From what, I neglected to consider.

There are rules of behavior in America, rules of conduct, rules that can change your luck in a country based on the rules of luck. For instance, after forty, never go anyplace you've never been before. Except on somebody else's nickel. Never go out at night unless you're wearing black. And never go anywhere in America without a gun and a little C-4 and det cord.

Rules work.

Everybody looks silly with camo paint slashed across their face. But so few people see you, it's not a huge problem. Swaddled in black sweats, painted like a black and white Comanche, I worked my way down to the highway, wrapped a string of det cord and C-4 around the power pole and the telephone pole just past the junction, then dropped them like bad habits. Cigarettes and cocaine, perhaps. Hardy's Gulch had no more alarm systems that night.

Put your money in bad dogs before good alarm systems. Technology is interesting, but nowhere nearly as effective as a couple of Rottweilers.

Somebody had already cracked the automatic gates at Joe Don's, as they had the front double doors, so I stuck my crowbar back in my pack. Once in the foyer, I shouted:

"Wynona! I'm a friend of Mel's from Snowy Lake! She . . ."

"Ain't no need to shout," she whispered from the darkness beside me. "I just got Lester to sleep, and if you wake him up, I'll kick your butt past good daylight."

"Sorry," I said quietly, flashing my light across her. The baby slept like a rock in her arms.

"You're Sughrue?"

I didn't bother to deny it. "I don't know what sort of mess you've gotten yourself into, girl, but they know you're here."

"The Mexicans? Shit," she said. "Shit, where have you been? Mel said you were dogging me and were bound to find me. Eventually," she complained in a soft semi-southern accent.

"Mel didn't exactly give me a map, girl."

"If you'd waited a day, she would have," she said. "And besides, I turned the fountain on hoping you'd see it. If you were being cautious."

"Sorry" was all I could say. "They saw it, too . . ."

"I knew they were watching," she said. "The first time I opened the refrigerator before I unscrewed the light, they were here in a couple of hours. But we heard them and hid . . ."

"Where?"

"I grabbed the diaper bag, and we hid uphill until they left."

"That was smart," I said.

"Mel said you were smart, too, she could tell, and that I could trust you. My bags have been packed for five days," she whispered, then pointed to a backpack and a duffel stacked on a hallway table. "So let's get outa here. If you'll get those, I'll tote the diaper bag and the car seat," she said.

"And Lester, of course," I said.

"Of course, dummy," she said.

So we gathered her gear and struck off up the dirt track to Norman's van. We made it just before moonrise. Without any idea that my foray was going to work, I hadn't made any preparations to leave. While Wynona played with the briefly fussy Lester, then filled his mouth with her left breast, I strapped everything down, washed my face, then cut a piece of netting large enough to cover the van's windows and chrome and taped it down.

"You ready?" I asked when I got ready to coast the van out of the arroyo and onto the uphill road.

"There ain't no seat belts back here," she said from the back, "so I'm gonna have to put Lester in my seat." She strapped Lester's car seat down, then curled between the seats and looked up at me, her eyes shining in the muted moonlight. "No more shooting? I got to watch out for Lester, you understand."

"Shooting?"

"When that second bunch of Mexicans took Mrs. Pines from that first bunch," she said, "I never heard nothing like it."

"Where was this?" I asked, popping the clutch to start the engine and turning the van onto the dirt road that led over the ridge and into the next drainage.

"Up there at Joe Don's big place. You know, the one by the golf course," she said.

No wonder the FBI didn't want me inside the house. Now that I thought about it, the housekeeper looked less like a Mexican domestic than a feminist Chicana lawyer.

"There was so much blood and noise," Wynona continued, "that me 'n' Lester didn't have no trouble getting out. Lester was a good boy—he never even made a peep," she said calmly, as if firefights were everyday occurrences in Lester's brief experience. "What's all that stuff on the windows for?"

"Well, it ain't bulletproof, girl, but maybe they won't see the moonlight reflecting off the windows."

"Mel said you were probably as tricky as any Mexican."

"What else?"

Wynona giggled.

"What?"

"She said she'd a probably gone to bed with you, but you seemed so 'worldly.' That's a kinda nice word, don't you think? You know, with all that gunk off your face, you kinda remind me of Magnum PI. 'Cept you're some older." Then she giggled again. "And shorter. She told me you looked like a cop but you didn't act like one. Are you?"

"Say what?"

"You don't have to treat me like the village idiot, Mr. Sughrue. Are you a cop?"

"No. A private investigator."

"Then why're you looking for Sarita?"

"You wouldn't believe me if I told you," I admitted.

"Try me."

"Not just yet," I said, long past the moment when I knew when, why, or if I could tell the truth. Or even recognize it should I hear it again in this lifetime. "Just as soon as I know how you're involved in this fucking mess."

"You don't have no call to cuss in front of a sleeping child, Mr. Sughrue." Wynona sounded hurt.

"Sorry," I said, then glanced at Lester. He slept like a saint. "But I would surely like to know what's going on."

"Well, I'll see if I can tell you," she said, tucking the blanket around Lester's sweet face. "Where should I start?"

I suggested the beginning, always a mistake.

"My daddy used to take care of bird dogs for Mr. Pines. Down in El Paso. Well, in point of actual fact, just over the line in New Mexico. 'Til he got killed. My daddy, that is. Dona Ana County sheriff said it was a suicide, said my daddy took a hatchet to his bird dogs, then to Sr. Bones, then . . ."

"Sr. Bones?"

"His pet monkey," Wynona said as if everybody had one. "He might a killed them pointers if'n he was really drunk, but he wouldn't have ever killed Sr. Bones. No matter what. And he never took no cocaine, either. My mama never had a good word to say 'bout him, but she always told me that he never did no drugs of no kind.

"Sheriff said Daddy did that to the animals under the influence of cocaine, then cut his own tallywacker into four pieces before he cut his own damn throat. That sound like any suicide you ever heard of?"

After we topped the ridge, I rolled the window down, grabbed a handful of netting, and jerked the whole piece loose from the masking tape. Once I stowed it behind my seat, I turned on the van's lights, then watched the road for a while.

"Where are we going?" Wynona said, finally breaking the silence.

"Where you want to go?"

"Aspen."

"Why?"

"I got a place to hide out there," she said, "a place where me an' Lester can lie low 'til this shit-storm blows over . . ."

"You're not planning on hiding out with those Mexicans from the Quirky Arms, are you?"

"Just me and Lester. No more Mexicans, even though Sarita got me a job there." Wynona gave me a look as if she suspected I might want to share their safe place.

"Good," I said. "There's some folks in Aspen I want to see."

"You got any music? Lester sleeps better with a little music."

"I'd rather hear more of this story," I said, "more beginning, more middle, and more ending."

"It's kinda like the story of my life," Wynona said, a rueful smile flickering across her face, then she frowned. "You don't have any idea what's going on, do you?"

"Just what I read in the papers," I admitted. "And the part you told me about Sr. Bones."

"Shit-a-brick," she whispered.

"I didn't think we were supposed to be cussing in front of a sleeping baby," I said.

"Shit-a-brick ain't cussing," she calmly maintained, "it's a condition." Then she paused, thinking. "I got some cross-tops, man, so we can drive straight through."

"You're dodging the question, girl," I said, "which gives me the terrible feeling that we had best keep our wits about us and take the long way to Aspen."

"Do I have any say?"

"Not unless you want to walk."

"That's no choice," she said, but not talking to me. "Hellfire, I ain't had no choice in my life, except for having Lester, and to do that I had to hang out with a bunch of pro-life dumbfucks for six months . . . So I guess we'll get there when we get there."

"That's right," I said. "I don't think those *vatos* from Aspen saw me but I suggest we go the long way around, take it slow and safe, and watch our back trail . . ."

"Shit-a-brick," she whispered. "You won't sell me out, will you, Mr. Sughrue? Please say you won't."

"Girl, I wasn't even looking for you, remember? I was looking for Sarita Pines. So why would I sell you out?"

"I don't know. I just don't know what's happening," she gushed. "But I swear on Baby Lester's head that if you get us to Aspen safe, I'll tell you everything I know and help you find Sarita. Please."

"Okay," I said, and she held the blanket aside so I could place my hand on Lester's soft head.

"Swear," she pleaded, and I did.

I also noticed that Lester's blanket had been hiding a port wine stain that covered the upper right side of his face. Like a seal on this mad bargain. I left my hand resting on Lester's little head long enough to feel those shockingly resilient bones, the throb of blood, the bass line pulse of life. Over the years I had worked for blood, pain, bone-ache love, and sometimes money. This was the first time I ever went to work for a baby.

It took us until daybreak to thread the mining trails and Forest Service roads back to Sun Valley, then we went to Aspen the hard way, north to Stanley, over to Boise, then down into the Nevada and Utah deserts, then into Colorado on I-70, edged around Grand Junction, then down through Delta and Gunnison, then finally ran out of energy about three in the afternoon a day later outside of Buena Vista, some sixty-five miles south and east of Aspen.

Wynona and Lester had done some road time together before me. They were great travelers. As far as I could tell, either Lester was a fucking miracle or coming down with something. He only cried when he was hungry or sleepy, and even then he did it quietly and quickly. Sometimes he would fuss briefly until Wynona shifted his seat or changed his diaper. He always seemed grandly amused. About almost everything. I couldn't tell how old he was, and didn't want to admit my ignorance to his mother, but he always looked me in the eye as if he thought I actually knew what I was doing. He'd take a giant grunting dump in his diapers, looking quite serious but faintly amused, then he'd glance at me, cock his head, then smile in relief. He'd laugh when I touched his tummy and sometimes fall asleep holding on to one of my fingers.

"He really likes you," Wynona said once as she was changing his diaper on the floor.

"Wait until he gets to know me," I joked, "then he'll really like me. We'll be running buddies, chase women, annoy fish, and . . ."

"Please," she said.

When I glanced down from the endless highway, she was

crying without movement or sound. Just tears. That's the hardest way, I think. Shit, here I was full of myself, acting like Uncle Dad. Lester was just a lark for me. But he was Wynona's life.

"I'm really sorry."

"You are, aren't you?" she said, brushing at the wet tracks of her tears on Lester's chest. "You know, Mel was wrong about you . . ."

"Wrong?"

"She said you were worldly. Bullshit."

"I take it we've taken to cussing in front of the baby even when he's awake," I said.

She slapped me on the thigh, the first time we had touched, except for the accidental moments of close quarters. "You ain't worldly at all. You just act like that. You're just some good old boy who done forgot where he came from. A sucker for every bird dog pup and shitty-bottomed baby that come down the pike." Then she laughed, brushing at her own tears. "Next time Baby Lester takes a dump, Mr. Sughrue, I'm gonna make you change the diaper."

"You think I'm afraid."

"No, I don't think you're afraid," she said, serious again.

"You sound as if I should be."

"You look tired, man," she said. Somewhere along the way I had made the change from "Mr. Sughrue" to "man." "How much farther now?"

"Girl, I think we should crash up here in Buena Vista. Catch up on the z's, then hit Aspen just about daylight. The bad guys live such bad lives that they're never worth a shit in the morning," I said. Of course, neither was I. "How does that sound?"

"Can we have a cheeseburger, extra fries, and a strawberry malt?"

"Sure," I said. "What about Baby Lester? Can he tell what you've been eating?"

"That's an awfully personal question to ask a mother."

"Well, excuse me," I said, "I'll see if I can't find two restaurants and two motels . . ."

She grabbed my arm. "No. No. Just get two beds. Lester and

me, we won't be any trouble. I promise. But please don't make
us stay in a room all by ourselves. Please."

Who could argue with that? I found a motel that looked as if
it had once been a motor court just across a gravel lot from a
cafe. Above the small town, way the hell up among the rocky
heights of the Collegiate Peaks, winter raised tufts of its cold,
gray head. But down where we stopped to rest, the sun still
worked. Even the broken glass scattered through the gravel spar-
kled like jewels, and the cafe smelled like the place they invented
cheeseburgers.

I don't know how long Wynona had been snuggled against
my back when she shook me out of the sweaty depths of another
nightmare. Or dusk-mare. The gray light slithered around the
thin curtains. The small room could have been underwater or lost
in an evergreen jungle. Even after she woke me, I couldn't move,
any more than I could remember what had frightened me. Wynona got a towel, sopped up the greasy sweat, then opened me
a beer from the cooler. I guzzled the beer, as cold as ice cream,
then grumbled about the ache in the top of my palate.

"You always act like that when a woman climbs into your
bed?" she asked as she popped another beer.

"I don't know," I confessed. "Not too many women climb
into my bed . . ."

"Well, I suspect that's 'cause you don't want them."

". . . and none like you, girl."

She kissed me for a long easy time, lifted my hands from my
sides, made me touch that creamy skin, so soft and thin that I
could feel the hard muscles working beneath, the milk-hardened
breasts. When she let me up for air, I managed to struggle out
of her arms long enough to sit up and pull on the beer again.

"You don't owe me anything," I said, "for the ride, and I've
survived bad dreams before, but I haven't made love to a woman
in a long time . . ."

Wynona pulled me back down with a hard no-nonsense jerk,
her mouth working softly against mine. Something important
inside me leaped into her arms. "What have you been doing up

there in Montana? Helping sheep through fences?" she whispered, laying out the old joke. I started to answer, but she hissed, "Just shut the fuck up." And I did.

Later, she told me secrets devoid of narrative.

"Oh, goddammit," she moaned when I laid my tongue in the fold of her thigh, then she giggled, "Watch out, man, I come too easy and too hard." A threat, or a promise. Whichever, she kept coming until she stuffed a pillow in her mouth to keep from waking Baby Lester.

"You know," she said in the darkness above me, later, her breath harsh and gasping, "you're . . . the first man I've . . . made love with . . . since Lester was born." Then she moved against me again, leaned into my face, french fries and strawberry malteds redolent on her night breath.

When she kissed me, she came again, sucking my lower lip into her mouth, her throat, her heart. Just as I considered dying a wonderful relief, she stopped again, then sat up.

"Hey, man, don't fall in love with me, okay?" She had the same tone in her voice that she used when she talked about Lester. "Guys do that shit to me all the time. Fall in love with me. They think that because I come all the time that I love them or something. It's just something my body does, okay? Love's a hell of a lot more complex than that. Right now it's me and Lester against the fucking world. I mean it's not like we don't trust you, you know, but . . ." She paused, stared at me as if I wasn't nodding my head quickly enough. Then she lifted her hips, eased down, once slowly, twice, then so slowly I knew I was going to die. At least somebody in the room moaned like the living dead.

"Stop that," she said. "What the hell's your first name?"

"I don't know anymore."

"You tell me your name, or I'll quit," she said, then did it again. "I mean it."

"C.W." was about all I could strangle out.

"All of it," she said, riding me again and again until the pleasure became pain.

"Chauncey Wayne," I stuttered, and she laughed. "But you can call me 'Sonny.' "

"I'll bet your mama called you 'Sonny,' " she said, then went after me with sweet vengeance. "But I ain't your mama, sweetie pie," she added, unnecessarily, then proved it.

Just before dawn, Wynona, Lester, and I were cuddled against the head of the bed watching cartoons.

"My Dad loved Tom and Jerry," I said.

"Who were they?"

"Before your time."

"Oh, back in the old fart days," she giggled, then snuggled against me. "Is your daddy dead?"

"Both my folks."

"Mine, too. Maybe that's why we get on so well," Wynona said. "We're both orphans." Then she fell sad. "I hope Lester never has to be an orphan."

"No you don't," I said.

"What's that mean? Goddammit, you've got no call to say that," she said, then flopped away from me.

Lester was propped between a pair of pillows, watching us as if we were aliens. I patted his mother on the hip. Sometimes she seemed ancient and wise; sometimes, like now, a child with a child; sometimes her small hard body seemed so easy and soft that it didn't have enough skin to contain all that passion; sometimes she retreated in pain and fear until she seemed just skin and hard-rock bone-hurt.

"Girl, the only way he can keep from being an orphan is if he dies before you do," I said softly, then tried to kiss the cusp of her neck.

Wynona rolled over and talked into my chest. "I ain't stupid, Mr. Worldly. I knew what you meant. But I don't care. I don't want Lester to ever have to be an orphan," she said, but we both knew she was talking about herself.

The cartoons played out in front of us. Lester, his purple scar shining like ancient wisdom in the flickering light of the cathode-ray tube, would gurgle a small laugh, then stare over my chest toward his mom. Then he pulled himself across me, clump of hair by clump, to his mom, then he whacked her on the smooth, lovely forehead.

"Jesus, baby, what do you want?"

Lester laughed as loud as he could, then cut loose a wet, stinky, endless fart, and whacked his mom again.

"This is your chance, cowboy," Wynona murmured just before she sighed and rolled away from us. "Don't blame me if he pees in your face" were her last words of advice before sleep overwhelmed her.

I didn't blame her. And I didn't blame Baby Lester, either. I hoped they wouldn't blame me for going through their gear.

PART THREE

PART THREE

We weren't going to make Aspen by dawn, not the way Wynona was sleeping, but I figured I'd let her sleep while I changed Lester. So I propped the baby on my hip, and he slipped right off, reminding me that sometimes women's parts had multiple uses. Trying again, I draped the little sucker over my shoulder, picked up the diaper bag, and eased into the bathroom.

The diaper bag seemed a bit heavy and when I set it down, it made that dreadfully dramatic thump against the tile floor. I'd known women—several, in fact—who carried guns in their purses, but usually something cheap, light, and easy to handle: a .25 automatic or a .32 five-shot revolver. But Wynona was the first woman I'd known to fill her diaper bag with a silenced Colt Woodsman .22, weapon of choice among some professional killers, and a Glock 10mm semiautomatic, handgun of choice among some of our esteemed FBI agents, and six loaded clips for each. At least the .22 was empty and the Glock had a trigger lock so Lester couldn't blow us away.

I left the pistols in the side pocket. In the middle of the bag, the package of disposable diapers seemed a bit heavy, so after I changed Lester and washed my face, I dug deeper and found a package the size of a large cantaloupe swaddled in bubble wrap and mummified with strapping tape. It rattled dully when I shook it. I didn't think it was a baby's toy. I shook it again, and Wynona murmured in her sleep.

It only took a moment to slip Lester beside her; he gave me a wonderfully happy grin, then suckled merrily away. I sure as hell didn't remember having that much fun when I was a baby. While they slept, I went through the rest of Wynona's things, and found nothing to show that she wasn't exactly who she said she was: a single mom on the run from god knows what. Except for the key to the Glock's trigger lock.

She had promised to tell me where to find Sarita Pines once I had them safely to Aspen, and I thought perhaps she might be more help if I held up my end of the bargain, but she and Lester made such a picture together, I fell asleep watching them.

Three hours later I woke from a seamless nap, cool and ready to kick ass, but Lester's diaper had come unfastened, and the little dickens had peed all over my side.

After I showered again, we packed, then trekked on toward Aspen like a small happy family. Wynona searched the radio dial for a station that penetrated the mountains, then rattled through Norman's tapes looking for anybody she had ever heard of before. Lester endured his mom's restlessness with minimal fussing, but as we climbed higher and higher up Independence Pass he became more and more agitated, then when we topped the pass, he went insane. At first, he screamed, clawed at his ear, and tried to break out of his car seat. Then he got serious.

"Jesus," I said, startled, "I think Baby Lester's had enough of this driving around . . ."

But Wynona was too busy digging into the diaper bag to answer. "Oh, Christ," she finally muttered, "it's his ear . . . the altitude . . . I should have been nursing him . . . but I hate to take him out of the seat . . . Goddammit, where's his medicine . . ." Then she stared at me, all the tough calm lashed away by the whipping frenzy of her baby's pain. "I can't find it."

Once in the bush our company hit a cold LZ on a ridgeline somewhere close to Cambodia. After we set up a perimeter, we were joined by a batch of battalion S-2 brass and some of those sun-glassed guys whose fatigues lacked insignia. They seemed like a bunch of Rear Echelon Motherfuckers out for a lark or another cluster on their Vietnam service medals, standing around catching an overview of the war.

One of the majors, a tubby little guy, sat down on the grass while the hard-assed head-hogs conferred. Then he made a pillow of his helmet and leaned back to catch some rays. Instead of a tan, though, he caught the green-slivered strike of a bamboo viper just under his right eye. One of the snake's tiny fangs must have penetrated into the major's sinus cavity because the snake was stuck there, hanging like a decoration from his cheek.

Operating bolts slammed shut all over the LZ when the major screamed, slapping and jerking at the small green ribbon dangling from his face. Then for some reason, panic perhaps, surprise, terror, the major darted into a tight tangle of brush at the edge of the clearing, where he managed to grovel and growl and scream for at least five minutes as he wrapped himself in the endless clutches of wait-a-minute vines. The new company CO looked at me, and I looked at my oldest hand, Willie Williams. He shook his head, a gesture I didn't have to convey to the captain.

When it was finally quiet, Willie turned to the captain, spit on the dusty grass, and said, "The major must've been some kinda tough, sir." The captain raised an eyebrow. "Most guys, sir, get one a them little green fuckers on 'em, they sometimes get one step, maybe half another, then hit 'the mud dead. If the major could've straightened out his trail, hell, he'd a made it a couple a klicks. Course somebody should've told him this ain't no place for a picnic."

The captain agreed without comment. He wasn't a great officer, but he did know enough to listen to the old guys. Even that, though, didn't keep him alive long enough for us to learn his first name. Or even remember exactly how he died.

But nobody ever forgot the major. Nobody felt sorry for him, though. The fucker didn't have to be there, and nobody cared if his wife got his Purple Heart. But pain and plain fear like that is hard to forget. It took a squad of engineers thirty minutes with wire cutters to get the asshole out of the vines. The hard guys never even took off their sunglasses when they watched the body bagged. But for those of us who lived in the bush, it was the sort of moment that made a lively addition to our nightly entertainment of bad dreams and shitty sleep. Now we had something else to worry about.

But Baby Lester was a different deal.

"What can I do?" I pleaded with Wynona, her face already dull from Lester's pain. Sympathetic milk poured from her breasts, seeping through her sweatshirt.

"One more favor," she wailed, jerking at the straps of the car seat. "One more."

Well, more than one actually, but I did them all as best I could. First, I had to hurry, but be careful, she explained as she jerked up the car seat and hurled it into the back of the van. Second, I had to follow her complex directions to the safe house and I had to remember the way back. Because she would try to ease the pain in Lester's ear and she would call a doctor Sarita had recommended and he would call the pharmacy and I could pick up Lester's medicine. She jerked up her sweatshirt and tried to get Lester to at least nurse, but he fought like a tiny madman.

When we finally dropped into Aspen, both exhausted by the baby's screams, Wynona shouted the directions at me in a voice as desperate as her child's.

The directions were complicated, but eventually we turned off a paved street onto a dirt trail. Fifteen or twenty yards up the trail, the road switched back, became paved, and led to a serious locked gate. Wynona shouted the code at me, "Eighteen-forty-seven-eleven," prayed I could remember it, then urged me forward. "The front door code is the same but backward!"

We followed the paved road to an oversized A-frame set on a daylight basement next to a three-car garage at the top of a heavily timbered knoll. Wynona leaned over to give me a quick hug and kiss that got more nose than mouth, then smeared my face with Lester's milk-soaked chin in lieu of a kiss, then grabbed her purse and leaped out of the van and ran for the house. Lester's screams echoed back down the driveway.

It didn't take forever, but it did take some time. Aspen has more pharmacies than a small town deserves, but fortunately the first one I tried called the others until they located Lester's prescription. Then more directions. Then a try at backtracking myself. It almost worked. I ended up at a cul-de-sac on the next knoll over, just a small creek away.

Your heart doesn't sink or leap into your throat, but something happens inside when you know it's gone bad, something scientists can probably explain with chemical and neurological changes in the body, but that's just some scrawls on paper. When I stared across the small distance to the A-frame, I knew it had gone bad. I got the field glasses out of the glove box in time to catch the rear end of a Chevy pickup truck as it dropped down the driveway. And two numbers off the New Mexico license plate. I took a moment to dig out my Browning and strap it on under my vest, then fasten the Airweight to my ankle.

Of course, by the time I backtracked to the right knoll, there was nobody to shoot. That's how it usually happens.

The house was more than empty. Not a sign of Wynona and Lester, of course, not even the echo of a scream. And not much of anything else, either. Not a bill, no mail at all, not even a piece of paper except in the bathroom on a roll. Nothing on the walls, not even a number on the telephones, not even Wynona's fingerprints there, I would bet.

She had been there long enough to make the telephone call to the doctor, whose name I had on the prescription bottles, and then disappeared. Hell, I didn't even know whose house I was prowling. I could find out, sure, but that would take time, which I didn't think I had.

I left it like I found it, climbed back into the van, then drove into Aspen. I kept the pistols strapped to my body, the drugs in the false bottom of the propane tank, and the diaper bag on the seat next to me. I unlocked the trigger of the Glock, slammed in a clip, and jacked a round into the chamber. If I couldn't find Wynona and Lester, at least I could kill somebody with their pistol.

At the last moment, I stuffed Lester's medicine into my vest pocket.

*　*　*

They hadn't even bothered to hide the black Chevy pickup. It was parked right in front of the open doors of the Quirky Arms. Dagoberto even sat at the bar, alone, as if he were waiting for me. David and Chato sat at a table in the rear, flanked by two other *vaqueros de farmacia*. Nobody bothered to hide their feelings about my presence, but at least I didn't see any pistols around. Maybe because several tables of rich tourists picked at an early lunch.

"I thought you must be around somewhere, man," he said as I hitched up on the stool next to him. "Let me buy you a drink. *Hola, Roberto*. A Dead Solid Perfect Martini for my friend here." Then he leaned his elbows on the bar, smiling at himself in the mirror as he lifted his drink.

"No, thanks," I said, then dug my thumb deep into his exposed armpit and held on for dear life. Give him this: that hold hurts way down in the viscera; but he only spilled a few drops of his drink. "People who fuck with my friends usually end up sorry."

"Shit, man," Dagoberto hissed between clenched teeth, "people who fuck with me always end up dead." Then he tried to laugh. "But the two of us should be *amigos*, we have so many friends in common." He set down his drink, carefully, then I tightened the hold. He just grunted and tried to smile. "Roberto, please."

The bartender stepped over to hold the swinging doors open. A swarthy guy in a chef's hat checked a large soup pot while Wynona chopped onions with a large knife. Somewhere deep in the bowels of the place, Lester's faint cries drifted toward me. Then the doors slowly closed. A moment later Wynona walked out smiling under her red eyes, wiping her hands on a cloth towel.

"If you'd put a kitchen match in your mouth," I said, "the onions wouldn't make you cry."

"I'll bet your sweet mama told you that," she said. "I'm so glad you found us, Mr. Sughrue," she said, "we just missed you at the pharmacy." I handed her Lester's medicine, and she thanked me. "He'll be fine now. We'll both be fine. Can I get my gear out of your van?"

"Sure," I said.

"These two Meskin boys," she said, nodding over her shoulder, "will help us." Chato and David stood up and strolled over.

I led our little group, followed by Dagoberto, out to the van to unlock it. I reached for the diaper bag in the seat, but Wynona jumped past me into the back, saying, "I see all my stuff back here. Thanks." Then she handed her gear and the child seat to Chato and David, and without another word, she followed them back to the Quirky Arms.

"I hope Baby Lester's all right," I said to her back.

"Thanks," she said without turning.

Dagoberto smiled at me. "Hey, *vato*, I don't know why, but I like you. I got no reason. You come into my place of business wearing a gun, not just once but twice, and you tear the heart out of my armpit with some old judo hold, but still I like you. So let's have that drink."

I considered my options: I had my hand on the Glock under the diaper bag, so I could try to bluff him into the van, but I didn't think that would work; or I could step back into the spider's web and see what was shaking.

"Why not?" I said. "I'm a professional. I can have a cocktail with the enemy."

"Believe me, Mr. Sughrue," Dagoberto said seriously, "I am not the enemy. Like you, man, I am just a hired hand."

Which told me nothing. Or everything.

Roberto did a pretty good job with the martini. I sipped mine, but Dagoberto gunned his like cheap tequila.

When I stared at him, he said, "Man, I have hated gin since the day I got to the U.K." I looked a little more amazed than disgusted. "My old man sent me to Oxford. I hated every moment on that foul little island with those pasty-faced pricks. 'Cept for the women, of course; they were fine. But I made this place look like it does to remind me of those bad times."

"Never had the pleasure myself," I said.

"Forget it," he said.

"I never forget anything," I said. "Mel, Wynona, Lester— they're like family to me. Their health and safety are your personal responsibility."

"You make friends too fast, my friend," he said, smiling at his own frail joke.

"Hurt them and you're dead," I said, then finished my drink. "No matter how long it takes, I'll find you and gut you with a *punji* stake and you'll take a long, hard time to die."

"You old farts," he said, "still mucking around in that war. Hell, you guys lost the son of a bitch, and that's the real story, fucking old news, so get the fuck out of my place, man, or we'll see who dies . . ."

It wasn't a great right hook, a little too short and a bit off center, but he was a small, rich Mexican and probably hadn't been hit in the face in his life. It lifted him off the stool and staggered him into the nearest tourist, a tall, stately type. "See you around, pepper-belly," I said, in my best Texas twang.

The stately type helped Dagoberto to his feet, then turned on me with one of those educated Texas accents, the type that defies shit to melt in their mouths, and said, "Sir, you're the sort of Texan who gives the rest of us a bad name."

"Thank you, sir," I said.

David and Chato wanted to laugh, but Dagoberto, who couldn't even get his eyes focused in time to shout a parting threat, was the boss.

But nobody followed me out to the van, so I assumed they were going to leave it alone for the moment.

If only the FBI would have.

Cromwellington and his twin brother picked me up when I left the Quirky Arms, followed me about town until I found a service station with a hydraulic lift, which is no small feat these days, then bribed the gas jockey to let me look underneath the van. The FBI didn't seem to mind. They drove past to park down the street and read the morning paper like innocent bystanders. I found the transmitter fixed to the side of the gas tank and pried it off. Then I called Solly.

". . . then what is my legal position," I asked as soon as he stopped lecturing me for losing my only lead and I stopped criticizing his read on Dagoberto and his merry band, "with a bug like this?"

"I don't know, Sughrue, but I don't think it comes under the federal wiretap regulations."

"So what should I do with it?"

"If it belongs to them," he answered, "they might bust you for destroying government property."

"Are you serious?"

"I'm a lawyer," he said. "Is there a voice bug inside the van?"

"I don't know," I said. "I'll have it swept when I get to Denver."

"What the fuck's in Denver?"

"Backup," I answered, truthfully I hoped.

"Norman's been bugging me. Maybe I should send him and some of his boys down to help," he said, then added, laughing, "or I could show up again."

"Norman got me into this mess," I said. "Let's keep him at a safe distance, okay? If he really wants to get involved, he can find his own fucking mother."

"Sure, but what about the women and that kid?"

"That's my problem," I said. "If I hurry, the stupid fuck won't even move them. I've got an old buddy who's a cop in Denver . . ."

"The big guy from Nam? What was his name? The Big Tamale?"

"Super Nacho," I said. "But what should I do about the FBI?"

"Worst they can do is pick you up as a material witness, and I'll blow that bullshit right out of the water. Without a warrant they can't do a thing except act tough and stupid," he said, then added, "so piss on them."

As much as I wanted to, I didn't. I made do with a pound of roofing nails scattered on the interstate entrance ramp as they tried to follow me to Denver. Their tires went flat all around, as did those of a battered gray pickup just behind them. Down the interstate I tossed their transmitter up against the side of a cattle truck, but the magnet didn't stick. We all know what "good enough for government work" actually means.

* * *

Denver used to be one kind of place, a link between the Great Plains and the Rockies, but now it might as well be Minneapolis. When you can't see the mountains for the smog, every place is the same.

I found a local electronics guy to sweep my van and verify that it was clean, and in spite of the traffic and the new street scheme downtown, I still made it to the main station by midafternoon. The desk sergeant, as usual, wouldn't have told me his name without his name tag, but he was a vet. After I showed him my driver's license and my reduced and laminated DD 214, separation papers from the 1st Cav, he relented slowly, a grin spreading across his face.

"Detective Sergeant Vega. Sure, fellow," he said, the grin growing, "he's working juvenile. If you hurry, you can probably catch him at this address." He scrawled an address for me, then gave me directions.

When I got there, I had to look at the address twice. It was an elementary school. After a bit, I saw Nacho shamble down the steps in a suit way too large for him, followed by a flock of little kids who didn't seem exactly impressed by his size or his badge, which still dangled from his coat pocket.

As he stalked past the van, I stepped out on the sidewalk to say, "Hey, Blood, you lookin' downright skinny. You been humping the bush without your fearless leader?"

He stopped his giant, gaunt frame, saying as he turned, "By the Rio Pocomoco, slowly I turned, and step by step . . . ," then began to advance upon me, his outstretched hands poised to crush my throat, but at the last moment, threw his arms around me, picked me off the ground as if I were a child, and swung me around and around in the brilliant October air while the children watched in amazement. They'd never heard of Abbott or Costello. Which was their loss.

Franklin Ignacio Vega was either the luckiest man I had ever known or the unluckiest. Born in El Paso to a half-German half-black father and a half-Mexican half-Samoan mother, Nacho grew up with no place to call home, no race, creed, heritage, picked upon by everybody on the street with the slightest trace of ethnic purity. His soldier father was killed in a bad jump at Fort Campbell before he could marry Nacho's mother, so the Army gave them nothing except his last name for Nacho's first. She cleaned houses on the west side, while Nacho shined shoes and fought every street kid on the east side. Luckily Nacho was nearly as big as a house, early on, which is why football looked as if it were going to save his life.

During his teens he played ball at a high school so poor they couldn't afford to buy shoes big enough to fit his feet, but even slipping around the dusty fields in cheap tennis shoes he managed a scholarship to Colorado, where he made the All-Big Eight second team at defensive end three years in a row, where he might have made the first team if he would have talked to reporters, but he didn't. As far as they were concerned, he was just a big dumb good-looking Mexican kid. And the white girls fell all over him, which never helps.

The pros called before he finished his degree, but he got cut at Boston because he didn't have enough downfield speed. "Cut by a fucking clock," he used to say, "without ever playing a down from scrimmage." So he went to Canada, where he was cut to meet the Roughriders' American quota. "Then cut for being an American," he used to say when we were stoned in our hooch. "Do I look like a fucking American to you, Sarge?"

Not a bit. As far as I was concerned, Nacho looked like Tarzan of the Apes should have, like the man who ruled the jungle. Of course, that's where the Army sent him, shortly after he was drafted. "Maybe if I'd stood up straight that day, they would have cut me, too." Nacho got in under the Army's height standards by one-eighth of an inch.

That's the unlucky part.

The lucky part: Franklin Ignacio Vega survived two combat tours with the 1st Cav carrying an M-60 machine gun, two *full* tours without suffering a scratch, a scrape, or a day on sick call. That luck followed him into the Denver Police Department: Nacho had never pulled his revolver on duty. Now it looked as if he never would, since his job was to convince inner-city kids that the police were their pals.

After I got my breath back, Nacho suggested catching up over a beer, so we climbed into the van and headed west.

"Hey," he said, "let's see if we can't find that little ant turd, Gorman. The little fuck has probably already run through his route and is dying for a beer and a jukebox."

"*El Hormiga*, the fucking ant is in town?"

"Hey, where you been, Sarge? Jimmy's been in town for years. Works for the post office. Turn right here."

Jimmy Gorman was a tiny Irish kid from Philly who walked point for us. Unlike Nacho, Jimmy had joined at seventeen and wouldn't have passed the short end of the height test if he hadn't spent the night before hanging from a head harness to stretch his spine.

When we got to the post office, Nacho flashed his badge, and the window clerk told us that Jimmy hadn't shown up. But some confused old woman from Jimmy's route had. She claimed that the mailbox on her corner was singing. The supervisor was on his way.

Nacho and I pushed it as hard as we could, but the supervisor was unlocking the green route storage box as we parked beside it. When he pulled open the door, Little Jimmy tumbled out, his transistor radio clasped in one hand, and a nearly empty pint of Jack Daniel's in the other. It would have been better if he had been dead instead of merely passed out.

His supervisor addressed Jimmy in official tones and Jimmy responded like a true postman.

"You can't fire me, you asshole!" he shouted.

The supervisor just smiled. Jimmy was about to split him open like a pig in a slaughterhouse, but Nacho wrapped his long arms around Jimmy and made peace with the official world. After he had gotten Jimmy locked in the van, he tried to explain to the supervisor that Jimmy was on stakeout for the Denver Police Department. The supervisor's smile changed to laughter.

By the time we got to the nearest bar Jimmy was cutting the post office patches off his uniform.

"Chill your jets, Jimmy," Nacho said, then shambled off to the latrine.

"It's not like you got busted, kid," I said. "Hell, the government never fires anybody."

"That's the fucking trouble," Jimmy shouted, then looked at me, his drunken eyes finally realizing who I was. "Jesus, Sarge, what the fuck are you doing here?"

"Night ambush, kid. You up for it?"

"Don't kid around, okay?" he said seriously.

"I came to see the Super Nach', and he said we should . . ."

"Jesus, you know, where have you been? Nobody's called Frank that in years," he said. "And you, you know, I spent—what?—six months in the bush in your squad and I can't fucking remember your name . . ."

"Sughrue," I said, holding out my hand. "Let's drink to civilian life."

"People like us, Sarge, we never get to be civilians," he whispered, then added suddenly, "You didn't get hit, you got arrested, right? For fraggin' that family. Just bad luck. That's what I told the CID guys. What the hell, though, didn't I hear that you went to Leavenworth for that? That true?"

"Not exactly," I said, "I went to graduate school." Then changed the subject. "What's wrong with Nacho?" Then quickly wished I hadn't.

"Ah, fuck, Sarge, he's dying. Cancer. He's eat up with it. Started in his gut, but now it's everywhere." Then Jimmy hit his beer hard. "Don't let on like you know, okay? Nobody knows but me and his ex-wife. The cops don't know. He don't have another physical for four months. So he's trying to build his retirement check for his kids. Not that the little fucks deserve it. Poor bastard married the worst white woman in America and believe me when I say that I know what I'm talking about."

Before I could say anything, Nacho came back to the table, grinning through the gray pallor lurking like a lie beneath his rich brown skin.

"What are you girls gossiping about now?"

"Just catching up, Frank. We ain't got to old times yet," Jimmy said, laughing and punching Nacho on the shoulder with so much affection it brought tears to my eyes.

* * *

The rest of the night was like an ambush: close, dirty work in a frenzied scramble. One of the few clear moments I remember came as we exchanged a narrow crowded yuppie bar for a Mexican jazz club. We were in an alley somewhere down by the train station. Somehow we had garnered a couple of women passengers, a giant Jamaican doobie, plus an extreme desire to all piss at once.

One of the girls wanted to know if it was all right to piss in this warehouse alley. She had already hiked up her tight skirt and was skinning out of her panty hose and hanging on to a sign so she could lean backward. This was no yuppie chick; this woman had pissed outdoors before.

"This is perfect, ma'am," Nacho, whom I had started to call "Frank" already, said. "This is a 'coop,' lady."

"A coop?" she said, pissing neatly.

"Where patrol units, cops, come to sleep late on shift. It's too early, so we're clean and green right here."

"Not me," the other woman giggled from behind a loading dock, where she tried to be modest. "I think I just pissed on my new come-fuck-me's, Linda."

"I told you how to do it, hon," Linda said, struggling back into her clothes. Then she walked over to Nacho. "How do you know that?" she asked. "About the cops?"

"I am a member of the Denver police force, ma'am."

"Why aren't you arresting us?"

"I'm off duty," Frank said solemnly.

"I'm off base," Jimmy added.

"And I'm off, period," I said.

"I've never been exactly regular," Linda said, then laughed wildly.

I dug out the cocaine while the doobie circled the shadows, then Mexican food sounded a little heavy after that, so it was Chinese in what looked like an Italian place way out Colfax.

Somehow about daylight Frank and I were in the middle of an argument in a suite at an airport motel. I put up the money and Frank put up his badge. I think he told them we were on a stakeout. Whatever, we were high enough up on the east side of the motel to watch the sun clear the eastern horizon. Jimmy had collapsed in front of the television. The girls—ah, the girls— had gone into the bedroom together.

I guess it happens that way sometimes these days. Good-looking women prefer each other to asshole men. Linda explained it to us in a long cocaine speech about sensitivity, thanking us for the drugs and drink, trying to compliment us by saying we weren't bad guys for men, and that sometimes they went out drinking around men just to remind themselves what they weren't missing, but now they were tired and sleepy and half-horny, would we excuse them.

Frank and I looked at each other after the bedroom door closed behind them. That's when I opened the drapes to watch the sunrise.

"How come I don't give a shit?" I asked Frank.

"You always were a fucking hippie," he answered, which started the argument. "I knew that when you took over the squad, and I know it now."

"What the fuck does that mean?" I said, not exactly sure where this attack was leading. "Shit, we smoked dope together every off-duty moment we could manage it. Why does that make me a hippie and not you?"

"Because you're a white guy," he said calmly, "and I'm a Mexican. It's okay for us to smoke *mota*, but you white guys take it too seriously. You smoke dope, it makes you a hippie."

"You're not a fucking Mexican," I said, "you're a New World, Old World, third world mongrel. And I've never been a very fucking good white guy, anyway."

"That's no excuse," he said, "for being a hippie."

"You asshole, I'm a fucking licensed and bonded private investigator working for a world-famous drug lawyer. That captain we plucked out of the bush, Rainbolt, you probably knew him when he practiced down here . . ."

"I knew him, Sarge, and only a fucking hippie would work for a beefstick like that," he said, smug with cocaine happiness. "He was our most wanted. That's how *real* cops felt about him."

"Frank, I may not be a cop but at least I don't have to go around to grade schools to tell little kids that the policeman is your friend." I think I was shouting by now.

"That's *police officer*, you sexist pig," he said with a straight face.

When we stopped laughing, Frank asked me what I was working on. I guess I told him a good version of the story, because as soon as we were able, we were on our way to Aspen, a dying cop, an alcoholic mailman, and a licensed and bonded private dick working for a world-famous drug lawyer. I knew if I told him about Norman, Frank would call me a hippie again.

I probably shouldn't have, but before we cleared the suite, I peeked into the bedroom. Women look a lot like men after thrashing drunkenly around the bed, except they always seem to be prettier. They looked kind of sweet. But when I pointed that out to Frank as we drove out of the motel lot, Jimmy sleeping curled in the back of the van, Frank, of course, just smiled as if that was exactly what a hippie scumwad would think.

Before we left, we finished our chores. Frank cashed in some comp-time, Jimmy took a suspension without pay until his termination hearing, and I loaded the van with camping gear. Nobody ever expects the bad guys to show up in a tent, and I suspected that whatever happened in Aspen, we were going to be the bad guys.

When I explained that wrinkle to Jimmy the second time between hangover naps, he said, "No problem, Sarge. I've already been the bad guy once."

"When?"

"When I came back to the world, this fat broad in San Francisco—I went over to the Haight in uniform on purpose to give them a chance to pick on me—called me a baby killer to my face. You know what I did?" I shook my head unable to imagine it. "I pulled a string of Chinese mushrooms out of my pocket, told her they were baby slope ears, then I started to eat them." Then Jimmy laughed as he drifted back to sleep. "Fucking bitch fainted so hard she bounced, then rolled down one of them slick, steep streets like she was gonna roll 'til she lost some weight . . .

And fuck if some hippie chick didn't step outa the crowd, put her arms around my neck, and start to cry . . . My first wife, man, and the best . . . so let's go grab this broad and her kid back, and fuck bein' bad guys . . ."

As he fell asleep, I thought about revising my opinion. Perhaps only people who followed the letter of the law, instead of the spirit, would think of us as bad guys. Recently, it came to me that the letter of the law was a dollar sign, and the spirit a ghost of her former self.

Since Dagoberto and his minions knew me, I stayed out at camp while Jimmy and Frank spent a day in town in a rent-car chasing paper and casing the Quirky Arms. I communed with nature in the quiet empty campground and listened to the last game of the Series over ten cups of cowboy coffee. Then I remembered Lester's diaper bag.

I set it on the picnic table, went through it again with the same results. I leaned my head back in the thin fall sunshine, watched the smoke from our fire, a straight column baffled by the skinny arms of the pines. Wynona wanted me to have the bag for some reason, maybe trying to help me chase down Norman's supposed mom.

I hadn't forgotten my job, but I wasn't about to hurry, either. My mad father taught me from the beginning that you kill more deer with patience than energy. Also, you usually didn't have to drag the carcass quite so far to the pickup. Maybe my best hope would be to stand still and let the FBI flush her into my arms.

So I turned to the bubble-wrapped package with the sharpest and thinnest blade of my Case pocketknife, the one that said "meat only," whatever that might mean. Slow and easy, cutting just the strapping tape, I removed the first layer. Then the second, then the third. Then I set it on the table and stared at it for a long time, as if watching it closely might make it talk.

After a while, I realized that if it did talk, it would speak in an ancient tongue I wouldn't understand. It was a bird, a pottery bird of some sort in a colorful fired glaze. Pinkish-orange legs, which seemed impossibly thin for pottery this old, held up a rusty body with a black belly and a white stripe along the edge of the wings. It looked something like a duck, or a goose, and somehow Mexican, something I had never seen before, but something I knew, if I could just think of what it might be. The bill looked as brightly coral as a teenage girl's lipstick. A thumb-sized hole, encrusted with a black substance like hardened tar, pierced the middle of the duck's back, and another hole, straw-sized, also tarred shut, stuck in the center of the duck's pink puckered bill, puckered as if to whistle . . .

Fuck, I thought, *a Mexican Tree Duck*. A flock used to summer in the mesquite scrub along the *resaca* behind my mother's house, the remains of a slough off the Muddy Fork of the Nueces. When I was a kid, I thought them the dumbest ducks in the world— all they did was stand around in trees and look silly. I seemed to remember that they had teeth, too, and sure enough when I looked at the pottery duck I saw tiny rows of teeth scratched in the glaze.

I felt like a real detective instead of a maniac, for a change, so I picked up the duck and held it softly. When I shook the duck, something inside rattled with dull, padded thumps like a large marble or a lump of clay. I set it back down on the table, cracked a beer, and proceeded to watch my duck.

That's how Frank and Jimmy found me a couple of hours later.

By then I had a stack of beer cans and roaches beside my duck and I knew every crack in the old glaze, every minor imperfection in the clay below it. I had begun to talk to it and cuddle it like a baby or a very old dying man. It had an air about it, a cruel ancient dignity, a stern implacability, a pitiless gaze that had survived the centuries.

I was reminded of a trip to D.C. years ago, during my first hitch in the Army, from Fort Bragg to play a football game in the Capital, Fort Belvoir or Fort Meade or some other fucking fort, and they gave us an afternoon off the day before the game. Our only requirement was to show up at the mess hall that night sober. We were all sweat hogs and flakes, so that was a major chore, but playing football was such a lazy, crazy way to serve the Army time, we took the coach's order seriously. Somebody, the quarterback probably, suggested we tour the Smithsonian, so we trekked over that way and herded into the first giant building we saw.

But it was the National Gallery. Everybody wanted to leave except me, and I couldn't leave. Not yet. It was the first time I'd ever seen a painting that hadn't been executed on black velvet. Rembrandt, Van Gogh, Moran—I don't remember all the names, but they couldn't get me out of there. First, they tried pleading. Then threats. Then they meant to carry me away bodily, but in my younger days I had a reputation for being both mean and crazy, and they let me be.

It would be a perfect story if I had dropped the first guard who told me that the gallery was closing, but I went along as docile as a pet lamb. That was one of the most important days in my life. I didn't become a painter or anything like that, but I stopped being whatever it was I had been before. I had found some other way besides violence to be calm. That day led me out of the Army the first time, back to college, thinking I could play football just for the money, and then into some other nonsense, in and out of the Army twice more, to Vietnam, eventually to jail, then to graduate school and somehow to whatever life I was living thirty-some-odd years later. Whatever trouble that day in the National Gallery caused, I never forgot the way I felt, nothing ever sullied that day. Or matched it.

Until this silly goddamned duck.

"So what the hell is that?" Frank asked as he carried another six-pack out to the table.

"A Mexican Tree Duck," I said. "It was in the package in the diaper bag."

"Now that I ain't gonna be hounded by piss-tests," Jimmy said, "I was kinda hoping it would be a pound of Peruvian flake or some of that Humboldt sinsemilla. I've been looking to expand my drug experiences."

"We've got plenty of drugs, kid," I said.

"I can't tell you how *glad* I am to hear that," Frank said.

"Take it easy, you big bastard," Jimmy said to Frank, "it's time to have some fun and stop being the most serious Mexican I ever met."

"I'm more than a Mexican," Frank said.

"And you, Sarge, quit fucking calling me 'kid.' I'll never see forty again."

"Then you stop calling me 'Sarge,' " I said. "I made PFC again three days before my discharge. I think they were trying to get me to re-up."

We all laughed at the notion, though at other times the idea hadn't seemed so strange.

"So tell me, boys," I said.

Frank straddled the bench across from me as Jimmy cracked three cans of beer, then Frank took his little notebook out of his back pocket and began ruffling the pages.

"The gate code you gave us for the house didn't work today," Frank said, "but I boosted Jimmy over the fence . . ."

"They had changed the code on the front door, too," he said, circling the table like a midget Hollywood Indian, "but they forgot to lock the garage doors. House looks exactly like you said. 'Cept the phones are dead."

"No way to come up with the owner, C.W.," Frank said. "Paper trail ends at a holding company whose only address is a lawyer at an offshore bank. We'll never break that one."

"These are some rich, smart dudes, man," Jimmy said. "Why the hell are you holding that fucking duck like a baby?"

I put the duck back into his plastic nest and began carefully replacing the wrapping.

"After a pretty good look at your pal Dagoberto," Frank said, "as far as the Denver police computer can tell, he is the sole owner of the Quirky Arms. There's no note, his bills are paid promptly by a national independent accounting firm, as are his taxes, local, state, and federal. I didn't see the books, but if he's washing money through there, none of the obvious signs are around." He paused, then shook his head. "On the other hand, when we had a couple of drinks there, I noticed some interesting things. I couldn't place the accent but I'd swear some of the other guys are not any kind of Mexican that I know. We don't see enough Colombians in Denver for me to be absolutely sure, but I thought I recognized several Colombian accents, at least something Central or South American. The cook, maybe the bartender, one waiter. But the oddest thing, Sughrue: I can smell criminal activity. And right now I'm smelling trouble, not cocaine."

"Wish to hell I was smelling some right now," Jimmy said, "up close and personal."

"Just wait," I said.

"But even stranger," Frank said with a cop's sense of the dramatic, "when my buddy ran Sr. Reyna's name through the system, he came up completely clean. Not just in our computer files, but also in the NCIC."

"I can't believe that," I said as I finished taping my duck safely into his nest. "What the hell does that mean?"

"One of three things, I suspect," Frank said, closing his notebook. "Either he's clean, which I truly doubt. Or he's got friends in high places. Or . . ."

"Or?" Jimmy and I said together.

"Or he's a DEA asset. Stranger things have happened with our brother officers in the drug war."

"Fuck that version," I said. "What sort of friends could he have in high places? Maybe Joe Don Pines? He ran for governor in Texas, didn't he?"

"And got beaten so badly he moved to New Mexico," Frank said.

"But he works for the President, right?" I said.

"That's oil and energy shit, C.W.," Frank said, "wrong area code. Plus, he just doesn't feel right in my gut . . ."

On that we all fell silent together, then all tried to talk at once. Jimmy won through sheer energy.

"That Joe Donny Pines, he was a fucking officer in Vietnam, wasn't he? Some kinda head-hog in Saigon?"

"Sounds right," Frank said, "but I gotta drain my lizard."

Jimmy and I watched the big man shuffle toward the latrine again. I opened a couple of beers for us. "Isn't there anything he can do?" I asked as I handed him the can.

Jimmy turned on me, his eyes so angry I thought he was either going to shout or hit me, then they just got sad. We sat for a moment listening as the valley lost the sun, cooling, drawing the wind down. The trees rattled, rubbed, and squealed, needle against needle, bark against bark.

"The biggest target in the fucking bush, man. He shoulda died a thousand times over there," Jimmy said softly, "a thousand times."

Thirty minutes later the sun had disappeared and we all sat around in down vests staring into cups of murky coffee, something besides beer to drink after a couple of hits of Norman's biker speed.

"Neither hide nor hair," I said, "of Wynona or the Cisneros woman?"

Frank shook his head. "We followed him home, glassed his house good, then followed him back, followed the flat-nosed guy around, and the fat one some, too. But nothing. If they've got the women, we didn't see them."

"So what now?" Jimmy asked.

"You guys have to go in and take Sr. Reyna out," Frank said, "see if he might join you in an intimate conversation."

"You guys?"

"Sarge, if I'd put in my papers before I left town," Frank said, "I'd go with you. But if we get caught, my kids lose the retirement."

"Makes sense," I said. "What about you, kid?"

Jimmy stared up at the blue sky fading to black, then said, "Wish we had a helicopter . . ."

"What the fuck you want a chopper for?" Frank said.

"Carry that little bastard up about ten thousand feet and hold him in the door," Jimmy said, still looking up. "Usually they can't talk fast enough at that altitude."

Frank looked at me and said, "Jimmy did a few weeks with the ARVN Rangers after you left the outfit. The uniforms fit, and he liked being the tallest piece of shit in the company."

"They had the best whores, too," Jimmy said, smiling into the heavens.

"But let me point out something, you little fuck," Frank said, then reached over the table and picked up Jimmy by the back of his vest, "we're already at ten thousand feet."

Without a pause, Jimmy said, "Then we'll throw him off your shoulders, you big fuck."

"I can't be involved," Frank said, taking charge anyway, "but I'll cover the front. You guys park on the street. I'll go for a drink, see if the slimebag is there, then come back and give you the setup, then go back in and order another. You guys go in through the alley."

"What if the door's locked?" Jimmy asked, shuffling from foot to foot.

"Wait until somebody brings out the garbage, you worthless little Harp," Frank said. "But don't bring him back here. Please. And don't tell me where you take him. Okay?" Jimmy and I nodded. "I'm treading the line as it is . . ."

"Don't fuck *the job*," Jimmy said, heading for the pisser, "and the job won't fuck you."

"Right," Frank said, watching the little man hump through the darkness as if he could see.

"He can still see in the dark," I said.

"You know what the little jerk did after you left the outfit?" Frank asked me. "He went a little batshit, you remember, after Willie got wasted, so the green machine wouldn't let him extend for another tour. So they sent him home. When he cleared division, he went AWOL and hitched back to the company, said they'd changed their mind at the last minute. Usual Army fuckup. Dumb-ass. It took 'em six months to find him, then they didn't know quite what to do . . ."

"They couldn't get rid of me quick enough," Jimmy said from the shadows, still as quiet on his feet as the old days. "An MP rode me all the way to Travis. I was a civilian two hours after my feet hit the runway. But I fooled 'em."

"Jerkoff used his cousin's birth certificate to enlist again," Frank said. "You ever hear anything like that?"

"No," I had to admit.

"My own mother turned me in," Jimmy squealed, "just after I finished basic—you'd be amazed how easy basic is after a few months in the bush." Then he laughed. Jimmy had enlisted the first time after his older brother came home in a box, so I couldn't blame his mother. "So I said fuck it, went back to San Francisco . . ."

"Where you fucked up again," Frank said, then paused. "Let's do it before the place closes and one of you hippies loses his nerve."

So we did.

After Frank came back out front and laid the details on us, we walked around to the alley, two guys in gray overalls and watch caps that pulled down to become ski masks. Jimmy carried a clipboard in one hand, my spring-loaded sap in his other; I toted a new toolbox full of rocks and the silenced .22 Woodsman loaded with hollow points in my long pocket. Just a couple of working stiffs on a late night call.

I don't know about the old cliché of soldiers following a good officer into the gates of hell; but my experience had taught me that you could follow a good point man and trust him to keep you out of the shit. And Jimmy had been good. Maybe walking point was like riding a bicycle: you never forgot. The jittery, jumpy Jimmy disappeared as he led me down the alley; he was in charge now.

Jimmy stepped over an untidy spew of garbage, mouthing "sloppy fuckers" at me, then checked the door. Unlocked. Jimmy seemed as calm as if he was stopping by his mother's for corned beef and cabbage, but as we checked our watches—two minutes tops inside, we'd planned—he stopped to look again at the garbage. Suddenly, he crouched, as I did, then we pulled down the ski masks and went in the back door in a quick silent duck walk, as I covered Jimmy's advance with the .22.

We found the first body, a busboy, just inside the hallway. Somebody had gutted him.

What is it about human viscera that makes it stink so bad?

Jimmy rolled his eyes, tried to breathe through his mouth.

Why is the taste of death in the air more palatable than the smell?

Since I had the weapon, I eased around Jimmy, careful to keep
my feet out of the blood and entrails, trying to act calm as I
peeked into the kitchen. Nothing moved. A longer look revealed
two bodies in cook's hats, one shot through the eye crumpled in
front of the prep table, the other frying his brains on the grill.
A busboy bowed his head into the bloody water of a sink. I
couldn't see where he'd been hit, but like the others I was sure
he never knew what had hit him.

"All of them," I whispered to Jimmy. "Silencer."

"Frank?" was his soft question. To which I shook my head.

The produce room door was open. But before we could look
in, a waiter carrying a plastic tub of dirty dishes and a very
haughty, angry frown came through the swinging doors. I covered the waiter, motioned for him to put the dish tub down, and
when he started to stand up, Jimmy laid the sap neatly behind
his ear, then used the unconscious body to block the doors as I
dove into the produce room.

Chato at least had time to stand up before he had taken three
small-caliber jacketed rounds through his face and spread-eagled
among flats of fancy lettuce. You could have covered the entrance
wounds on his forehead with a silver dollar. You could have
covered the three .22 wounds behind the ear of the dead cocktail
waitress on the couch with a quarter.

She looked familiar, even with her ankles and wrists bound
with dish towels, her mouth gagged with a bar rag. It was Mel
from Snowy Lake, her open eyes *dead*. What the fuck had she
been doing here? I reached for her eyelids to close them, but for
the first time in my life, I couldn't touch a dead body. Wynona
and Baby Lester were nowhere in sight, their only spoor a dirty
diaper I couldn't even smell after all the blood.

Back in the hallway, Jimmy motioned me toward the open
door of Dagoberto's office, and I obeyed.

They wanted Dagoberto to see it coming. Somebody had jerked
out a couple of handfuls of his thick hair and stuffed an onion in
his mouth before they cut his throat so deeply his head hung
backward over the desk chair. The room was so full of blood I
could only venture a couple of steps inside the door.

Jimmy followed me out into the fresh air of the alley, where

we unmasked, then strolled like two guys on our way to a beer.
I glanced at my watch: in and out in less than two minutes. And
not a sign left behind, nothing but more bad dreams carried
away. A long two minutes.

In the van, we tore out of our overalls, stuffed the .22 under
my belt, then walked calmly to the front door of the Quirky
Arms.

"You get Frank the fuck out of here," I said to Jimmy at the
door as I shoved a wad of cash in his hand. "Then you guys get
in the rent-car, take it to the Denver airport, pay cash for the
day and the drop-off fee, and tell them to tear up the credit card
receipt. Then you guys go home. You don't need this shit."
Jimmy opened his mouth, but I shut it with a look.

Two couples sat over coffee and drinks at one of the back
tables, and another couple billed and cooed over a bottle of white
wine at the bar. Frank was the only other customer and he had
sense enough not to give me a funny look as I walked past him
toward David at the end of the bar. He was Jimmy's problem
now.

David looked a little surprised to see me, but I nested the
silencer into his chubby ribs before he could complain.

"Don't say anything," I said calmly, "just fucking listen.
We're in deep shit . . ."

"You're in deep shit, Sughrue . . ."

"Shut the fuck up, David," I said, "or I'll pull the trigger
right here. Shut up and listen. Everybody in the back is dead."
David jerked off his stool, but I kept the silencer screwed into his
side. "If I'd done them, we wouldn't be having this conversation,
understand?"

"Everybody?"

"Except Wynona and the kid . . ."

"They were out of here this morning," he said, briefly confused, then composed his face to ask, "What about the other
broad?"

"It's all a fucking mess," I said, "three times behind the ear.
Professional job."

"Shit. You didn't call the cops?"

"I assumed you wouldn't want the cops running an investigation team through this place," I said, watching Jimmy and Frank exit.

"Are you kidding? We have to clean up this shit ourselves, then pray it's clean."

"Then get rid of your customers, and let's work a deal," I suggested, then stuffed the .22 under my vest.

It took longer than it should have, and I, no surprise, had two more large Scotches than I should have. The whisky didn't make me drunk, it made me sick. But the knots in my gut wouldn't be purged by retching. While David eased the customers out, I introduced myself to Roberto, assuming that one should know the names of people with whom you were about to commit multiple-count major felonies.

"Roberto Reyna," he said, no longer exactly a bartender.

"C. W. Sughrue," I said, extending my hand.

"I know your name," he answered in unaccented English, then smiled sadly as if that weren't all.

David locked the front door, stepped over to the bar, then sighed. "Let's have a couple of shots of Herradura, Bob, and a couple of cans of Listón Azul." Then he turned to me. "How about you, Sughrue?"

"Why the fuck not?"

We gunned the shots, then washed them down with the cold clear beers. I was willing to do anything to get Mel's eyes out of my memory, knowing it would never happen.

"So how bad is it?" Bob asked David.

"Everybody," David said. "Or so he said."

"Mr. Sughrue is here, David," Bob said, "so I guess we can assume that he's not going to lie to us." Then he turned to me, gave me one of those sadly resigned smiles of a guy who had seen far too many bodies. "Is it bad?"

I didn't even have to answer.

"Shit," Bob said. "Can you stand it again?"

"I'd rather not," I admitted. "But I will. If you'll pour some of that tequila for me."

"Sure," Bob said, then poured shots for all of us, and they went down like the last hope of a dying race.

We had another sip of beer, then went back to the killing ground.

Whatever he did in his real life, Bob wasn't a bartender, but, considering Frank's suggestion that Dagoberto might be a DEA asset, Bob wasn't a cop, either. Whatever he was, though, he was used to command and dead bodies. After he calmly checked the scene without disturbing it, we followed him into the alley.

"I wish I still smoked," he said.

"Ditto," I said.

David handed us his cigarettes, so we stood in the alley smoking. After a minute, Bob said, "Pretty fucking slick. You were inside only two minutes?"

"Maybe a little less," I said. "So they were in and out in less than five minutes. And they knew we were coming."

"They wanted you to take the rap for this?"

"I think so."

"How could they know?" Bob asked.

"I don't know," I said, "I just don't know."

"Maybe your friends . . ." David began.

"No way," I said. "They're both wild cards. I didn't even know I was going to use them for backup."

"But you won't tell us their names?" Bob said.

"Not a chance," I said. "I trust them with my life, and guarantee their lack of involvement with it."

"Believe me, you have," Bob said. "But what about you, Mr. Sughrue? Is it possible you're the betrayer?"

"How could I be?" I said. "I still don't know what the fuck is going on."

"Perhaps if you would tell me what you know, I could help you find out for both of us," Bob said.

"I'm looking for Sarita Cisneros Pines. Just like I said at the beginning," I said. "And Wynona now."

"Do you know where Mrs. Pines is? Did the girl tell you? She wouldn't tell us," Bob said softly, then when I shook my head, he added, "David is a skilled man with a question. But he has this thing about women."

"Can't stand to see them cry," David said. "But men, man, I don't give a fuck. They answer my questions."

"Fuck that shit," I said. "Nobody asks questions from the grave."

"Or answers them," Bob said. "Are you that quick?"

"Quick enough," I said, "and mad enough." Then stuffed the .22 under his nose. "I don't know what Mel was doing here, but she's dead now. We could have been friends. I don't mind starting payback with you guys. So let's fucking see how many twenty-two rounds you can take before you can get your hands on me." They didn't like that much. For a moment I thought they might, but it was just blood and adrenaline.

"Her presence was a regrettable mistake and I am deeply sorry about her death, and you must not feel responsible, Mr. Sughrue," Bob said. "She showed up looking for a job. We hired her. Then we caught her in the office files. We had to restrain her until we could find out who she worked for . . . It was not your fault."

"Believe me, asshole," I said, "*responsible* is not what I feel. And who the fuck is *we*?" I asked.

"Unfortunately, I'm not at liberty to discuss this matter with you," Bob answered.

"Which bunch of Mexicans are you?"

"I beg your pardon," Bob said.

"The ones who took Sarita Cisneros from the first bunch? Or the first bunch?"

"I am not sure that I understand your question, Mr. Sughrue," Bob said, then added, "but it gives nothing away to tell you that the health and safety of Señora Pines is of paramount importance to us."

"Right, but why?"

"That's none of your affair," Bob said. "If I were you, I'd give up this case and go home."

"Sure," I said. "Just as soon as I find her, make sure Wynona Jones and her baby are safe, and gut the motherfucker who did Mel. Then I'll think about it."

"Please," Bob said. "We'll clean up this mess. Just go home.

No bodies will appear on your doorstep. If you don't go home, I can promise we can fill your bed with dead bodies."

"What the hell," I said, "I live in a morgue. And you dudes are cold bastards even for cocaine dealers," I said.

"Believe me, my friend, this isn't about cocaine," Bob said. "You may have been an adequate soldier in a bad war a long time ago but you're just a civilian in this one. Retire from the field, go home. War is a young man's game but only an old man's memory. Go back to Montana, resume your place at the bar, on the stool or on the tap, but go, enjoy your middle years . . ."

I put a round between his feet, but Bob didn't jump.

"Some years ago in Denver," he said calmly, "I understand you put a round in the foot of a pornographer just to get the answer to a single question. Now you shoot near my foot . . . I hope my point is well taken."

"It was two rounds," I said, "from a derringer, .22 shorts. Just made him walk funny. This fucker is full of long rifle hollow points. The doctors will never be able to glue all those little bones together. And you may never walk again . . ."

I let off another round close enough to shatter asphalt under the soles of his black leather sneakers. "I hope my point is well taken. I ain't gonna retire until I finish my chores—now one of them is Mel—or I'm fucking dead."

Bob frowned, but not in fear; something closer to consternation, or maybe mild irritation. I was dealing with one tough, committed son of a bitch. Committed to what was the question.

"I can see that this is a wasted conversation," Bob finally said, "and David and I have a full night of chores. We'll discuss these matters again. I'll call you in a few days. Agreed?"

"I'll see how I feel wherever I am when you want to talk," I said. "Call Solomon Rainbolt. Tell him your name is Dagoberto."

David snorted with something like laughter as I backed down the alley.

"What the fuck's funny, asshole?"

"Dagoberto was my brother," Bob said.

"I knew that," I said, lying and enjoying it, even if I didn't know if I was lying to the good guys or the bad. "All you Reynas look the same."

* * *

Back at the campsite, as usual after the stress ended, I went directly into mental overload, and tried to achieve a chemical balance without any light and with only the drugs at hand. I needed a couple of long hits off the Jamaican roach to breathe deeply without hyperventilating. Then the speed calmed me as if I were a hyperactive child. A line of coke sharpened my focus. Three beers burned up some of the adrenaline. And the half a dozen cigarettes from a pack I'd bought on the way back to the campground satisfied my death wish.

Since I had lost more adult friends to cigarettes than to drugs, alcohol, or gunfire, I hated to start again, but the evening didn't seem to leave me any choice. What I really wanted was a Tuinal and a platoon of bush vets for a bodyguard. Maybe my heart would stop banging on my stomach wall then. But I did what I could.

In the moonless dark, a cold wind moaning, fear warming my gut and freezing the sweat on my face, just as I tugged a sleeping bag out of the tent, planning to drag it over to a rock face where at least nobody could get behind me and the Browning, I heard a car turn off the road into the campground.

It came toward me. When the headlights flashed down the track to our campsite, I rolled across their beams, my eyes tightly closed, crashed into a tree with my forehead, but managed to keep my eyes closed until I took cover looking away from the bright lights.

"Pretty good, Sarge," Jimmy's voice cackled from the car as the lights switched off. "I didn't know you had it in you."

Jimmy opened the passenger door, the interior light snapped on, and I put three 9mm rounds into the pine branch above his head.

"Motherfucker!" I screamed.

Jimmy scrambled under the car while Frank laughed behind the wheel of the rent-car.

Even before the echoes of the gunfire had faded, some disgruntled tourist shouted, "Hold it down over there!" He must have made camp since we had left just after dark.

How did I know it was a tourist? A reasonable person wouldn't have shouted at me after just hearing three rounds thunk like a double-bit axe into the tree. But tourists are brave, not reasonable. In fact they are the bravest people in the world. They leap into giant vehicles and haul oversized trailers into places that most intelligent people wouldn't take a D-9 Cat and at speeds most people wouldn't attempt in sports cars. They try to sit their children on black bears with bags of marshmallows, they try to photograph the nasal passages of buffalo and moose, and they blunder their way up trails closed by grizzly bear signs, flouting their chocolate bars and menstrual pads, so they are so brave they scare the shit out of me.

Which is why I didn't lay a couple of rounds over the heads of whoever decided to camp nearby. Or maybe it was because Frank took the pistol away from me before I could pull the trigger.

"My god, you look like shit," Frank said a few hours later during breakfast at a truck stop outside Grand Junction.

As soon as I could settle down we broke camp and fled, Jimmy driving the van, Frank following to make sure we weren't tagged when we left Aspen. Once I had accused Jimmy of not talking much for a fucking Harp, he stopped talking altogether, leaving me to try to destroy my mind by myself.

Even in the truck stop, he wouldn't talk to me. But Frank wouldn't stop.

"You never even looked this bad in the bush. Guess you ain't as tough as you used to be," Frank said, dumping syrup over two pancake sandwiches. "Or as smart. You know, when you came into the company, we all knew you were some lifer football pogue who had decided that the war was some way to justify your worthless and wasted life."

"Sigmund Freud on the M-60."

Frank took a large bite of pancakes dripping syrup and egg yolk. I don't know why I didn't puke. Or why I hadn't yet.

"Any asshole with a room-temperature IQ could tell it," he said when he finished chewing. "But you weren't stupid, you humped your own gear and dug your own holes, and you weren't some dumbshit lifer. So we kept you alive until you were able to hump your own weight." He paused, his large black eyes, those eyes that had seen it all from all the genetic directions. "So what the fuck happened?"

"Maybe I needed a longer break between wars," I said, then laughed my way into the hiccoughs, then hiccoughed my way into tears. Which I took outside. Then puked, finally, the bile, the acid, the tears scraping out my throat like a wire brush.

"You okay now?" Frank asked when I slid back into the booth.

"What are you motherfuckers looking at?" I said to the truckers who had turned to watch.

"Guess not," Frank said, then stood up. A large man of dubious hue holding a badge is an impressive sight. The truckers, who had stood up, sat quickly down.

"What if we hadn't been here?" he asked as soon as he sat down.

"I'd have had my ass kicked," I said, semi-lucid, "but they wouldn't be getting a cherry."

"And what if we'd been the bad guys driving into camp instead of us?" Frank said.

"They would have been fucking sorry."

"And you would have been dead."

"Tell me somebody who might give a shit," I said. If you're going to dip your toe into the false warmth of self-pity, you might as well put your whole foot into the sloppy brew of true sentimentality.

"Beats me," Frank said. Then continued with his breakfast until it irritated me.

"I don't know how a dying man can eat like that," I said to Frank, who merely smiled like a man who had been told his zipper fly was open. But Jimmy grunted like a man hit, and when I managed to focus my drunken, stupid eyes on his face, I gathered enough sanity to apologize. "I'm sorry," I whispered.

"Me, too," Jimmy said to Frank, his anger gone immediately. "I was drunk, I guess. I just thought he should know, or some other stupid shit . . ."

"No problem, James, no problem," Frank said, then stared at me, holding the last disgusting hunk of his breakfast on a fork. "Remember when you figured it out, Sughrue?"

"What?"

"That staying alive had nothing to do with you," Frank said softly, "that it was all luck."

I looked out the window. On the interstate people were going places I'd never been, people perhaps with a future, people whose lives were lived without looking always backward.

"When Willie went down," I said.

"The baddest of a bad bunch," Frank said. "First Squad, Charlie Company, Third of the Seventh, First Air Cav. Nobody did it better than we did, and none of us were as good as Willie. And he died like a fucking jerk. Right?"

I nodded.

"So I'm dying now, Sarge," Frank said, "and when the time comes, I'll eat my piece and try not to make a mess, but until then, I'm alive." Then he looked out the window. "It's fairly simple, man, it's how you live, not how you die." Frank looked at me a long time, then reached over the table for my plate. "If you ain't going to eat your breakfast, I will."

After a second, I took my plate out of his hands, and ate every bite of the cold, withered omelette.

We crashed at a nearby motel, taking a single room with two double beds for the normal-sized people and a rollaway at our feet for Jimmy, circling the wagons, setting up the night defensive position. I looked around before switching off the lights: Jimmy grinned like a child curled on the rollaway; with his arms propped behind his head, against the white sheets, Frank seemed dark and large, ominously huge, except for his large white smile; I suspected I still looked like shit.

"Sorry about your friend, C.W.," Frank said seriously, "and sorry about coming down on you so hard, but it sounds like you're in some kind of big-time trouble, and you got to keep your wits about you, or we're all dead."

"No problem," I said, "I got a handle on it. And thanks for taking care of me." I switched off the lights. "Why didn't you guys go home?" I asked in the darkness.

"Hate to leave even a dumbfuck lifer behind," Frank said.

"Thanks."

"If you guys are gonna jabber all fucking night," Jimmy said, "you take the perimeter guard and I'll take the nap duty." After a long pause, Frank said, "Fuck the duty, Jimmy, let's get some sleep. The war will still be out there tomorrow." As far as I knew, we slept like the dead. For a change. Perhaps we all felt as if somebody were watching our backs. For a change.

At noon the next day, over another truck-stop breakfast, I tried to talk Frank and Jimmy into going home. Not too hard, I admit.

"So what's next?" Frank said, another gooey pancake sandwich in front of him.

"If you want to stay, you've got to go back to Denver," I said, "and put in your papers."

Frank nodded. "It's time."

"Take the rent-car back to the Aspen airport, turn it in, and you guys fly back to Denver and wait for me to call," I said, then looked at them. "Either of you guys ever spent any time in El Paso?"

"Why El Paso?" Frank said.

"That's where the Cisneros woman lived," I said, "and her hubby, Joe Don."

"I got a tattoo there once," Jimmy said, pulling up his shirt sleeve to reveal a blue blur that had once looked like the sailor on a pack of rolling papers.

"You know I grew up there," Frank said, "but the only person I've stayed in touch with is my mother."

"And you don't want her around this shit," I said flatly.

"Nowhere near."

"I met a guy there," Jimmy said, "in jail . . ."

"This before or after the tattoo?" Frank wanted to know.

". . . in Juárez. Before. Anyway, this guy's a vet, a Navy guy . . ." Obviously Frank and I sneered because Jimmy quickly added, "A riverboat commander and a SEAL, Barnstone, one bad dude."

"So what was he doing in jail in Juárez?" Frank asked.

"Getting this buddy of his out, some redneck college professor or something," Jimmy answered. "And he saw me in there, so he got me out, too. Paid my *mordida*, took me home, got me fucked up—and tattooed, by the way—then loaned me the money to get back to Denver." Then Jimmy pointed a stubby finger at Frank. "And your people kept my fucking car."

"What for? Samoans don't need cars, man. We ride the waves," Frank said.

"No, some Detroit niggers," Jimmy hissed, "you asshole."

"You do this shit often?" I asked Frank.

"What?"

"Lie?" I said. "And defame your ethnic heritage. You told me the other morning that you could smoke dope without becoming a hippie because you were a Mexican."

"Patently true," Frank said, as innocent as a gull drifting on an ocean breeze.

Jimmy and I looked at each other. "Sometimes I find myself regretting my full Irish blood, just like I regret my RVN medal, my Purple Hearts, and my Bronze Star. What about you, Sughrue?" Jimmy said, then picked up his ice water.

"Scotch-Irish," I said, "and don't forget it. And not even a good-conduct medal. My father had a DSC and a Purple Heart but he was most proud of his claim to be half-Comanche, but I think his mother was Czech or German or something, and the only metal she had was in her teeth. Who knows? You know how those people are, always changing their borders so they can change their names. Remind me of anybody you know?" Then I pointed out the window. "Maybe that guy."

Frank looked. Jimmy leaned over and poured the cold water into Frank's cop shoe. "Jesus fucking Christ!" Frank shouted, and jumped up so quickly that he nearly tore the table from its moorings.

Jimmy and I laughed, but one of the truckers at the booth behind us, the biggest one, of course, who had taken an interest in our multi-ethnic scruffy crew since we first sat down and picked up the Army talk, leaned over and said, "Why don't you children grow up? And forget the war. You assholes are the kinda vets who make it hard for the rest of us. Just fucking grow up."

Jimmy stood up quickly. "You wanna teach me how to grow up, you worthless, gear-grinding Rear Echelon Motherfucker."

"Uh-oh," Frank said to me. "Let's see if we can't at least get it outside."

We almost didn't. As the big trucker's buddy held the door open with mock politeness, Jimmy kicked him in the shin so hard he nearly fell down, but I managed to shove him outside so he could limp after Jimmy, who was walking fast after the big trucker.

Frank tried to keep it fair, just Jimmy and the big driver, holding out his hands at the other five truckers, but they could see that the big trucker had as much chance of hitting Jimmy as kissing his elbow, and even if he could hit him, it would be like hitting a big rubber band. Jimmy had raised knots all over the trucker's face with his hard little fists, so one of the other ones, unable to get his ethnic slurs together, called Frank a "spigger," and took a swing at him.

Frank had been a cop too long to ever hit a grown man in the face with his fist; he just dodged the roundhouse, let the punch's momentum spin him around, quickly applied the time-honored choke hold for the few seconds it took for the guy to start "doing the chicken," then dropped him to the pavement. That's when everybody decided to take part.

By rights we should have had our asses kicked—they were twice our number and most of them half our age—but Jimmy was insane, Frank a large gentleman with lots of practice, and I . . . well, I don't fight fair.

I ripped an antenna off the closest truck, whipped one guy across the ear, which left a welt like forty wasp bites, then got the remaining one a couple of times on the arm and once on the neck before he ran over to his tractor to grab his tire-thumper.

I stuck my hand under my vest and shouted, "If I have to pull this motherfucker, man, you are dead."

He thought about it, but luckily Frank's two guys were twitching all over the pavement. When Frank moved on him, he let the wooden club fall to the ground.

The guy Jimmy had kicked in the shin had wisely restrained

from the melee, and the only reason the big trucker wasn't supine was that Jimmy held him up by the collar.

"No harm, no foul," I said. Everybody agreed but the guy in the worst position, the big guy with his hands over his face.

"No harm, my ass," he mumbled. "I think the little fucker kicked one of my teeth out."

"He didn't kick you," I said. "You don't really look old enough to be a vet . . ."

"MP," he muttered, "Long Binh. Nineteen seventy-two."

"You're lucky he didn't kill you," Frank said.

Jimmy jerked the trucker up as if to land another on his already swollen eye, but he raised his hands, saying, "Okay. Okay, man. You got me."

"Say it," Jimmy said.

"No harm, no foul."

"Thank God for the Denver Nuggets," Frank said.

So much for planning.

Jimmy drove the van on the way back to Aspen, and I rode with Frank in the rent-car to see if we couldn't come up with some sort of notion about what had happened and why, but all we had were guesses, until just outside of Rifle a battered gray GMC pickup went around us like a rocket and pulled up behind the van. The engine sounded like a Cadillac, well tuned and roaring, and the pickup sported four new tires.

"I know that truck," I said. "They were following the FBI when the FBI was following me. Let's try something. Let me borrow your piece."

"What piece?" Frank said.

"I thought the law required you to carry a piece all the time," I said.

"Only in Denver," Frank said, "and I never even do that. I haven't carried a piece on the job since I . . ." Then Frank paused a long time, staring at the road. "Look, C.W., I wasn't just in that schoolhouse telling them little kids that the policeman is their friend . . . I was also talking to a nine-year-old girl who thinks she's her daddy's wife. She has thought that since her mother died when she was four. She cooks, keeps house, and warms the old bastard's bed at night. I was trying to convince her to testify. I work child abuse cases, too. You don't need a piece for that, man, just a cold heart and a strong stomach. If I carried a piece, C.W., somebody would be dead . . ."

"I'm sorry," I said, "I didn't know."

Frank slapped me on the thigh with a giant hand. "Don't worry," he said. "When it doesn't work out, it's the worst fucking job on the job. When it does, it's still the worst fucking job on the job. My shrink . . ."

"Your shrink?" I said, amazed.

"What the fuck? Can't the third world enjoy the benefits of analysis?"

"I, ah, just assumed you natural folk weren't in need of that sort of witch doctoring."

"Well, I used to beat drums and dance naked and bite the heads off chickens, bro', didn't think I needed any of that intellectual shit until the night I found myself eating my piece without taking the time to write a note to my kids or even think about it. And this was before I knew about the cancer," Frank said, then smiled. "My job is too tough to do alone, C.W., so I got some help. Anyway, my shrink says I've got to stop blaming the cancer on the job, but you can understand how I might."

"I'm sorry," I said. "Maybe I'm stupid to lose my shit over a woman I just barely knew. But dammit she was dead and I didn't think I could stand it. She was a fine woman and a great bartender."

"Sometimes being scared and hurting is the right thing. It's like evidence that you're still alive. And we all need that. Sometimes," Frank said softly, then raised his voice and slapped me on the knee. "Goddamn, it's good to see you. You know how it is. Sometimes you forget how much you miss people when you don't see them around."

"Yeah," I said, "I guess I should thank you for putting it into words."

"Don't get too fucking sensitive on me," he said, "I won't trust you anymore."

"Thanks, asshole," I said.

"So why'd you want a piece?" Frank asked when he stopped chuckling. "I thought you were carrying."

"Bluffing," I said. "I'd like to talk to those guys in the pickup and I want a a better choice of weapons than a tire iron and a radio antenna."

"Want me to pass Jimmy and take the next gas exit?"

"Read my mail, old man, read my mind," I said, then added a question. "How'd you feel back there, tussling with those truckers?"

"Old" was his simple answer.

"Yeah, me, too," I said. "You know that asshole Mexican bartender told me that war was a young man's game. We couldn't go back in the bush again, could we?"

"Not a chance," Frank said. "You know what, though? If they'd do it the right way this time, I'd give it a try."

"What's the right way?"

"Let the guys who do the work run the job," Frank said, but I think he was talking about more than Vietnam.

After ten minutes of duplicity at a convenience store just off the interstate at Rifle, which the gray pickup watched from a service station across the highway and which I spent prone in the backseat, we took our little band back on the road. Only this time, I had the Airweight strapped to my ankle, the Browning under my arm, and the 10mm Glock in my hand.

"You got enough firepower?" Frank asked as we roared up the exit five minutes after the gray pickup.

"Hey, as long as you can carry it, there's no such thing as too much firepower," I said. "When you catch up to the pickup, pull up beside it. I'll see if I can't get them to stop."

"Without gunfire, I hope," Frank said. "My papers ain't in yet."

"Of course," I said.

Fat fucking chance.

Frank pulled the rent-car up beside the pickup that didn't sound like a pickup at all. I showed the Mexican driver Frank's badge, which we had sullied beyond the point of shining, and made the motion of rolling a window down. Which he did.

"Are you guys the good Mexicans," I shouted, "or the bad ones?"

The driver didn't answer, he just showed me the twin dark holes of a sawed-off 12-gauge shotgun.

Conversation was out of the question. I jammed my foot over Frank's, and we smoked to a stop on the left shoulder of the interstate. Only one pellet of the buckshot skipped off the hood of the rent-car.

A big rig blasted past us, its horn blaring. I hoped it wasn't one of the truckers from Grand Junction. We had already ruined their day enough.

"What the fuck?" Frank sighed as the burnt-rubber cloud enveloped the car. "What happened?"

"Sawed-off," I said. "Good driving. Now, go, man, put your foot in it."

I had always loved cars as only a country boy can. Cars are freedom, romance, and true, true love. But I haven't been able to tell the makes apart since I came back from Southeast Asia. So I didn't know the make of the rent-car—something American full of rattles and bad plastic—but when Frank put his foot to the floor, that Detroit iron roared while I checked the 10mm clip again.

Up the highway, the pickup sped toward the van. I saw the dark blunt shape of the shotgun pass from the driver to the passenger. I grabbed the Airweight, shot four holes in a square pattern into the windshield, which deafened us almost beyond hearing, then tried to kick the safety glass out.

"What the fuck are you doing?" Frank screamed.

"The assholes are going to do Jimmy," I shouted back as a chunk of the windshield tumbled into the slipstream, then leaned into the wind. "Get me closer, goddammit, closer."

I didn't know how fast we were going but was amazed that three cars and a semi whipped past us during the shoot-out. What the hell, it's America; nobody dies, they just pass on the right. So I couldn't complain. Besides, the flying convoy kept the pickup out of the left lane long enough for me to draw a bead.

"Don't fucking shoot anybody!" Frank, in his capacity as a minion of the law, shouted.

"Not a chance," I whispered, then fired half the 10mm clip at the pickup, praying for a lucky shot.

Like most prayers, it was wasted. I should have been praying for a lucky ricochet. I missed the rear tires, but it was a tough shot for anybody at any time. So I got ready to try again. Frank didn't have any advice this time. We were close enough to see the passenger lean out his window with the shotgun.

Before I could pull the trigger, though, a cloud of oil and auto parts destroyed the remainder of our windshield and a roil of smoke spewed from beneath the pickup and it stopped without benefit of brake lights. The two Mexicans piled out of the cab, their gear flapping, and headed off the interstate highway, hopped the fence and headed up a low ridge, then turned right along the crest and headed south into the mountains.

By the time we parked behind the pickup on the side of the interstate, the smoke still hadn't completely cleared. But we could see them rapidly diminishing up another ridge hill as they chugged toward the higher ridgeline and invisibility. I watched their remarkable advance as Frank squatted to peer under the pickup.

"Lucky fucker," Frank said when he straightened up.

"Me?" I said.

"No. Jimmy," he said. "Looks like your round keyholed through the pan and busted the crank."

"He was always lucky," I said, but watching the incredible progress of the two men. "Frank."

"What?"

"Maybe those are the good guys," I guessed.

"Why?"

"Because the bad guys always have tanks and choppers and planes and that kind of shit," I said. "Only the good guys can hump Indian Country like that."

PART FOUR

PART FOUR

While Jimmy drove the van down to Albuquerque to wait for us, Frank and I flew from Aspen to Denver—cash tickets, assumed names; who knows what computers the FBI can read?—where he stayed long enough to turn in his retirement papers and take his children to dinner and where I caught the first flight back to Meriwether, a long silent flight.

"So what do you want from me?" Solly asked as he poured another four fingers of his expensive Scotch into my crystal tumbler. The sun had just dropped behind the Hardrock Peaks, and suddenly it was too cold to be sitting on Solly's deck. "Want to go back inside?" he asked, dipping the end of his Cuban cigar into the Scotch.

"It's fine," I said, watching the clear valley air cloud with woolly puffs of woodsmoke. "You could check with some of your bureaucratic pals in D.C. and find out why the FBI is dogging my tracks everywhere I go."

"Can't you think of something else?" he suggested. "In order to come up with that kind of information, Sughrue, I'd have to call in some markers so heavy that it would cause more trouble than it's worth."

"I suppose you'd have the same answer if I wanted Joe Don Pine's FBI file?"

Solly just stared at me, then smiled. "He's a lying, no-good, worthless piece of shit," he said.

"I take it you're not fond of the gentleman, speaking personally?"

"We crossed paths," Solly said, "several times. But the first time was enough for me. The first time I shook his hand in Saigon, I wanted to take a shower."

"I always wondered what you officers did with all that shower time," I said. "What was wrong with him?"

"Professional Texan, for starters. Starched and tailored fatigues. Talked a hell of a game but his sunlamp tan faded every time the air-conditioner compressor changed tunes," Solly said.

"We all saw a lot of officers like that," I said. "What's new?"

"He worked for the Defense Intelligence Agency."

"So did I," I reminded him.

"Yeah, but that was just to stay out of Leavenworth," Solly said. "That's different."

"I hope so," I said, meaning it. The DIA had seen too many spy movies and was completely out of control in those days, doing the jobs that not even the cowboys at the CIA would touch, roaming across the world in whatever manner suited them, bureaucrat-warrior-spies. "And since then?"

"Well, I hit a clipping service in D.C. for you," he said, then tossed a file folder on the table. "Usual oil and politics shit. Got rich after the war playing the international market. Then went public and lost all his stockholders' bread. Joe Don would have come out all right, but some slick lawyer proved that he was trading on illegal insider information, so the judge stripped him of everything but the desert ranch his grandmother left him in New Mexico. And that ruined his political ambitions. Again.

"Luckily, he married the Cisneros woman just about that time, and her relatives' money bought him a little junkhouse exploration outfit, and he hit a couple of wildcat holes on the Overthrust Belt, so he's about to go public again. Plus, his wife opened a fat farm on the southeast corner of the ratty-ass ranch where the rich, famous, and politically powerful who haven't taken up public confessional chic can dry out in seclusion and luxury, which gives him a lot of clout in all the right places . . ."

"Except among the voters of Texas," I said, "who are renowned for their resplendent political accuracy."

"Don't sell them short," Solly said. "They're known to be half-right half of the time."

"It could have been California," I admitted.

"So what's next?"

"Replenish the trinity of twentieth-century power," I said, "then confront Joe Don in his lair."

"Why?"

"I'll bet he hasn't told the FBI everything," I said.

"What makes you think he'll talk to you?" Solly asked, then changed his mind. "Don't tell me, okay?"

"Just call one of your secretaries—that great-looking blonde will do—and tell her to open the safe and meet me at the Riverside with the rest of Norman's cash."

"What's Norman going to say?"

"Nothing," I said, "if you don't tell him."

"Shit, Sughrue. How the hell did I get to be your lawyer?"

"Same way you got to be my friend, Solly. Luck and geography."

He laughed a little, then asked, "What's the trinity of twentieth-century power?"

"You don't want to know," I said.

Cash, drugs, and firepower, I thought as I hoofed down the steps toward my rent-car. Millard, the goose, had circled it for the hour I had been at Solly's, but had been unable to find a single sliver of chrome with which to admire his manly reflections. He followed me screaming down the driveway, anyway. He made friends too easily, too, but he had no luck.

Norman didn't sound surprised when I called and asked him to meet me at the Riverside for a few minutes' conversation— guys like Norman are too cool to be surprised—but he groused when I told him what to bring.

But he wasn't so mad that he wouldn't give me a little space while I chatted up Solly's secretary at our small table by the river where she had consented to have one tiny drink, a Campari and soda. Norman raised what looked like jellied gasoline from the bar, then smiled. I ignored him almost completely.

"I don't believe I've ever known a woman named 'Whitney,' " I said, trying not to look too deeply into her bright blue eyes. "Or, hell, even a man for that matter."

"You've never heard of Whitney Houston?"

"Who's that?" I said, realizing that I had never gotten really serious about a woman with blue eyes.

"You're such a card, Mr. Sughrue," she murmured. "Everybody at the office thinks so, you know. First, you did that crazy thing with the jukebox and now you're living in the basement and Solly just thinks the world of you . . ."

I guess I smiled.

"Oh, here I am running on and on," she said, then smiled. "You lead such an exciting life, you must be bored to death with my idle babble . . ."

I caught myself before she could blast me with another of those perfect smiles, shook my head, and realized I was out of my depth with this woman. If she wanted marriage, children, all my money—well, Norman's money—or just an idle, boring afternoon of rabid and wet sheet wrinkles, she could have it. I shook my head again, looked away, and said, "I take it you brought the cash?"

"Silly," she said with another lovely smile, "of course."

I glanced in the envelope she placed between us, said "Thanks," then tried to look out the window where large dry snowflakes swirled into the dark waters of the Meriwether River.

"Looks like a great year for skiing," she said to the side of my face. She smelled so good I could almost taste her, but she wasn't my sort of woman, and I vowed to stay away from her. "Maybe we could hit the slopes sometime," she said, "when you're finished with this case, of course."

"Absolutely," I said quickly. "I'll give you a call when I get back. First thing."

Whitney stood up, smoothed her skirt, and said, "Just walk upstairs, silly. I'm there almost every day." Then she smiled and ankled toward the door, a rose on perfect stems, an orchid feeding on mountain air, a . . .

Shit, I hadn't been on skis in years. And even in my youth, I wasn't any good. Couldn't figure out how to turn. Christ on a crutch, I'd be dead or crippled in a hospital bed before I could get her to make the beast with twenty toes.

Norman, as usual these days, looked as normal as he could in jeans and a flannel shirt, as he plopped into the chair across from me. "That stuff's not for road-dogs like us, Sughrue," he said. "That's somebody's private stock. And besides, a taste would probably kill you."

"She asked me to go skiing."

"See what I mean," he said. "You found my mom?"

I shook the bullshit ski lodge, mulled wine, kisses like frozen limes in the snow blizzard of dreams out of my head. "No, Norman, but I did find a bunch of shit. And lots of Mexicans, some alive, some dead, and a new friend popped three times behind the ear with a .22 short . . ."

"Jesus, man, you're one unlucky bastard. I'm really sorry," he said as if he meant it. "What's this got to do with my mother?"

I told Norman everything I knew. Except the names. And the places. If my clients were going to lie to me, I was duty bound to return the favor.

"You think she's in deep shit?" Norman asked.

"Norman, anytime the feds can't find you and your friends start finding people with holes in their heads or their throats unzipped, you're probably in very deep shit."

"Why the fuck are they following you? They think you know where she is?"

"It takes a major criminal mind to figure out the FBI," I said. "Unfortunately, I'm just a minor player."

"So what now?" he asked seriously, then gunned another shot of nearly frozen vodka.

I left the manila envelope with the money on the table and placed another one on top of it. "Here's the rest of your cash and my time sheets, expenses, and the bill," I said. "You can walk away from it right now."

"What about you, C.W.?"

"It's like World War II, man, I've been drafted for the duration."

Norman didn't even pause. He pushed both envelopes at me, saying, "Anything else you want, let me know."

"Thanks," I said. "This is personal now, and I may end up in more shit than Solly can cover."

"I still got some connections . . . Where you headed now?"

"El Paso."

"That's why you wanted the birth certificate? And the adoption papers." I nodded. "You think I might be lying?" he said. I nodded again. Norman handed me a sheaf of papers, smiling as he said, "I may be a fuckup, man, but I don't lie much. Not to my friends."

"Just in case," I said, gathering up all the paper and money.

"How can I get hold of you?" he said.

"I'm crashing at a place in the Upper Valley," I said, "but I can't remember the guy's name. Some ex-SEAL or something."

"Barnstone, I bet," Norman said. "He used to be connected to one of the border biker gangs. Not a member, but a safe housekeeper for brothers and vets. A solid guy. How do you know him?"

"I don't," I said, and Norman left it at that. I didn't like the connection, but it would bear watching. "He's a friend of a friend."

"From what I know, man, he should be god, or at least President, he's that straight," Norman said sincerely. "Tell him I said hello. And, you know, I've got a couple of AKs stashed in the 4Runner. You want them?"

"There's other people involved now," I said, "and I can't take a chance of getting busted on the airplane. But thanks for the thought."

Norman raised his empty glass at the waitress, then turned to me. "You want another go?"

"It's your money," I said, and Norman laughed as if it might be well spent.

* * *

The Dahlgren boys were laughing, too, as we stood in their storage warehouse while I suggested a list of weapons they might be able to supply.

"There's only three of you?" the one I assumed was Joe asked. "One BAR and two M-1s. Not bad. Two Thompsons and a grease gun. Sure. No problem. And I've got a lovely Sako sniper rig," he continued, but I shook my head. "Let me suggest a couple of the M-1A carbines with the automatic-fire option. Less power than the Thompsons, but a little more range. And light as a bamboo spear."

As if to illustrate, the other twin grabbed one off the wall and twirled it like a drum major. "Nice piece."

"How much unregistered shit do you have?" I asked.

"Oh, just tons and tons," Joe said. "Of course, we keep it out at the farm."

"If we had been interested, we could have been arms dealers," Frank said with a trace of sadness.

"Well, you're getting close," I said. "How much?"

The boys looked at each other, grinned, then one said, "We'll let you have it for exactly what we paid for it."

I must have frowned because the other quickly added, "Absolutely nothing."

"I can't do that," I said.

"Of course you can," one said. "The General would have loved it."

"Okay. Can you ship it to El Paso without any trouble?" I was learning how to ask for things, I guess. And it worked. They had a friend with a fish store on the east side of town who would hold a crate of fish tanks for me. "You guys got any hand grenades?" I asked after the details were settled.

"We had some but we had to dispose of them. Too old and unstable."

"We couldn't guarantee them," the other added, then they both blushed.

"You fucking guys were dealing, weren't you?" I accused them.

"We only sold off the stuff that was about to go bad," one said.

"And we only sold to people with the right politics," the other amended.

I didn't want to know what that meant.

"Besides," the other said, "a stick of forty percent in a twelve-inch length of capped cast-iron pipe works nearly as well. And anybody can buy dynamite, right?"

I had to agree, then Frank had to go back to the store. Joe asked me to wait a moment. He had something he wanted me to see. I had the names straight now because Joe said, "You know, I'm worried about Frank."

"Why?"

"Well, it's sort of complicated," Joe said, and I leaned back against the Sherman. "In lots of ways, Mr. Sughrue, hiring you was one of the smartest things we've ever done. I don't know exactly how it happened, but you changed our lives. You didn't treat us, you know, like freaks, and you took our concerns about the fish seriously. We both know what sort of picture we make and we both appreciated your treatment of us. And when you took us along out to Mr. Hazelbrook's place . . .

"Well, I hope you don't mind if we think of you as a friend. Our lives have opened up again. We're no longer caged, you know, by our size, and we no longer feel as if we're two little fat boys playing with our father's guns. We feel as if they are our weapons now, and we couldn't have been happier when you called, but . . ."

"What's the trouble?" I asked, afraid I already knew the answer.

"Well, we've been out to Mr. Hazelbrook's several times, to see the fish, you know, and . . . well, I'm afraid Frank has not just fallen for little Mary, which is reckless enough given the sort of person, you know, Mr. Hazelbrook seems to be, but he seems to have become addicted to cocaine."

"I thought he looked like he had shed a few pounds."

"Almost thirty in a week," Joe said. "And it's changed him. I flew a couple of professional women up from Las Vegas, really tiny women, almost midgets. Frank has always loved tiny women. Compensation, I suppose. But he wasn't even interested.

All he wants to do is sit in the office and snort coke and feel sorry because Mary is marrying that animal.

"What should I do?" he almost wailed.

"I don't have a clue," I admitted. "He'll either get over it or not."

"But isn't there anything I can do?"

"If you can't take him to a shrink," I suggested, "join him for a while. Take a road trip. Go someplace strange. Vegas, maybe. Get naked and get weird. You can afford it. Get a high-roller suite, dance, drink, gamble, and feed your head. It'll either kill him or cure him or change your life. Whatever, nothing will ever be the same again."

"You think so? What about, you know, diseases? And what if one of us dies?" Joe was deadly serious now.

"Wear a rubber, man, tell Mona to feed your bodies to a tank of piranhas, act like arms dealers," I said, hoping I hadn't ruined their lives by random chance. "But get his power of attorney before you go."

"Thank you, Mr. Sughrue," Joe blubbered, "thank you." Thanking me endlessly, as if I had found the cure for cancer, or saved somebody's life.

His brother Frank was trying to kill himself; my brother Frank was dying for no fucking good reason; and I couldn't stop any of it. But my hand remembered the feel of Baby Lester's skull, the pulse of his life, the sound of his laughter as he peed in my face.

"Don't thank me," I said, "please. I should thank you, Mr. Dahlgren. Trust me, I'm in your debt."

Then I went back to work.

I flew back through Denver and picked up Franklin Vega at the airport. Seeing his kids for what he assumed was the last time had kicked his ass hard, and I remembered why I had avoided children like the plague, so he ranged between false drunken hilarity to deep sad silence as he watched the desert clouds search for a reason or a shape or a single drop of rain.

We had a white telephone page waiting when we walked

into the terminal. In spite of getting to Albuquerque from Aspen on every back road he could find, Jimmy picked up a tail outside of Bernalillo when he turned onto Interstate 25. A red Cadillac convertible, of all things, carrying four dark-haired guys in big cowboy hats, which meant somebody didn't give a shit if we knew, and another damned anonymous government sedan.

"Fuck 'em," I told Jimmy over the telephone. "Pick us up. Let's see what *La Gloria Azul* will do."

"*La Gloria Azul?*" Frank said.

"Norman's van."

"Norman?" Frank said. "Who the fuck is Norman?"

I told him as we waited for Jimmy to pick us up, then we were silent until I picked up Interstate 40 and headed west with the hammer down and the speedometer needle buried while Frank stretched out in the back estimating our speed and Jimmy screamed like an insane child in the passenger seat.

At about 135 mph, the Cadillac had become a red dot, the gray sedan disappeared, and dozens of reconstructed hippies on the freeway had Owsley acid flashbacks as the van bombed past twice as fast as memory allowed.

We made the turn onto State Highway 6, and never saw the sedan again, but the driver of the Cadillac, who was pretty good, managed to follow us. Jimmy had grabbed a handful of maps, which served us well as we blasted down the dirt tracks toward the Alamo Reservation and Magdalena on the other side. But we couldn't escape our dust trail, or the red Caddy tied to it.

Heading up Mesa del Oro, we stopped around a long curve at the top of a switchback. Jimmy stayed with the van, Frank grabbed the glasses and a sleeping bag for a rest, and I loaded the three 10mm clips with full metal jackets.

As the Caddy swept around the lower switchback curve, I leaned on the rolled sleeping bag and fired half a clip while Frank spotted my shots. We were so far away, the guys in the Caddy had to put the top down to be sure they were really hearing gunfire. Frank finished the clip while I spotted, but I didn't recognize a soul in the convertible, and Frank didn't shoot any better than I did. But face it, a hundred yards downhill with a pistol is mostly luck.

"Remember those fat boys I told you about?" I said to Frank as I reloaded. He nodded. "They're shipping us a couple of BARs. I could make them boys down there do the Bunny Hop. Two switchbacks ago. I used to hit shit with the BAR at a thousand yards. Regularly."

"A BAR. Hell, man, I used to see those ARVN cruds lugging them across paddies, but I never fired one."

"Hey, you fucking new guy, I enlisted back in the brown-boot Army, when the M-60 was just some bureaucrat's dream."

"I could never shoot that son of a bitch worth a damn," Frank said, "but boy could I make a lot of noise."

"You could carry the pig," I said, "and that was the hard part." Then I fired another few rounds.

This time I got close enough to scatter rock dust on their windshield. Everybody but the driver unlimbered some sort of stamped tin assault rifle burdened with a suppressor. They sprayed the hillside at random, but didn't have much more range than I did. Then the driver made the mistake of stopping to look around. My first two shots were high, but the next three went dead center into the hood. The Caddy stopped for good, and the men scrambled out of the car. Then I put the rest of the clip into the trunk lid, hoping to hit the fuel tank.

Whatever I hit wasn't the gas but it went off like a bomb. The blast knocked the four guys off their feet and set fire to one guy's hat, but they didn't pause to look back, they just came up the hill like four heavy-duty professional grunts assaulting a bunker, covering each other, and moving pretty good for guys in cowboy boots.

I threw the sleeping bag down the slope. It took two bounces before they shredded it with automatic fire, covering the slope with petrochemical fibers.

"Don't look like feathers to me," Frank said.

"Trying to save money for my client," I said.

"False economy," he said, "goose down's the best."

"Glad to know that," I said. "Now what should we do about these assholes down there?"

"I'd suggest we get the fuck out of their way," Frank said.

We slithered back through the scrub brush, careful not to raise a bit of dust, then both leaped into the van as Jimmy hit it.

We eased the long, slow way down to Santa Rita, skirting the Gila, nobody talking much about the young professional soldiers on our asses. We waited outside Santa Rita past midnight, then worked our way south toward Deming, where I really had been born in a motel, then down to Columbus, where Pancho Villa's dream really ended with the massive mistake of the night attack on the American troops. Jimmy claimed to know a back way into El Paso, a notion that neither Frank nor I bothered to dispute.

We were content to chug slowly through the desert, driving by moonlight, trusting our point man to find the pale tracks through the spiked cactus and the night. Jimmy found the remains of the Jamaican roach and managed to roll a fairly substantial joint out of it, which we smoked through the night. Frank and I opened the sliding door and sat on the floor of the van watching the moonlight spill across the sand.

"This is really stupid," Jimmy said dreamily from the driver's seat. "We've got no edge at all. Maybe we should do some coke, Sarge."

"Now, that's a really stupid idea," I said, giggling, then arranged it.

"Not a great edge," Frank said later, "but an edge, nonetheless."

Because of the flight, Frank hadn't brought a piece, but he carefully loaded my entire arsenal and spread it out on the carpet around him. He looked like a heathen god who had just discovered gunfire. He tossed the Airweight to Jimmy, who stuck it between his legs. "This is about your size, pissant." Then he stared into the night for a moment before he turned to me. "We did the right thing to boogie," he said. "Those guys were going to kick our ass."

"I had the twelve-gauge, man," Jimmy said, "and they would've paid fucking dearly."

"You know," I said to Frank, "he's right. Maybe they would've kicked our butts, but maybe they wouldn't have paid the price."

"I don't know who the fuck trained those guys," Frank said, "but they were fucking pros. They would've gone through us like thin shit through a tall Swede."

Jimmy got the giggles and wanted to know how fast that was, and we riffed that number for a while, until Frank got serious.

"Face it, guys, we're old."

"Fuck you," Jimmy suggested.

"Then why the fuck didn't we stick?" Frank wanted to know.

"Because it's not the fucking same!" I shouted.

Jimmy stopped the van, and I stepped outside into that layer of desert night where the ground still seeps heat like a dying sun and the air is as cold as moonlight. I think maybe I was crying again. But they listened.

"It's not the same, not now," I whispered. "We fucking ran from those guys because we didn't want to kill anybody anymore. Four pistols, one pump shotgun, plenty of ammo, great cover, and the high ground. Fuck it, we could've kicked their butts in a Waxahachie minute. And you assholes know it." Then I paused, and Frank said it for me.

"But we didn't want to," he said, then handed me a beer, and we climbed back into the van to crawl across the desert track, without speaking until Jimmy wanted to know just how long a Waxahachie minute was, you know, compared to the thin-Swede real-shit thing. Then we laughed and crossed the night.

Occasionally, the shadows of mountains mounted the horizon, suggesting mazes of rock and thorn. Or the muffled engine would fall quiet and the squeak of a windmill or a bat could ring through the moon-spill. I wanted to stop, build a tiny, smokeless fire, and chant the words my crazy father had taught me so long ago, chant until his grandfather shades rose from the sand to dance before me. I remembered the words but could not say them even under my breath. I tried to fill that failure with more smoke, jokes, and laughter, trying to stifle that sad moment of seriousness when we had to admit that we were no longer what we had once been. We could still sleep in muddy holes, still stand back-to-

back, as Solly and I had that ambush afternoon, and fight without
fear, but we could no longer kill without . . . without . . .
without rancor, or reason, just for the simple yet complex act of
possible survival.

Just about the time I nearly had it worked out, just as we
could see the city lights of El Paso polluting the night and three
drilling rigs to the southeast horizon, a phantom, wrapped in
camouflage and sporting an M-16 at port arms, stepped out of
the creosote brush with his hand raised. Jimmy stopped the van
as if this were an everyday occurrence. The sentry stepped over,
swept the interior of the van with a red-lensed flashlight, and
said, "Shit, that *mota* smells good. Jamaican, huh? You guys got
a roach, maybe, and a cold beer? Hey, and by the way, you mind
waiting here for a little while?"

After a long silence, Jimmy said, "Well, fuck, if this is an
ambush, boys, it's too good for us." Jimmy tapped the Airweight
barrel on the door frame. "You put your gun down, son, and I'll
put mine down, and we'll party quietly through the night."

The kid didn't even hesitate, but leaned the M-16 against the
van. "You guys seem cool, so it's okay with me," he said, "but
there's twenty of us, so let's be friends."

"Sounds good to me," Frank said, then clicked the shotgun's
safety back on.

So we sat there in the middle of nowhere watching the track
in front of us while a reinforced squad dressed in combat fatigues
and carrying state-of-the-art automatic weapons rigged with
night scopes crossed the desert with two low-boy semi-tractors
and trailers loaded with a wrecked C-47 and hundreds of bales
of marijuana, as silent as ghosts and as serious as rattlesnakes.
The crossing completed, the phantom kid ate the roach, handed
his empty beer can to Jimmy, then picked up his weapon.

"Pack it in, pack it out," he said. "You dudes take care," he
added politely, then jogged after the low-boys and the troops.

None of us moved for a long time, then Jimmy found his
voice. "What the fuck was that?"

"What?" Frank said.

"That!" Jimmy shouted, then threw the empty beer can out
the window.

"Yuppie drug dealers," Frank said, "and if you don't pick up your litter, pissant, they'll kill you, your family, and all your friends, supposing you have any."

Jimmy got the beer can while we laughed, and as he drove away, I said, "I don't know why I didn't shit my pants. I haven't seen anything like that in a long time."

"I know why I didn't," Jimmy said.

"Why?" Frank wanted to know.

"Because I had about three pounds of seat cover up my asshole," Jimmy shouted, then laughed finally himself.

"Nice of you to pick a road not taken," Frank said.

"How the hell did I know the fucking Free Texican Air Force was flying tonight?" Jimmy said. "Peter Rowen fucking forgot to tell me, man."

"Too true," Frank shouted, and we butchered the song until dawn.

Dawn found us wallowing in a windmill-fed steel tank on the edge of the desert above the Upper Valley. The salt cedars growing along the seep killed the morning breeze as the sun's fireball rose over the Franklin Mountains. We were dark and red and glistening in the morning light, sun-struck and stupid, maybe, but dying full of life as the sun reared its head and filtered through the dew-damp spiderwebs threading the thorny brush.

One of the too few times my father garnered me for a summer, we went back to Deming to see an old war buddy of his. After all these years it seems his name was Lawson, or Layton, and he had been wounded several times wading to the beach on the third wave at Tarawa. The .25-caliber Nambu rounds had stitched his stomach, and the puckered scars grown large and frightening as his beer belly grew. He'd married a Mexican woman whose family owned a piece of ground with a spring out toward the Florida Mountains south and east of Deming where they raised melons and peppers and truck-garden vegetables. And he had a daughter named Marta.

While our fathers were drinking, she took me into her bedroom to play Kitty Wells on her 45 rpm changer, which played through a ten-dollar plastic radio, the only thing her mother left when she fled back to Crystal City, Texas. After she played "An Answer to the Wild Side of Life" about ten times, Marta spent about an hour teaching me how to French-kiss.

I might have been eleven, maybe twelve, just old enough to have an erection but too young for ejaculation, and she was perhaps thirteen, but we were hotter than two-dollar pistols.

The next sunrise morning she rapped on the side of the pickup bed where I slept wrapped in canvas and one of my grandmother's quilts. When I looked up, she had her finger to her lips. Not that our fathers would have heard us from the small fire they tended in the backyard, the fire they had tended through all the night of serious drinking.

I followed Marta out to their bulldozed dirt tank, where we took off our clothes, slipped into the muddy, shallow water, and without swimming a stroke began touching each other. She didn't exactly have breasts, just nipples and bumps, as she said, and she didn't have much more pubic hair than I did, but we did what we could to make the world safe for sexual freedom.

In the dawn light the desert mountains reared wild and rough against the sky, ancient yet young, an endless reminder of our transient youth and promised demise. But it seemed so far away at that moment.

Though coming fast. Shortly afterward I had my first real wet dream, and it was of Marta, standing in the reflected dawn fire of that scummy pond.

Of course, nothing is ever that simple.

We made love the night after she buried her father in Las Cruces twenty-some years later, then again when I buried mine after a motorcycle wreck outside Falfurrias, Texas, the very next year.

But it never went anywhere. She blamed that first morning, the water shining with tiny rainbows as it dripped from her hair, her hand soft on my prick as hard as a mesquite root. I blamed the deaths. Whatever, it never went anywhere. She married a melon farmer outside La Junta, and they had a dozen kids. I didn't.

*   *   *

Later, dripping and semi-sane, Frank, Jimmy, and I climbed out of the tank and stood drying in the sun. Jimmy wanted to talk about the day we stood in the rain, but nobody would listen to him. I insisted on finishing the drive out of the desert—driving sometimes settles me down—so Jimmy guided me straight to Barnstone's place, just over the Rio Grande River levee, nearly in New Mexico, and beautifully situated on a knoll in the middle of a pecan grove. Barnstone's place looked like home. His main house, two stories and a dozen rooms, was stone instead of adobe, as was the wall around his two acres of yard. Inside the wall he had half a dozen small stone apartments, a small stable and barn, and a three-car garage, each of the stalls filled with Morgan convertibles in various stages of restoration.

When we pulled up to the back gate, a tall red-bearded bald man was standing in the compound with a bowling ball in one hand and a beer can in the other. About thirty feet away, a tom turkey, wings spread, eyes glistening, faced him.

"Be quiet," Jimmy recommended, "this is serious."

"What the fuck is this?" Frank asked, kneeling between the seats. "An attack turkey?"

"Bowling for Turkeys," Jimmy said, and about that time the tall man launched his ball.

The turkey waited until the last moment, then hopped casually into the air and shit on the ball as it trundled below him. The bowling ball rolled to the edge of a raised bed garden where another tall man in a conical straw hat and black pajamas toiled at the weeds with a short hoe. The turkey stalked over to a bathtub full of beer cans, where it perched like the national bird Benjamin Franklin meant it to be.

"Goddammit, Carney," the red-bearded man shouted, his deep voice rich in the damp river morning, "it's your turn."

The man in the garden glanced from under his Vietnamese hat and said quietly, "He shit on the ball again, Barnstone. It's not my turn."

We climbed out, beers in hand ourselves, and leaned on the white gate. Barnstone walked over to the soiled bowling ball, then noticed us when he leaned over. Two bantam roosters crowed

from the corral, and a white duck scuttled to Barnstone's knees.
He watched us carefully as he stroked the duck's back. The duck
quivered as if about to lay an egg, then squatted in the grass and
shuddered as if overwhelmed by an orgasm, then staggered àway.
"It's not polite to watch sex with animals," he said.

Hacienda Barnstone had some rules we couldn't exactly live
with—like no guns on the place and no hard drugs, unless they
were the "people's drugs," which meant stingy didn't cut it—
but his neighbor down the road had no such qualms. He rented
us his empty garage to stash the van. Then Barnstone loaded us
into his desert camouflage WWII Power Wagon ambulance and
drove us over to a place called Victor's, where we were assaulted
by a squad of *huevos rancheros*. Mostly we just ate and sweated,
guzzled Tecate beer, then repeated the process. But Jimmy
stopped long enough to ask:

"What's with that Carney dude? He having delusions of Cong
grandeur?"

"No," Barnstone answered seriously, "he's paying a great
karma debt."

Frank nearly spit eggs and peppers across the table, and I had
to grin.

"You a Buddhist?" I asked.

"A label implies a path; a path, a desire. Whatever I may be,
my friend, I am without desire," he said, his huge freckled face
as peaceful as stone.

"What the fuck did what's-his-name do," Frank asked, "that
we didn't all do?"

"Carney's his name, and his debt is not incurred by the act
but by the refusal to acknowledge the debt," Barnstone said.
"Arthur was a balls-to-the-wall stockbroker in Dallas, a man with
all the toys—boats, cars, north Dallas women—then he found
the ultimate toy. Cocaine. Some can, some can't. He couldn't. I
couldn't. We found each other bleeding in the same cathouse
piss trough over in Las Palomas, and put our feet to the ground."
Barnstone picked up the breakfast check in one hand, his beer in
the other. "My debt seemed lighter. At least I can still smoke a

little dope and drink the occasional beer. The last time Carney had a beer, he ended up in Ohio." The way he said it, Ohio sounded like the seventh circle of hell. "Breakfast is on me, gentlemen. After this you're on your own. Times are gentle right now, so I can give you three small apartments or the big place which sleeps four. Pay what you can as long as you can. No questions asked."

"The big place," Jimmy said quickly as if afraid to split the fire team, "and thanks, Barney. This time I can pay."

"And you remember the rules."

"You dirty it, you wash it. You break it, you fix it. You fuck up, you walk," Jimmy said, then Barnstone nodded and headed for the cash register and the merry, rotund presence of Victor himself.

"You didn't tell us this was some kinda religious fruitcake of a place," Frank growled as he finished his beer.

"Believe me, it's not," Jimmy said, then shook his head. "Fuck, it's the only place I ever felt at home except the bush," he added sadly.

"Let's try it," I suggested, then caught the tip and followed Barnstone.

"I got the tip," I said at the front.

"Thanks."

"An old friend said to tell you hello," I said.

"Who might that be?"

Standing next to Barnstone, his form black against the light, I realized how much he loomed over me.

"Abnormal Norman," I said quietly.

"Holy Jesus," Barnstone said, "is Mr. Hazelbrook alive?" Then he smiled, radiant as the sun. "I nearly killed him myself one Sunday afternoon. I had the shovel raised that would have sent him into a desert grave but I couldn't plunge it into his neck."

"He thinks quite highly of you," I said. "Says you should be either god or President."

Barnstone laughed and the whole room rumbled. "That was just his first mistake," he said.

"What was his second?"

"I don't exactly remember, my friend, but in those days it was very nearly worth his life," he said, then paused to chuckle. "How is Norman these days?"

"Almost respectable," I said, "looking at getting married."

"Then I suppose I should be glad I didn't take the fuck's head off," Barnstone said seriously. "I spent too much time around the killing, my friend, in the Delta, then in the drug business. Back in those days I guess I thought, 'What fucking difference can one more make?' But now I know the difference."

"Yeah, I've got a buddy back home," I said. "He did two tours and an extra eighteen months."

"Somebody should pray for him," he said as Jimmy and Frank joined us, then we took the ambulance home.

Although the three of us swore we'd never sleep again, the rumbling of the swamp coolers and the pecan grove silence of the Upper Valley morning had us sleeping like tired children within moments, sleeping once again without the dreams.

I woke first, changed into running shorts and shoes, then jogged slowly up the levee and walked back alongside the sluggish brown of the tamed river. On the other side of the border they called it the Río Bravo del Norte, and somebody once told me that down at Ojinaga the Río Conchos dumped clear cold water into the muddy river, but I had never been there and didn't know if I should believe it. But suddenly I wanted to see it, all of it, West Texas, Mexico, and points south, I wanted to see where my Mexican Tree Duck belonged. I wanted to go home someplace I had never been before.

When I got back to Hacienda Barnstone the sun hovered just over the rim of the valley, and my chest prickled with late fall desert air. Frank and Jimmy sat across a picnic table from Barnstone, who held his white duck in his lap as if it were a large sleepy cat. The horses cribbed noisily at the corral posts, their teeth like chisels, the chickens clucked aimlessly, and beyond the garden the turkey had a bantam rooster cornered in a fuck-or-fight position. Only god, or perhaps Ben Franklin, knew what the turkey had in mind. Nearby, on a rock cairn among the raised beds of the garden, Carney sat in the lotus position as still as a silk flower.

I showered, changed, then joined the boys at the table. Frank opened a beer, Jimmy passed me a joint, and Barnstone smiled. I hesitated.

"I think maybe we're running out of time, boys," I said.

"I know a little bit about it," Barnstone said quietly, "and I suggest a night of R&R. This is not Vietnam. A lot of rich people live in the Upper Valley; a lot of private guards watch over them. Run a scout patrol tomorrow afternoon around rush hour, nobody will notice you. Some people are coming over tonight. Take a moment. Please."

Frank took the joint from me, hit it, then talked through the smoke. "I know you're worried about the woman and the baby, Sughrue, but if we go off half-cocked, we'll fuck it up." He handed me the joint.

"Or half-stoned," I said, hitting it too, hoping we were right one last time, wondering what kind of people were coming.

Barnstone's dentist girlfriend showed up to tend her horses and lay out a couple of lines of pharmaceutic cocaine for his guests. She was a horsy blonde with an overbite and an East Coast accent that could have stripped paint off steel. Then a few college professors and some of their students arrived with a keg. Slumming I thought, until I realized that one of them, a potbellied jester of a history professor, was the guy that shared a Juárez jail cell with Jimmy, and another, a chubby perky redhead who latched on to Gorman's arm, was more than an old friend. Then some pepper farmers from Hatch showed up with half a dozen goat kids, which Barnstone slaughtered and butchered while Frank and I built a fire of pecan logs in the barbecue pit.

Three guys passing through on Harleys, on their way from Long Beach to Miami, dropped in to crash. They smelled like biker trash to me, but Barnstone laid his beatific rap on them and made them at home. A lady columnist from Austin, whose work I knew, came by to grab some local color, by which, it became clear, she meant Frank. A pair of homosexual bone surgeons came down from Albuquerque escorting a pair of lesbian dancers, by far the prettiest women at the party, but not the only ones.

By good dark, Frank and the journalist had settled the barbecue sauce debate and the *cabrito* simmered and sizzled over a bed of hardwood coals. A pot of beans the size of a sidecar had appeared, dozens of steaming tamales covered the table, and more people rolled into the yard. But if you watched, Barnstone occasionally turned people away, usually groups of young men or a hard-core ex-con or a biker without credentials or the wrong colors.

It wasn't a party that a Republican could understand—the marijuana smoke sweet on the air, the occasional cocaine sniffle, cold Mexican beer, good food, great conversation and laughter— but a Parisian deconstructionist scholar might find it about as civilized as America gets. Or at least the one I met, who was visiting at UTEP, maintained. Somewhere along the way, he claimed, Americans had forgotten how to have a good time. In the name of good health, good taste, and political correctness from both sides of the spectrum, we were being taught how to behave. America was becoming a theme park, not as in entertainment, but as in a fascist Disneyland.

"No facial hair, no false eyelashes, and no fucking fun!" the short Frenchman shouted, then stormed away toward a tequila bottle in the hands of a tough-looking Kiowa-Chicana breed with a single foreboding eyebrow dark as war paint across her face.

"I hope she doesn't hurt him," a woman's voice said beside me. When I turned, she added, "Barnstone said I should talk to you."

"Okay," I said. Whoever she might be, she had the prettiest pug nose I had ever seen, dusky rose skin, and a thatch of silver-blond hair that gleamed like stainless steel in the firelight.

"Let's take a walk," she said, holding up a joint, "and get to know each other."

"You got a deal," I said, holding out my hand to introduce myself.

"Dottie Milano," she said. She was short, almost petite, but she damn near broke my hand when she shook it. "Sorry," she said, "but I love to bring you big guys to your knees."

"Don't hurt me," I said, "it'll be my first time. On my knees, that is."

Dottie brayed, then headed for the gate, talking to me over her shoulder. "If it comes to that, Mr. Sughrue, we'll compare rug burns in the morning."

"What the hell do you do for a living," I asked, "that allows you to behave like this?"

She stopped at the gate latch, sort of a vision in a white off-the-shoulder blouse, a pale yellow skirt, and a bright red belt with matching high heels.

"I'm a deputy sheriff up in New Mexico," she said, then smiled, happy as a pig in shit, as we used to say.

Dottie was one of those women who aren't slowed by high heels. I don't know how they do it. After she fired up the number, I was walking too fast to smoke it.

"This ain't a race, is it?" I asked. "Because if it is, I'm already whipped."

"Sorry," she said. "I've just got too much fucking energy. Sorry, didn't mean to put it that way, didn't mean to lead you on."

"Go ahead," I said. "Lead me on. I'm a big boy. I can stand the disappointment."

Dottie gave me a shot in the ribs Jimmy would have admired. I nearly swallowed the joint.

"Sorry," she said again, then laughed. "Barnstone said you needed a tough broad, said you'd been hanging around fake tough broads." She took the number out of my fingers, hit it so hard, the fire flared among the shadows of the pecan trees. "He said you needed a strong dose of reality."

"You do everything he says?"

"We trade favors," she said.

"Are you really a deputy sheriff?"

"Wanna see my gun and my badge?"

"Sure," I said, nodding, and Dottie lifted her full skirt. The badge case was tucked into one of her stockings and the Ladysmith S&W .38 nestled beside the tight bundle of her crotch. "Jesus," I whispered.

"Excite you?" she asked. I guess I nodded. "Me, too," she said, then clicked down the hardpan road through the dark glade.

"Wait up," I stammered. "What the fuck are you doing here?"

She stopped and I bumped into her hard little body. "Sorry," she said. "I'm undercover."

"Not yet," I said, and she actually laughed.

"Thanks," she said, "I haven't done that in a long time, not like that, out of the gut." Then she giggled. "Of course, I'm stoned senseless. That's how stress works sometimes. Sometimes I can't get stoned on a *cola* the size of a horse's tail, and sometimes I start giggling just thinking about it." Then she paused. "Too much fucking stress in my job," she said, then sighed.

"I've got a friend who says that," I said.

"What's he? A dealer?"

"Good guess," I said. "But what are you really doing here?"

"Hey, asshole, I'm really undercover," she said, then laughed again, a husky little chuckle that lifted the hair on the back of my neck. She wasn't the only one stoned. "Barnstone used to move major weight across the border, and he never got caught. Until I popped him. So he belongs to me."

"He's still moving grass?" I asked, wondering why she was telling me all this.

"Barnstone hasn't bought or sold a single joint for eight years," she said. "He won't smoke it if he has to pay for it. But he still belongs to me. We've been friends for a long time, lots of favors over the years. He says you're cool, even though your name has been all over the DEA computer for the last week."

"How the hell do you know that?"

"The FBI told me," she said. "You'd be surprised what kind of women FBI agents have to marry," Dottie said, smiling. "The dumb bastards will give up their pieces, their snitches, shitty as they are, and their children just for the hint of a promise of an actual blowjob."

"So where do I play in all this shit?" I was beginning to feel as if I had been playing out of my league with women lately. "Exactly fucking where?"

"Don't get tough with me, cowboy," she said, turning delicately in the center of the road. "I know you're not packing, and if you fuck with me, I'll blow your nuts off." Then she grabbed her crotch.

"Promises, promises," I said. "If I tell you I love you, will you show me your gun again?"

"Absolutely," she said. "If you do it right."

"Dorothy, I love you," I said.

"You're good," she said. "You're fucking good, C. W. Sughrue. That's perfect. We're going to be friends. Thanks." Then she lifted her skirt, laughing like mad, then dropped it and kissed me so hard she nearly broke my neck.

After we stopped nibbling, stroking, and running our hands all over each other, I stepped back, rolling my shoulders and stretching my back, which had been holding her surprising weight all that time.

"What's the matter, cowboy? Little tough girls too much for you?"

"Goddamn, I hope so," I said. "I've been looking for too much all my live-long days." Dottie just grinned like a small mean animal. "But I have to know where I play in this fucking little game of yours, kiddo," I said as I twirled her little pistol around my fragrant index finger, then handed it back to her.

"Where have you been all my life?" she said, tucking her piece away. "Okay, Barnstone has great instincts about people. I've never seen him miss. So I'm telling you this because he says you're absolutely the straight-on decent goods. So don't fuck me over, okay? Word is, though, that somebody's about to move a huge shipment of cocaine across the border here—tons. I've heard two and I've heard ten. And you're the middleman on the deal."

"I don't know anything about that," I said, "but I've got a missing woman and a baby out there somewhere."

"Barnstone didn't say anything about that."

"I didn't tell him," I said. "But I'll for damn sure tell you something: I don't give a rat's ass about your cocaine bust. The best you ever do is ten percent, anyway, and I believe you people lie about that . . ."

"You people?"

"You fucking DEA people," I clarified for her. "You haven't survived this long undercover without major DEA connections."

She shrugged as if it didn't matter. "What do you want to know from me, lady?"

"So what do you know about the shipment?"

"Not a fucking thing," I admitted. "I started off on this thing looking for a friend's mother so he could invite her to his wedding . . ."

When I paused, she said, "What?" As if she didn't believe me. "Where do this woman and baby come in?"

"On the fringe, I think."

Then she wanted to know: "Who's your friend?"

"Sorry," I said, "I'm working for his lawyer."

"And you criticize me for my known associates?" Then she laughed. "Between you, me, and the bedpost, honey."

"Nice place," I said, even though I knew she meant the name, then I took a long breath and sighed. Well, I had to trust somebody eventually. "Swap?" I suggested, and she nodded vigorously. "His name is Norman Hazelbrook, and he claims Mrs. Joe Don Pines is his mother . . ."

Dottie shook her head and cursed under her breath, "Jesus, you must be crazy to fuck around even the fringes of an FBI kidnapping," she said, then leaned against me, her arms wrapped tightly around my chest, her head tucked under my chin. "I think her husband did it," she murmured, "but like every decent human being in this part of the country, I hate the prick." She breathed against my chest for a while, long enough so I could feel her warm, moist breath through my shirt. Then she sighed, much as I had shortly before, and said, "What's the lawyer's name?"

"Solomon Rainbolt," I said, then moved her back to arm's length so I could see her face.

"I'll see what I can come up with," she said, smiling, cuddling back into my chest, whispering, "and keep in mind, cowboy, that I can lie just as well looking you in the eye."

"I prefer to be lied to in this position," I said. "See what you can find out about Joe Don's dog boy, last name Jones. They say he committed suicide some years back . . ."

"I don't need the computer for that," she said. "Eloy Jones. But I need another small favor before I tell you the story."

"What's that?"

"If we're still speaking around midnight," she said, "I'd like to fuck you."

"That's romantic," I said.

"For me," she said. "Truth is, Sughrue, I'd like to fuck you right now."

Who was I to argue? The lady had a gun.

The rest of the R&R evening was just as magical as that moment. The food was wonderful, the conversation marvelous, the stars shining in the desert sky. Even the duck was happy, squatting and coming all over the yard as everybody petted her. And Dottie . . .

Well, sometimes stress kills sex like a snake, and sometimes it makes foreplay superfluous. We both had come so quickly and so hard that we were sure we had knocked pecans off the tree we leaned against. Back at the party, we watched each other like hawks when we weren't holding hands like teenagers, and when we finally went to bed, stoned and greasy with goat meat, it was like making love to an old friend.

We knew the same things. Not just that tomorrow it would be different, and we hated our inability to change it, but that because this was all we were going to have, we had to actually love each other. It might have seemed like casual sex to some people, but for us, that night, it was the beginning and the end of the world. Of course, most people can't tell shit from wild honey. That's one of the things we knew together. We could be dead tomorrow. That's one of the others.

Later, when I was finally on my knees, and she was stretched out across the bed, breathing hard, I asked her about the suicide of Wynona Jones's father.

She grabbed the back of my head and buried it deeper into her crotch, then moaned, "Just one more, man, and I'll tell you anything."

Well, neither of us believed that, but we silently agreed to do it that way anyway.

Afterward, she turned the light on, sent me for a bump of

cocaine and another cold beer, then let me have it. It wasn't a bedtime story, but it made me want to sleep on it.

The next morning, the women were gone and we all suffered from mild hangovers that made us a little edgy and more than a little mean as we helped Barnstone clean up the surprisingly orderly party debris while a huge pot of cowboy coffee came to boil over the barbecue coals. When we finished, Barnstone filled tin cups with coffee and started cooking breakfast in two old iron skillets set on the coals.

Fresh farm eggs, some still warm with chicken shit, shredded *cabrito* and tamale hunks crumbled into the mixture along with white onions and jalapeño peppers, in one skillet; *refritos* loaded with a large handful of *chiles pequins* in the other. Just as it came off the fire, Carney returned from town with fresh corn tortillas, which we flopped on the crusted grill.

Carney filled two tortillas with beans and headed back to the garden, disappearing into a tiny bamboo hut that blended so well with the foliage we hadn't seen it before.

We watched with amazement. Jimmy sat down at the table, saying, "That fucking guy makes me nervous."

"Me, too," Barnstone said.

"What was he?" Frank asked. "A fucking lurp?"

"We've never discussed it," Barnstone said, leaving it at that.

When we had eaten everything but the plates, Jimmy said it for us. "It wasn't pretty, Barney, and I wouldn't feed it to my cousin in Boston, but that's the best breakfast I've ever had."

"I suspect you're going to need it," Barnstone said, pouring more coffee. Then he turned to me, his voice flat and hard like a place Buddha might sit, but not for long. "So what the fuck are you guys really doing in my town?"

Frank and Jimmy stood up to get between us before it got western and ugly.

"First, Mr. Barnstone," I said, "maybe you'll tell me why you sicced that little DEA bitch on me."

"She's an old friend, Mr. Sughrue, and she asked me. That's why."

"What the fuck . . ." Frank started to say.

But Barnstone stood up, stepped over to the tack room door, and said, "Let me show you something," then he swung open the door. The bloody body of his white duck dangled from a nail. "That duck was a great companion," Barnstone said. "She came with a touch. Anybody's touch. A truly happy soul. And this piece of shit . . ." Barnstone whipped a scrap of canvas off a dead body, the throat cut to the neck bone, then he covered it up. "I haven't seen a dead body in ten years. You guys are here one fucking day, and I . . . Well, you can dig it, right?"

"You do that?" I asked.

"Carney," Barnstone said. "He was sort of fond of Annie, too."

"Who was the guy?" Jimmy asked.

"Just some *mojado* fresh off the farm," Barnstone said. "I know the asshole in Delicias who probably hired him. But I've been clean so long I fucking know this is not directed at me, so it would be nice if I had the whole story, and how some fucking heavyweight Mexican scammer knew you were here. Is that a problem?" Barnstone closed the door on the dead as if they had already taken their places on the great wheel of life.

"Probably found it out from the DEA," I said. "Dottie said my name was all over their computer, but I don't know how the hell they could make this connection."

Jimmy and Frank didn't know if they should run or fight, so they babbled questions until I told them I didn't have a clue. Except for the one Dottie had given me.

"And the kicker is, boys, they think I'm in town," I said, "to shepherd several tons of cocaine across the border."

"Competition. That explains a lot," Barnstone said.

"Yeah, but what the fuck does it mean?" Jimmy said.

That, of course, as always, is the question.

For another bundle of bills, Barnstone's neighbor rented Frank and Jimmy an old Corvette that sounded like an airplane but, as Frank said happily later, "When the light changes, everybody else becomes a flyspeck in your rearview mirror." They went into El Paso proper, should such a place actually exist, to see if the childhood part of Norman's story checked out.

Then Barnstone took me into his house, which was filled with the most wonderful collection of junk on the North American continent. A child's barber chair, a stuffed *javelina*, a life-sized color cutout portrait of Pancho Villa in a pith helmet that made him look a lot like Teddy Roosevelt. A horseshoe collection mounted on varnished plywood. A chopped Harley hog in front of a projection television screen. And that was only in the living room.

"Where'd you get all this crap?" I asked.

"I don't know," he said, "shit just sticks to me like fuzz bunnies to a cat." Then he straddled the Harley, reached into the off-side saddlebag, and came out with an old broom-handled Mauser automatic pistol. "Shit like this," he said, a soft threat like a small flame in his voice.

"I thought you didn't allow guns on the place," I said, sinking into a tooled-leather couch underneath a longhorn steer's mounted rack, crossing my hands behind my neck. "Or questions."

"Just mine," he said. "In emergencies. The duck and the dead body make it an emergency."

"The gun won't buy you shit," I said, "and you know it. How long has it been since you dropped the hammer on a guy in your living room?"

Barnstone looked at me for a long time, the Mauser unwavering in his hand. Then he laughed calmly and slipped the pistol back into the saddlebag. "Well, either you're the real goods, Sughrue, or you're too tough for me."

"Tough never counts," I said. "But Dottie said I could trust you. Let's have a beer and I'll fill you in on the various felonies I've committed on the way to El Paso. That's if you're still interested."

"I'm interested," he said, "now."

So we settled at the kitchen table with a couple of Tecates, and I told him most of the story. While he shook his head, I added that I also wanted a close look at Joe Don Pines; he nodded sagely, and asked, "You always live like this?"

"Whenever I can," I admitted. He smiled serenely, then I said, "You know anything about Joe Don and drugs?"

He gave me a look that questioned my sanity. "As far as I know, he's just a rich asshole," he said, "but there has been some talk. He does have a three-thousand-yard paved strip over at the ranch headquarters in Edwards Hole, and her family has a ranch in the Encantadas south and east of Big Bend with a two-thousand-yard hardened runway on it. That's all I know." He looked at me again. "Think about it, Sughrue. I have a *lot* of money, but Joe Don and his wife have a hundred times as much as I do. Why would they fuck with nickel-and-dime shit like drugs when they've got enough money to do big-time white-collar crime?"

"Two tons of cocaine ain't exactly nickel-and-dime, is it?"

"For them, sure."

"Barnstone, remember," I said. "Money's the ultimate drug. And desire the snake swallowing its tail."

"Hey, now," he said, smiling, "don't get oriental on me. Just be cool and we'll take a look. With open minds, empty of desire."

"I can't promise that," I admitted.

"Well, we'll just leave the guns at home," he said, then laughed as he dug up a small tripod, two sets of desert fatigues, and a pair of WWII German naval binoculars. "Grab your walking shoes, man," he said, tossing me a set of fatigues. "We're going to cover some ground."

An hour later we were easing down an arroyo just southwest of the Upper Valley not too far from the track Jimmy had followed. Barnstone had insisted on leaving the ambulance a couple of miles west of the fat farm, hidden in a small brushy gully an hour downhill and a canteen of water behind us. It was cloudy and late fall, but the desert still sucked the moisture right out of us. We rounded a bend in the dry wash and overlooked the Upper Valley lying peacefully between the prehistoric banks of the Río Bravo del Norte. Barnstone motioned to belly down, then we slithered up to the edge.

"Probably a lot of trouble for nothing," he whispered, handing me the glasses, "but better safe than sorry. Anyway, there it is. One of Joe Don's lairs."

The three drilling rigs I had seen the night we crossed the

desert sat along the banks of the valley about five hundred yards apart just above a new road that seemed to lead to a brand-new border crossing. A telephone crew with ditching equipment approached the checkpoint from both sides of the border.

Just before the crossing, a road branched off, and a sign announced: *El Rancho Encantada*. The fat farm lay in front of us, glistening white stucco walls and red tile roofs among a plague of golf courses and swimming pools, green and blue rampant in the middle of the desert. A Gulfstream jet touched down at the private strip just beyond the eighteenth hole, then parked among several of its ilk.

A platoon of men and women dressed in shining gray Lycra tights and either halters or singlets danced to music we couldn't hear, training for the war against excess. Some of the figures looked as if they could use the work, but several of them looked as carefully honed to tendon and bone as lifelong speed freaks. Three young women in red Lycra led the dance, their hard, square jawlines commanding the air.

The rest of the help—gardeners, serving folk, and random gofers—wore red jumpsuits and looked Mexican, but none looked familiar. I swept the spa several times with the wide-angle glasses, then went back over it again closely with my spotting scope.

I didn't see a sign of Wynona or Lester, though, not an armed guard or even a simple cell, nothing.

"I don't see her," I told Barnstone, "and I don't see anyplace they might be holding somebody against their will. Except the dance floor and she's not there," I said. "What are the telephone companies doing down there?"

"Joe Don is building a new border crossing," he answered. "Another of his shithouse mouse dreams."

"Has he got an office in El Paso?"

"Yeah, but I don't think we can work that one. Maybe we can try the main ranch tonight," he said, "but that's a fucking different deal, man. We'll have to low-crawl about five hundred yards."

"I can see why you were able to stay in business so long," I said.

"Betrayed by my basest desires, though," Barnstone sighed, then chuckled. "But she was almost worth it."

"I wouldn't know," I said. "My desires have always been simply way off base." I paused while he considered that. "And I think I'll visit Joe Don at the office this afternoon."

"He ain't gonna like that," he said.

"I hope to fuck not."

Overthrust Drilling and Production had offices on the top floor of the tallest building in downtown El Paso, an edifice of black glass striped with white concrete columns. It had taken me a couple of hours on the telephone and the persistence of a junkie or a lawyer to get through to Joe Don's personal assistant. Once I had her on the telephone I mentioned that I had some questions about his missing wife that I was sure he wouldn't want to share with the FBI.

Then I got some action. They kept me on the line long enough to trace the call, then gave me an appointment at 6:00 P.M.

By the time I hung up the telephone in my room at the Paso del Norte Hotel, where I had taken a room in the name of Eduardo Nueces, and walked down to the lobby they had three guys with earplug speakers and lapel mikes on my tail. Two were dark and swarthy and dressed like traveling salesmen, but they both looked like refrigerators in bad sport coats and their little piggy eyes glittered with the hope of violence; the other looked like an unemployed pimp. The fourth and fifth, a tourist couple, picked me up as I strolled up to the little square where they used to keep the alligators.

As I walked through the throng of bums, a slim character in pimp clothes from the thirties stopped me with a long, thin finger.

"Hey, man, you looking for some action?" he said.

Slightly taken aback since several thousand prostitutes worked just across the border, all I could do was look toward Juárez.

"Don't even think about going to Mexico," he said. "The girls there are all ugly, greedy, and diseased. But if you're interested in some big-titted white pussy—cheerleaders and pom-pom girls— I'm your man, soldier."

"I just want to know what happened to the alligators, man."

"Just walked away, soldier," he said, then broke into a bit of soft-shoe hustle in his pointed alligator shoes, "just walked away." Then he smiled and followed them. One of the refrigerators grabbed his arm, and the skinny guy broke into his smiling spiel. I hoped they didn't hurt him too much. But I didn't hope too much.

But the brief weirdness made me think I needed a drink. In Mexico. Which somehow manages, in spite of its madness, to be saner than America. So I hoofed down Stanton Street to the bridge, then crossed the border to Juárez. None of my tails looked anything like government agents and none of them bothered to call home before we crossed the border, didn't even hesitate, which probably meant that Joe Don was holding out on the Fibbies, just like I thought.

Walking felt right, down the crowded dingy Texas side, through the lovely tamale stench. Besides, I had stashed my rent-car in a high-rise garage, and once across the thick, muddy waters flowing between concrete walls, chain link, and razor wire, Mexico afoot seemed even better. I played it out for a while, pissed in a urinal filled with ice, then another filled with seaweed. Nervous pees, so I took a cab a block and a half to a place I'd heard about, the Kentucky Club, for margaritas and nostalgia. The bartender claimed to have played in the Mexican League back in the days when American baseball players were giants, before the Dominicans took over the league. After I stopped peeing, I wandered back to America with my little band tagging behind me. At least they had the decency to hide their earplugs and mikes before they crossed over through American immigration and customs. Then I took the fucks into the parking garage and lost them until I was ready to be found.

They took me down half an hour later when I stepped out of the elevator on Joe Don's floor a few minutes before six. I resisted just enough to get their blood in an uproar, hoping they might give something away. They were tough but professional, like ex-cops rather than hired thugs. Except for the woman, whom I had managed to kick in the shin. Although she was a redhead com-

plete with a scattering of freckles, she launched a string of curses
in slurred Spanish that I couldn't follow with my smattering of
Tex-Mex. She was about to kick me in the nuts when one of the
dark guys spoke sharply to her. In what sounded like Mexican
Spanish. But so quickly that the only word I caught was *gusana*.
Then they hustled me down the hall to see the wizard.

Although I had been searched carefully twice, led through a
metal detector, then manacled into cuffs, a waist chain, and leg
irons, when I was ushered into the presence of Joe Don himself
and shoved into a chair, a tall, well-dressed young man went over
me again. He did everything but shine a flashlight up my rectum.
And I told him so.

"Don't tempt me," he said.

I looked at Joe Don and said, "That's the way it is with the
help today. When they don't have their heads up their own asses,
they're looking for some other shitty place to put their face."

The tall young man blushed under his rich tan all the way up
to his blond hair combed sleekly back from his high forehead.
He ran a soft hand over his hair as if I'd mussed it, a gesture that
reminded me of somebody. He looked sort of willowy under his
expensively loose suit and he wore thin Italian loafers without
socks, thin enough to show the callused toes. And when he
slapped me, it nearly took my head off.

"Thanks," I said. "That clears up everything except my head."
Then I shook my head, and he laughed. "I may be dizzy, motherfucker, but I promise payback's going to be a bitch."

"What the fuck do you want?" he said, then slapped me again.
A little harder.

"An office like this, man," I said, looking around Joe Don's
corner lair. It was all soft leather, dark wood, and views. Mostly
east El Paso and Juárez, not views much praised for their aesthetic
values. Other than this, the only displays of money were a couple
of original Spanish oils on the walls and a glass case of pre-
Columbian artifacts. Most of the wall space was occupied by
artifacts from the Vietnam War. Weapons and official photos,
citations and medals, the phony debris of a foolish cause. This
fucker had believed. So I added, "And other people's money to
fuck around with."

The blond boy struck me again before Joe Don could stop
him.

"Touchy," I said when the stars got out of my eyes.

"That's enough, Len," Joe Don said. He had a deep, theatrical
voice that went well with his large, rugged face. Then to me:
"You've gone to a great deal of trouble to get into my office, you
want to tell me what this is about, Mr. Eddie Nuts? Blackmail?
Ransom?"

"Hey, Mr. Pines," I said, "when you check your telephone
tapes, you'll see that I just wanted to ask you some questions
without the FBI in my hair. That's all." I rattled my chains.
"My real name is C. W. Sughrue and I'm a private investigator
from Meriwether, Montana, and I spent some of my life as a buck
sergeant in the First Air Cav, so let's cut the shit, okay? Get
them to take the gift wrapping off me, offer me a drink like a
white man, and get rid of these overpaid jerks, then I'll ask my
questions, and we can be pals, a couple of vets talking over old
times, good Saigon pussy and bad times in the bush."

Joe Don stared at me for a moment, then smiled his open,
handsome smile. Even chuckled warmly. We chatted while his
goons unlocked my chains and the blond guy, whom Joe Don
introduced as Leonard Townsend, his adopted son and his chief
of security, poured a large measure of Herradura Gold tequila
into heavy crystal tumblers. Joe Don was heavy himself, on the
charm, but I managed to keep myself from kissing him on the lips.
Maybe it was the empty slot in the display case where my Mexican
Tree Duck had once rested between his pals. It was clear to me
that the other two ceramic ducks lacked the distinguished character of mine.

Maybe Lenny had slapped me harder than I realized. But I
didn't care. I knew Barnstone was watching from the roof of a
nearby bank building. Surely he wouldn't let the bastards kill
me without at least calling the cops.

"So why don't you fill me in, Mr. Sughrue?" Joe Don said
quietly.

So I did my best.

*   *   *

When I finished Norman's version of the story, Joe Don walked over to the glass wall and stared deeply into Mexico as the shadows of sunset lengthened over the desert, then he sighed and began to speak without turning.

"I suppose you've gotten deeply enough into my background, Mr. Sughrue, to understand that my marriage to Sarita was simply a matter of financial convenience, arranged between her grandfather and me. And believe me, sir, it has worked on those terms. Worked so well that we've become quite close. Sarita is a lovely, cultured woman, my friend, and what began as a marriage of convenience has become a real marriage, and I would do anything to get her back. Pay any amount of money . . ." Then he paused, turned to look at me. "But there has been no ransom demand," Joe Don said, and let it lie there.

"Any chance she took off on her own?"

"I can't imagine it," he answered.

"Or that she's actually my client's mother?"

"You know she was educated in the States," he said, "back when very few women of her class were allowed such freedom. She went to Smith, then took an M.A. at Cornell, and I know she also spent some time in El Paso, so it's certainly possible that she had a child out of wedlock, then left it at the orphanage," he said, then added, "but I can't believe that she would have raised the child until the age of six and then abandoned it. I can't see Sarita doing that. Not for a minute . . ."

Joe Don paused, then stepped over to where I sat on the couch. He lowered his large frame onto the coffee table, then placed his hand on my shoulder. "She's a wonderful woman. And I can't think something like that about a woman I love. But she's always kept her own counsel, so it's possible," he said. "But I can't imagine it . . ." Then Joe Don stood up and began to stride around the room.

"What makes you think you can find her when half a dozen law enforcement agencies can't?" he asked suddenly.

"I'm lucky," I said, "and I have connections they can't touch."

"Is that enough?"

"Sometimes."

"So what do you want from Mr. Pines?" Townsend asked.

"Just the answers to a couple of questions," I said, "nothing more."

"Let me hire you," Joe Don said.

"I've already got a client," I said.

"I'll pay you a bonus, anything you ask, anything."

"No, thanks," I said. "Too many bosses and too much money might confuse me."

"Len," he said, "let me have your badge."

"What? No fucking way," Len responded, standing up and sweeping his hand through his hair again. I realized who he looked like. "You're not going to give my special ranger badge to this asshole," he whined.

Joe Don stepped over to Len and slapped him like a petulant child, then reached into his inside coat pocket, extracted a badge case, and handed it to me. "This is a Special Texas Ranger badge. There are only fifty of them in existence and the bearer carries the full force of the law, so I want you to take this one, and . . ."

"No, thanks," I said, then hefted it in my hand. "I know who carries these fucking things." Joe Don looked confused. "Strikebreakers, bigots, and the hired ass-kissing lackeys of rich folks. I'm not a saint but I don't fit into any of those categories." I tossed the badge case to Len, who caught it, frowning, and gave me his best hard look.

"I guess I don't have anything to offer you, then," Joe Don said, then slipped into his chair behind the black walnut desk.

"Just answer one question for me," I said.

"What?"

"Well, I know you paid for the murder of Eloy Jones. I even know how much you paid the deputy for the cover-up. That part of the paper trail is clear. But I don't know who you hired to cut his dick off and slice it like a little sausage. Can you enlighten me on that part?" I said.

I got a reaction, but not exactly the one I had planned.

Len cursed and without hesitation leaped into a flying heel kick aimed at my head. I guess if it had caught me, that would have been the end of my day.

But I still remembered a few things from the old days: stay away from a knife fighter until you find a club or a gun; even with a gun, run from boxers because they're likely to knock you out of your socks before you can think about pulling the trigger; and with karate guys, get inside as quick as you can and bite their nuts off because they usually forget the countermove for that.

So I stepped inside of Lenny's spinning leg, got as close as I could, and caught his thigh with my arms and chest. When I tried to bite his nuts off, I missed, but my teeth sank nicely into his silk-covered hamstring.

When we stopped rolling around the floor, Joe Don stood in front of his treasures, his arms outstretched, and Len hopped around, holding on to his bleeding leg as if he'd been shot. He took one more try at me, somewhat hampered by his one-legged stance, so it was easy to duck my head and let the bones of his hand splinter against the top of my skull.

Even on one foot he still rang my chimes, so I had to finish it quickly. I stomped on his lightly clad toes, the ones on his good foot, with the heel of my cowboy boot; that usually helps. Then he sat down on the floor like a sick child.

Another piece of good advice I remembered: once you get a guy like Len down, you can't let him up. I broke his right collarbone with the expensively large ashtray. He dumped a neat puddle of puke between his knees, then tried to stand up again. Fuck it, this guy was as tough as he thought he was. So I hit him behind the ear with the ashtray hard enough, I hoped, to kill him. Which barely made him dizzy. So I did it again. Finally, he splashed face-first into his own vomit.

When I turned around, Joe Don had found a small automatic pistol somewhere and aimed it at me with a shaking hand.

"Get on your fucking knees," he said, reaching for the intercom, "with your hands behind your head."

"You guys have pissed me off, Mr. Pines," I said. "Either pull the fucking trigger, man, or give me the gun before I make you eat the motherfucker. You've already pissed in your pants, anyway," I said. When he looked down at his crotch, I took the pistol out of his hand. Then he peed his pants. I quickly unloaded and tossed it under the couch. "And quit looking at the intercom. You don't want your people to see you like this." He didn't, so he sat heavily in his chair and fell on his hands, defeated. Then he began to try to gather himself back together like a man who knew how through long, sorry experience. "Swollen prostate," he said, then stepped into a bathroom to change.

"You know, Sughrue, I had a really hard time over there," he said over fresh drinks, after Lennie had been removed and Joe Don chosen a new suit. He had washed his face, too, but he still looked like an angry child. "I just fucking saw too much, Sughrue."

"Yeah," I said, "I was a Jell-O salad from Travis to Tan Son Nhut. Then back. Guess I wasn't cut out for it." Joe Don looked at me as if I were a lower form of life.

"Right, some of us just couldn't cut it," he said as if we belonged to the same guilt and whine AA group. "How long were you in Indian Country?"

Indian Country, I thought. What an asshole. Joe Don probably said 'Nam, too.

"Nine months in the bush," I said, "scared shitless."

"Nothing wrong with being scared," he said, as if he hadn't been, "as long as you admit it." Then he paused. "Actually, my wife told me that."

"Smart woman," I said. "That's what my counselor says."

"Flashback?" he asked.

"Drug abuse," I answered.

"I'm sorry," he said.

"I'm not," I said. "You have any idea where I might find your wife?"

"Do you think I would be sitting here if I knew?" he replied.

"I don't know you well enough to know," I admitted.

"Trust me, I . . . ." Then he paused, a rueful grin flickering across his face. "I guess that's the wrong approach." He stepped over to his desk and took a large checkbook out of his desk drawer, then scrawled one quickly and handed it to me. "That's yours, Mr. Sughrue," he said, "just for looking for my wife. No strings attached."

He'd made it out for ten thousand dollars. That part was fun. The fact that he could spell my last name wasn't.

"You're missing a figure, sir."

"Oh," he said, then acting as if he were the coolest rich asshole in the world, he corrected it to read one hundred thousand. He even initialed the changes as if every teller was just waiting to cash a check like that.

"If it's a gesture," I said, "it's an expensive one."

"Trust," he sighed. "A man can't do business without trust. There's my evidence."

I stepped over to the desk, picked up his pen, wrote "for services rendered" in the memo space, then turned the check over and endorsed it and handed it back to Joe Don. "I don't work on the come, Mr. Pines. Come up with the cash and a letter of employment," I said, "then we'll talk about trust."

Joe Don flinched but he rang for his personal assistant, scribbled a memo and handed the check and the slip of paper to her, told her to cash it, told her to fill out a standard free-lance contract, then when she left, he offered me another drink. I had to decline. Townsend had knocked me silly three times, and the afternoon tequilas hadn't helped, either. Plus, I knew the night was going to be a bitch.

"I'll just wait for the cash," I said, then sat down prepared to wait silently, but Joe Don obviously wanted to chat. Silence made him nervous. "You've got a hell of a lot of security for an oilman," I said.

"Life on the border isn't what it used to be," he said. "When I was a kid my mother used to hire a maid from Juárez who would work for ten, maybe fifteen dollars a week, and she would no more steal from you than from her priest . . ."

As if that explained what I guessed at a half million a year on security. Or more. "I heard a rumor, Mr. Pines, that the last time you lost an election here, you promised to never set foot in Texas," I interrupted.

Joe Don chuckled expansively. He took no offense; he clearly loved to tell this story. "No, what I said was that I would never set foot on Texas soil again. I come in from the ranch or the spa in my limo. It delivers me to the basement elevator . . ."

"I get it," I interrupted again, then I glanced at the two remaining ceramic ducks. "What the hell are those things?"

"Nobody knows," Joe Don answered, his composure almost complete now. "They might be Olmec, they might be Mayan. Whatever they are, those tar-looking blobs around the back and the bill are human blood. We know that much. And when we had them X-rayed, it looked as if they contained three of the largest freshwater pearls anybody had ever seen. This anthropologist suggested that they were used in religious sacrifices. Pour the blood in the back, let the pearl purify it, then pour it out the beak." Joe Don was proud and arrogant again, almost benign in his pride of ownership. He pulled the nearer one out of the case, held it next to his ear, then shook it. Hard. Even from where I stood, I could hear the lump bounce and echo inside the ceramic body. Joe Don seemed a bit too happy about owning the Mexican Tree Ducks. He had a rich man's taste: he didn't give a shit about anything but the story and the price; and the fact that he had the only ones.

"The old blood doesn't stink?" I asked, and he acted as if his feelings were hurt.

"Of course not," he said, dismissing the notion.

"You find them in Mexico?"

"No, not at all," he said, serious again. "They were recovered a few years ago from a Spanish colonial wreck over on Padre Island. They had been buried high and dry in the dunes for god knows how long. I was over there with a lease man and we stumbled into them. I've spent a long ton of money trying to have them identified, but nobody seems to be able to place them into any known religion or tribe."

"Look like Mexican Tree Ducks to me," I said.

"What?"

"Mexican Tree Ducks."

"What's that?"

"Just a goofy bird I used to see in my childhood."

"No, no," he said. "They're way too old for that."

I nodded, then asked, "Where's the other one?"

"The other one?" Joe Don seemed confused now. He had more moods than a bad actress. "Oh, right. I did say three pearls, didn't I? You're quick, Mr. Sughrue. It's being cleaned and X-rayed . . ."

Just then, much to Joe Don's relief, his assistant came in with an aluminum briefcase, set it on the coffee table, then opened it so I could see the money. She looked like somebody's mother until she said, "I hope hundreds are okay? They didn't have enough smaller bills." This woman had carried money somewhere before. I told her it would be fine, then she glanced at Joe Don and excused herself.

"You want a bodyguard or something?" Joe Don asked.

"Your money buys some trust, Mr. Pines, but not that much," I said. "Besides, I didn't get where I am by being afraid of dying," I added just in case he might be wondering.

"Where's that?" he asked, smiling.

"Alive," I said, and left him standing beside the rest of my flock. Then I paused at the door. "Hey," I said, "tell Lenny I'm sorry."

"Oh. No problem. Kid always did heal quick."

"Not that," I said. "About accusing his adopted dad of killing his real one."

Then I finally left, hoping Joe Don thought he had seen the last of me.

When none of his help followed me from Joe Don's building to the airport, I stopped at a package shop, moved the money to a cardboard box, left the locator beacon intact in the briefcase, then went on to the airport to air-freight the money to Solly's office. I called to check in and was quite happy to talk to the machine. Then I dropped off the rental car, left the briefcase under the seat in the unlocked unit next to mine, and walked over to the airport curb where Barnstone picked me up in a junky green GMC pickup he had borrowed from his neighbor of many cars.

"Jesus, Sughrue," he said as I tried to find a place to sit where a spring didn't bite my butt. "You're a pretty slick piece of work, man, and you sure know how to have a good time . . ."

"Thanks for covering my back," I said.

". . . but you're a dangerous man."

"How's that?"

Barnstone drove north through the hard-time neighborhoods of east El Paso, thinking, tugging at the fringes of his red moustache.

"It's hard to explain," he said, "but the easiest way to try is to say that you've rekindled emotions I had forgotten how to have," he said seriously. "I saw the way you took Lenny out . . ."

"Just lucky," I said. "If I hadn't gotten my teeth in his leg, they would have gathered me up with a police mop."

"It's always luck," he said, "or moral inspiration." Then he stared into the traffic as we turned west on Transmountain Road, heading uphill toward the faint remains of sunset washing the sky above the Franklin Mountains. "That's what I never had," he finally said. "I didn't believe in the war. Fuck, nobody worth a shit believed in the war. Not for very long. And if they did, they turned out to be Ollie North." Then he paused to look at me. "Man, could I tell you some stories about what really went down in Nicaragua in those days. It's a shitty world when the fucking drug smugglers know more about politics than the pissant Congress. But don't get me started. Please."

I thought it kind of me not to point out that I hadn't.

We drove in silence to the top of the pass, then Barnstone pulled into the parking area. We climbed out, gathered up a couple of beers from a cooler in the back, leaned against the pickup, took long swallows, then watched the sunset die across the flat spiky miles of southern New Mexico.

"Tell me that part about Baby Lester," Barnstone said. "Again."

When I finished, Barnstone said, "How did you learn how to feel those things? I've been trying for years now, and patience is just about as much as I've learned."

"And persistence," I said, "perhaps a little kindness."

"Those are external things," he said. "It's the feeling part that's tough. Where did you learn it?"

"My father," I said before I could think, "he was sort of mystical and crazy." Then I thought, quickly. "And an old buddy of mine—my ex-partner—he was a PI, but now he's a dry bartender. And Frank, and Solly, and . . . Fuck, I don't know. That's just my best short list."

"Thanks," Barnstone said, then glanced at his watch. "Let's hit it. You guys will want to be off the ranch before moonrise, and we've only got about six hours until it clears the mountains . . ."

"How do you know that?"

"What?"

"When the moon rises?"

"I read the paper, man."

We laughed for a moment, then he got serious. "One favor, please," he said. "No. Two."

"Sure," I said. "What?"

"Promise not to kill anybody."

"I'll try," I said, thinking of the night we had crossed the desert on our way to El Paso, "but I won't let Frank or Jimmy or you die."

"That's okay," he said. "How long's it been?"

I didn't have to ask what "it" was. "I don't talk about it anymore," I said.

"And how long has that been?" he pried.

"Since I started dreaming about it," I admitted. When he didn't say anything, I asked, "What was the second favor?"

"Oh," he said as if he had forgotten. "I was going to ask you to let me come along, but you already answered that."

So we climbed into the pickup and moved on the ranch, racing the moonrise.

PART FIVE

PART FIVE

Frank and Jimmy were already installed at the picnic table in Barnstone's backyard. For reasons I didn't want to think about, we seemed to have taken to staying outside as often as possible, as if we weren't prepared for the confinement of four walls. I dumped a pile of brand-new night gear—black sweat suits, watch caps, sneakers, etc.—on the table. Jimmy and Frank looked at the gear but didn't have any questions. Barnstone and I sat down and opened beers.

As I explained as best I could to Frank and Jimmy about what had happened to me and the hunch that had grown out of it, I noticed Carney drift out of the shadows behind his garden to hunker at the edge of the light. For a moment it looked as if he were about to say something, then he lowered his face, and I looked back at the table and told them that Barnstone and I were going to hit Joe Don's ranch that night. They could come along if they wanted.

Jimmy and Frank gave me the sort of look you give a puppy that just shit on a white carpet, then jumped up to retrieve the van. Barnstone said he thought he had some aerial photographs; he headed for the house, leaving Carney and me to our silence. After five minutes or so, Carney's stolid presence caused me to suddenly need a smoke, which I couldn't find.

"You don't have a cigarette, do you, man?" I said.

Carney glanced behind himself but found only the turkey

sleeping among the bantam chickens roosted in the low branches of a mesquite, then he took his makings out of his black tunic and rolled me a cigarette. Then he brought it to me. Or perhaps "brought" isn't the right word. One moment he was squatting by the garden; the next he was standing beside the table, his lips parted as if to speak, and the cigarette extended toward me; then he was gone, as quick and silent as a mongoose or a cobra before my "Thanks" cleared the air.

Barnstone came out of the house just as Jimmy and Frank returned. He lit a Coleman lantern and spread his navigational materials—maps, compass, straightedge, and protractor—across the table. Frank carried all our weapons over to the table to clean and load them while Jimmy checked the van's engine and controls, then did his best to quiet the engine with steel wool and asbestos wrap before he joined us at the table.

Since I had the *moral inspiration*, I was in charge of the drugs, trying to come up with the right mixture of raw biker speed and Peruvian flake to keep us awake but not insane. Not an easy chore with people like us, trust me.

I also felt obligated to try to figure out what the hell was going on, given the recent events. Frank and Jimmy could only tell me that Norman's paperwork checked. As far as they could tell, he was who he said he was—as if anybody else would have claimed to be Norman—and he came from where he said he did. But in the short time they were downtown, they couldn't turn up a word about the woman who had dropped him at the orphanage.

Thinking over my adventures downtown, I decided I didn't harbor any illusions that Joe Don Pines had given me one hundred thousand dollars to look for his wife. My best guess was that he had given me the money not to look for his wife. And given the electronics in the briefcase, I also suspected he didn't really expect or want me to keep the money. But I had no idea what sort of plans he had for me. Hell, I had no idea why I wasn't dead. My second best guess was that I was supposed to take the fall for something. Perhaps the tons of cocaine supposedly moving toward the border. The only thing I knew, and I had no reason to know it, was that Wynona and Baby Lester were on the ranch, and I was running out of time to get them out.

While I was ruining my mental health, Barnstone plotted a course to an arroyo three miles from the edge of Edwards Hole, where we could stash the van, then cut across the desert to the edge of the Hole. Then he got off in a discussion of the geological explanation of these southern desert sinkholes. It involved limestone and water, not meteors. Frank and Jimmy and I acted as if we knew what he was talking about up to that point, but when Barnstone started talking about the size of the sinkholes, we had a little trouble with that part.

"Kilbourne's Hole," he said, "is nearly one hundred feet deep and contains over six hundred acres. Phillips is a little larger but not as deep. Edwards, on the other hand, is twice the size of Phillips and twice as deep as Kilbourne's. That's why it has better water closer to the surface." Then he slid a large aerial photograph from under the stack of maps. "This is what it looked like fifteen years ago. Joe Don has made some improvements, I understand, but what I don't know." Then he stopped to glance around the crowded van. "It sits right in the middle of a serious drug and wetback border corridor, so some of the improvements are bound to be along the lines of better security. If we get caught down there, we probably won't get out without some legal problems . . ."

In the pause, I suggested, "Or disposal problems."

Jimmy grinned. "Disposal problems?"

"Somebody has to do the body count," Frank said, then stepped back with a wide gesture. "Gentlemen, choose your weapons."

Behind me from the dark shadows of the reed hut, I heard the stropping of Carney's knife.

"How many people we looking at here?" Jimmy asked as he picked up the suppressed twenty-two automatic.

"I don't know," Barnstone said. "Joe Don's mother still lives there, runs a little truck garden with half a dozen old Mexicans . . ."

"No problem," Jimmy joked. "When Frank's an old Mexican, he won't be no problem . . ." Then he realized what he had said, so the three of us shut up long enough for Barnstone to look up and realize we had left him out of something. But he didn't ask.

". . . and there's bound to be some ranch hands, but for all I know these days Joe Don might have a reinforced platoon down there. We could wait another day, do an overflight . . ."

Jimmy picked up two extra clips as I reached for the Browning High-Power that I'd carried for twenty years and the Airweight for a hideout piece.

"Let's do it now," Frank said, and waited for Barnstone to pick up a weapon, then shrugged and picked up the shotgun, a bandoleer of buckshot rounds, and his service revolver. Barnstone still didn't move, so I walked over to the van, dug into the footlocker, and grabbed my spring-loaded sap. He took that, slipped it in the cargo pocket of his fatigues without a word, then reached into his backpack and withdrew a starlight night scope.

"Well," I said, "those things don't stick to you like a dust bunny unless you paste them on with a three-thousand-dollar bill."

"Never pay retail," Barnstone said, almost smiling.

Then I passed the lightly loaded blade point of my grandfather's pocketknife under our noses, and we snorted like communion scholars complaining about the Host. Then we climbed into Norman's van and headed for the sinkhole, middle-aged men dressed up for war. If I hadn't known better, I would have guessed that we were happy.

Three hours later we were back in the van, giddy with success, Wynona safely in my lap and my arms, Baby Lester sleeping on Frank's giant chest, Jimmy speeding across the desert under a quarter-moon, and even Barnstone grinning. We hadn't spilled any blood but our own. And most of that minor scratches and our fault as we stumbled among the thorny residents of the desert. Except for the clotted dribble leaking off my left ear.

It turned out that about the only place to slip over the side of Edwards Hole without climbing equipment was at the road cut down the side from the airstrip, which turned out to be lighted but unguarded. Slipping downhill toward the ranch buildings along the roadside ditches made us a little touchy but nobody seemed to be watching for us. Except for the REA outdoor lights, two windows flickering with the electronic reflections of television screens, and a little fire by a small outbuilding beside the corrals, the ranch buildings were dark.

When we reached the flat bottom of the Hole we could see that three men with rifles squatted around the fire, passing a tequila bottle and a joint around the small circle. The sweet smell of *mota* drifted like fog across the still air of the Hole.

When we got close enough to the fire, we set it up without a word, as if we had been running night patrols all our lives. Jimmy, Frank, and Barnstone bellied behind the small plank building beside the corral—a tack shed, more than likely—as I covered the movement. We all paused a moment, listening to the soft Spanish, the gurgle of the tequila, the slow smoky exhales, then our guys went through the slovenly guards like corn through a goose. Almost without a sound: the flat muffled slap of the sap; the strangled gasp of a choke hold; and the sudden gasp of the last guard as Jimmy put the suppressor between his eyes.

The guards were trussed and gagged with strapping tape and propped against each other around the fire before I could trot quietly over to the shed. The single window, blue with the reflection of the television, was too high to see through and the cracks in the board-and-batten shed walls too narrow. The hasp and the padlock on the single door were too large to knock off without too much noise, but Jimmy had found a key ring in one of the guard's pockets, and I finally found the right key.

As quietly as I could, I opened the door and stuck my head quickly into the darkness relieved solely by the small television, which saved me from serious damage. A silvery glint caught my eye, and I just had time to dodge before I took a glancing blow on my ear. I grabbed a smooth, hard arm and smothered the familiar body with mine.

Sometimes, if you're not willing to hit a woman as if she were a man, she can beat the hell out of you before you can stop it. Wynona did a pretty good job on me with the bridle and bit before I got her to the ground.

"Babycakes," I whispered. "It's me."

"Oh, god," she sighed, then tried to hug me to death.

When she finally turned loose, I lifted my head slightly. Baby Lester reclined like an eastern potentate in his car seat, a pacifier lodged into his mouth. When he recognized me, he jerked it out of his mouth, raised both little arms over his head, and gurgled happily.

"I think he remembers me," I said quietly.

"Of course, he does, stupid," Wynona said. "Where the hell have you been, Sughrue?"

"Coming as hard as I could," I said, which wasn't exactly true. Then she locked her mouth on mine and held on until Baby Lester complained.

On the way back to Barnstone's, he suggested that we stash the van among a drift of dunes, then settle in to fox any pursuit. We snuggled into the cool sand fifty yards from the van and waited for the moon to rise over the Franklins. Then we drifted back slowly, Jimmy driving again by moonlight. The pause and enforced silence eroded our giddiness. Suddenly, it was all business, the exchange of information, some of the hard stories.

Wynona sat on the van's floor between the seats, nursing Baby Lester while I explained who the rest of us were, then segued into what had happened at the Quirky Arms when we went in after she was gone. When she found out that Mel was dead in the back room of the bar, Wynona cursed her for the love and friendship. Then she wept so hard that Lester caught the confusion and joined her.

"Who the fuck . . ." she blubbered, "what . . . I told her not to worry . . ."

We gathered closer, helpless, until she was able to continue.

"Sarita said we'd be safe, me an' Lester, at the house in Aspen," Wynona began. "It belonged to her family, and nobody knew about it . . ."

"The Quirky fucks did," Jimmy interrupted, then excused himself and kept driving.

"I guess so," she said, "but I didn't know that. I was just supposed to have a job there. My big brother got it for me . . ."

"Lenny Townsend?" I asked.

"Yeah," she said.

"How come he's got a different name?" Frank wanted to know.

"My mom remarried," Wynona said, "you know, after my daddy . . . my daddy died, and Lenny took the name . . ."

"Then Joe Don took him," I said.

Wynona turned to me. "What the hell would you do, Sonny? Some rich man come by the house and say, 'Come be my boy, boy?' What would you say?"

"What did you say?" I asked.

Wynona paused, then answered, "I said, 'Fuck you, Joe Don Pines. I done got a daddy, even if he's dead.' " Then she paused again. "But my mama was on his side so hard I had to leave the house just to get some peace . . ." Then she was silent again, her face turned to me, the skin glowing in the moonlight. I touched her face briefly with the palm of my hand. Wynona shook it off gently, and I held it against Baby Lester's cheek, warmed by her breast. "Goddammit," she sighed, "I could sure use a beer. You boys got a cold one in this heap?"

Frank and Barnstone nearly crippled each other trying to get her one.

I let her have a good long hit off it before I asked:

"What happened after I last saw you in Aspen?"

She didn't hesitate. "Lenny came by, picked us up, and flew us down here on one of Joe Don's jets." Then she bowed her head. "Then they said I had to stay out there at the ranch . . ." She raised her face to mine. "They kept wanting to know where Sarita was. But I didn't tell them. And they kept saying that you were coming to kill me, Sonny . . . But I knew better than that, so I kept trying to leave the ranch. Even knocked old Mrs. Pines down. She's a mean old bitch. She hung on to my leg like a mad monkey 'til them Meskin boys could come. That's when they locked me in the tack shed."

Lester suddenly had enough to eat but he was too excited to sleep. He shoved his mom's breast aside, then reached for me, but Frank picked Lester up in his giant hands before I could move. Baby Lester seemed quite happy to snuggle on Frank's shoulder and watch the moonlit desert flow past through the van's windows.

I gave Frank a look, but he ignored it. He was deep into his baby fix. Then I scooted over on the passenger seat and lifted Wynona so she could share it. She turned away from me, staring out the driver's window.

"I've got two really serious questions," I said, "and I have to know tonight." She nodded without turning her face toward me. "Do you know where Sarita Pines is?" Once again, she nodded silently. "Is Joe Don Baby Lester's father?" This time she nodded so slowly she might have been carrying a stone on her head. Or in her heart.

We planned to drop Barnstone at his house and crash at a motel near the airport to at least make it a little harder for Joe Don to find us—if he were looking, and I couldn't imagine that he wasn't—but as we pulled into Barnstone's backyard, we were greeted by an amazing tableau.

A blazing fire roared in the pit. Carney hunkered in its shadows, one of those ugly new automatic rifles with a bulky suppressor rested on his knees, his face dark beneath his conical hat. Little Mary and Norman sat like posed figures on one side of the picnic table, Solly on the other, the duct tape shining on their wrists and ankles.

"Who the hell is that?" Wynona asked, taking Baby Lester from Frank.

"A lawyer, a biker, and his intended," I said. "Barnstone, get Wynona in the house. Frank, Jimmy: you guys cover me."

"Jesus Christ," Barnstone whispered. "Watch the son of a bitch like a snake, man."

Jimmy stopped the van sideways to the table as Frank slid open the door. They exited the van, rolling into the dark cover of the barn and our quarters as Barnstone hustled Wynona and child around the stone fence toward the front of his house. I climbed out, took the Browning out from under my arm, and walked into the fanning circle of firelight, the pistol dangling from my hand.

"Hey, Carney," I shouted. "What's happening?"

Carney just lifted his head enough so I could see his eyes

glinting in the firelight. His eyes looked dead blank, but with tiny flames burning inside, as if he had died a long time ago but hell was still in his future.

I moved a few steps closer, but Carney just looked at me. Until I raised my pistol. Then, moving like a cobra, he covered me dead with the assault rifle. "Just putting it away, man," I said, then reholstered the Browning as slowly as I could. But he still kept me covered, so I stayed where I was.

"What's the matter, man? You didn't know who these people were?" I said softly.

Carney nodded, his hat moving, but not his eyes.

"They're friends of mine from Montana, man," I said. "They're all right. Promise. The one guy there . . ." I pointed with my chin. "He's got a goose named Millard Fillmore. Annie, she would've liked old Millard. He's one boss goose . . ."

Carney's eyes came to life with glittering red tears. I was either dead now, or alive for a time. He nodded swiftly, then disappeared as I was blinking. The flickering night filled with sighs. Even Solly, Norman, and Mary managed to sigh around the raw eggs stuffed into their mouths.

A few minutes later, introductions made, apologies tendered, we gathered around the fire and tried to fill the adrenaline gaps in our systems with a more peaceful chemistry.

". . . but the worst fucking moment," Norman shouted, "was when the son of a bitch selected—fucking selected—the proper-sized eggs to stuff in our mouths . . ."

"Of course, they got turkey eggs," Mary wailed, laughing, "and I got what looked like an apology because he didn't have any banty eggs."

So it was we restored peace among us again. Miracle of miracles, I watched Norman apologize to Barnstone for past transgressions, which Barnstone shrugged off as long-ago and faraway, though I gathered they had taken place in this very yard. Mary and Wynona passed a giggling Baby Lester back and forth so many times they finally wore him out; he went to sleep in mid-pass. Solly drifted around the garden to Carney's corner, squatted there talking so softly it almost sounded as if he were engaged in apology, talked until I saw Carney's grimy hand extend from the shadows and grasp Solly's in a shake of fierce brotherhood.

Then Solly strolled back from the dark toward me. Jimmy and Frank pulled up beside me. I asked Solly what the hell he was doing in El Paso.

"You know how long it's been since you checked in?" he said quietly. "I can see you're in good hands, but I got worried. And Norman wanted to come along. He is the client, you know, and we're his minions." Then Solly laughed, looked at Frank and Jimmy. "You guys look a lot healthier than the last time I saw you." Only Frank laughed. Jimmy muttered something under his breath that might have been "fucking officers," but I couldn't tell. Then Solly turned to Frank. "Remember that black kid? What was his name? The one Sughrue dug the mine out from under."

"Willie Williams," Jimmy answered flatly.

"Right," Solly said. "What the hell ever happened to him?"

"Did his tour," Frank said, "then went home."

Norman joined us in the resulting silence. "You guys swapping war stories?" When nobody answered, he slapped me on the arm. "You find my mom yet, Sughrue?"

"It's a long story," I said, "and we better tell it someplace else . . ." Then I turned around to find Barnstone, asked him, "Think we're too hot here?" He thought about it for a minute, then nodded sadly. "Got any ideas?" I asked.

"Ideas, hell, I got a place," he said, "the perfect place."

Like all successful smugglers, Barnstone always had trouble accounting for his money. The pecans were good—he could fudge weights and the costs of maintenance and capital improvements—but the damned trees kept making so many nuts he couldn't make them lose money every year. Then he discovered water. Or perhaps water discovered him.

Barnstone bought an old chili farm in New Mexico, between Las Cruces and Hatch, put in a small processing plant, then drilled a water well. That's always a great loss. Except Barnstone discovered a mineral hot springs with water that stunk so badly it had to be good for your health. So he started a small hot springs resort, which grew successfully into a motel-restaurant-golf-course-destination resort, a place so expensive he flinched every time he acted like a paying customer, a place so popular it overwhelmed its orginal purpose.

So he drilled another well. This time he hit clear, cold artesian water, perfect water, just about the time Americans decided designer water was the way to go. This time he had the perfect money laundry. Nobody could account for water. And Stone Wash Springs also gave Dottie a perfect cover and another career, as she worked her way from bartender to bar manager to running the lodge.

As the sun topped the San Andres Mountains, all of us, except for Carney, who stayed behind to watch the place, were clean and sober, tucked into huge rooms with stone fireplaces and even larger bathrooms complete with Jacuzzis and saunas and showers as large as small dance floors. Then we met for breakfast and a council of war.

Dottie gave us a private dining room, had breakfast with us, then gathered up Baby Lester and retreated so she wouldn't have to listen to our compounded felonies. Wynona had the floor, but before beginning she stared at Norman, who was trying to look as normal as possible, for a long time, then said tartly, "You don't look a thing like Sarita, man."

Norman blushed and stared at his coffee. Mary came to his defense. "It ain't his fault," she said. "Them niggers in Leaven-worth worked him over pretty good . . ."

"That's a jolt I didn't know about," I said.

Norman blushed again, then said, "I got popped in Crystal City, Texas. Right in front of the statue of Popeye. With a trunk full of Mexican brown. I pled on the federal charge so I didn't have to do life in Huntsville."

"Good choice," Solly said.

"Well, he still don't look nothing like Sarita," Wynona said, then without further preamble, she launched into her story.

"Sarita was always sweet to me, you know, 'cause I think she knew that Joe Don was always sucking around me, ever since I

was a nubbin. My mother wasn't too swift. I hate to speak badly
of my mom but, truth is, she was a couple of cans short of a six-
pack. She was sweet, man, but she wasn't quick enough to stay
away from Joe Don. Sometimes I think that's why he murdered
my pop . . ."

"If it's any help," I said, "Dottie agrees with you. She says
they had a line on the deputy who did it, then covered it up, but
he got shot by his brother-in-law down in Parras before they
could make a case. And they could never trace the money back
to Joe Don."

"The son of a bitch," Wynona muttered. "If Baby Lester wasn't
such a sweetie I could almost hate him, I hate his daddy so
much . . ."

"What happened?" I said.

"Oh, fuck, my mama died," she admitted, "and after the
funeral I let Lenny talk me into having a drink with the son of
a bitch and his pissant mother . . ." Wynona paused. "I guess I
shouldn't be talkin' down my mom. Sometimes my elevator don't
go all the way to the top floor, either. Joe Don put something
in my drink, and when I came to I was covered in sweat, spit,
cum, my twat so sore I couldn't hardly walk. And if that wasn't
bad enough, I was pregnant."

"You could have gotten rid of it," Mary said softly, reaching
over to touch Wynona's arm. Then when Wynona began to cry,
Mary gave her a shoulder.

"I guess I just ain't built that way," Wynona sobbed.

"I can understand that," Mary said, then looked at the men
around the table as if all this pain had been our fault. We, all
five of us, stared at the floor as if we agreed.

Finally, Wynona sat up, scrubbed her face with her napkin,
then continued. "And I think Sarita knew, too. She was especially
sweet to me when we ran into each other up at Snowy Lake, and
when she found out I was heading for Aspen, she asked if she
could hook a ride . . ."

"Nobody kidnapped her?" Solly said, bent over his leg to
remove his prosthesis and scratch his stump.

"Not then," Wynona said, with a wide-eyed stare at Solly's

foot, which he held in his hand as if it were as mundane as a shoe.

"When?" I said.

"In Sun Valley, silly," Wynona said, "at Joe Don's place. I told you about the gunfight."

"You did," I said, "but I guess I didn't understand what you were telling me."

"You were looking at my tits," Wynona said, "instead of payin' attention."

"Sughrue's like that," Solly said.

"So excuse the fuck out of me," I said, "and tell me again."

"Well, there was these Mexicans," Wynona said breathlessly, all memory of her tears seemingly gone, "those *pendejos* from the Quirky Arms waiting at the house . . ."

"Who the hell are those guys?" Frank said suddenly.

"Well, I'm not sure," Wynona said, "but they acted like her friends but they had guns and wouldn't let her go. Seems they had some business with Joe Don. And Sarita, too."

"Cocaine?" I said.

Wynona thought for a moment, sweeping the froth of blond hair out of her face, then said, "I don't know, but I don't think so. My Spanish ain't the best, but from what I could tell they spent most of the time talking about Mexican politics."

"Politics," several of us said at once.

"Sorry," Wynona said, "but that's what it sounded like."

"Fuck a duck," I said as I stood up, knocking over my chair. "Excuse me—I forgot about Annie," I said to Barnstone, "but I'm flat-ass running blind."

"Sounds familiar," Jimmy said softly, then we all laughed.

"Anybody else want a beer?" Frank said, then ambled toward the exit and the bar beyond it.

"Fuck a duck?" Barnstone said quietly, then the laughter broke out again.

"You guys are nuts," Wynona said as she stood up. "Where's my baby?"

"I'll get him," I said, then followed Frank out of the room.

I caught him at the bar where he was filling a tray with cans of Coors. "Hey, Officer Vega," I said, "you okay with Solly being here?"

Frank thought about it for a minute, then opened two beers and shoved one toward me. "Look, man," he began, "I know you two guys got tight coming out of the bush, and give him this, when we got hit crossing the river, he stood there toe-to-toe with fucking Charles and went to the ground with him, and I know you two were back-to-back when it was over and up to your asses in dead Cong. That'll make asshole buddies out of anybody, man, but I just never trusted the son of a bitch, okay, and nothing I saw while he was practicing in Denver did anything to convince me otherwise.

"There's something dirty about him, Sughrue. He was a fucking spook officer in the bush, part of the problem, and as far as I'm concerned he still is." Then Frank paused to hit his beer. "But he's your bro', man, and that's good enough for me."

"Okay," I said, "just asking."

"Thanks," Frank said, "but why in the hell does he want to know about Willie?"

"I don't know," I admitted, then drank some of my beer, too. "It's funny, though."

"Funny?"

"We told the same lie."

"It's a good lie," Frank said. "I just wish it was true." Then he sipped his beer, staring out the glass walls of the bar where a guy started a riding mower and began to cut the lawn grass. "That ain't all the bad news, either," he said.

I turned all the way around for a good look. "I don't like that worth a shit," I said. It was the phantom road guard from our night ride across the desert, the one keeping company with the crashed DC-3 and the numerous bales of marijuana. "Maybe one of us should take a look around instead of a nap."

"Okay," Frank said, then he carried the beer toward our dining room, and I followed him toward the sound of Baby Lester's laughter.

Dottie, hard-core, longtime undercover cop, lay on her back in her office, holding Lester up in the air so he could play flying baby. She stopped laughing long enough to hand him to me, then bounced up like a gymnast, her tight, agile body completely under control.

"What is it about babies that makes fools of grown people?" Dottie said.

"I don't know any grown people," I said as Baby Lester tried to tear off my nose.

"She's way too young for you, Sonny," Dottie said, smiling, "but you two make a pretty couple."

"I don't think we're exactly a couple," I said.

"You're sweet, Sonny," Dottie said, touching my cheek, "but sometimes you're dumb as rock."

A few minutes later we had reconvened around the table and Baby Lester had attached himself to his mother's breast with such sounds of marvelous contentment that we were all envious. Mary leaned over to whisper in Norman's ear, but as she did, Baby Lester detached and glanced up so we all heard what she said.

"We could adopt . . ." Then Mary realized we were listening and hearing, and she blushed like a maiden.

"So," I said to Wynona, trying to cover for Mary, "what happened in Sun Valley?"

"The usual," Wynona said as Lester fell on her breast like a starving man, "she shopped, I watched. She played golf, I watched. She showed me shit, like the other house, and I watched. Ever notice that: rich people need an audience. Hell, maybe we all need an audience."

"Better than a crowd," Jimmy said.

"It was fun, you know," Wynona said to Jimmy, "good times. Sarita is really a class act. Maybe because she's a Mexican. Sometimes it's like, you know, they're raised better. Or something. I don't know. But it was great times for a couple of days . . ."

"You guys were there for days?" I said, then looked at Solly. "When was the kidnapping reported?"

Solly thought for a second. "As far as I know, that night."

"This shit don't scan," Frank said.

"And those guys from Aspen were there all the time?" I asked Wynona.

"They were there when we got there," Wynona said.

"And when did the other bunch show up?"

"The second night," she said. "We were eating *fajitas* when they killed the two guys outside, then rolled into the house. It was a shit-storm, Sonny. Just like the fucking movies. Them that didn't run, fucking died. Shotguns and silenced Uzis, or some such shit." Wynona looked at us as if she expected us not to believe her. "Me 'n' Lester hid under the cover of the hot tub. These guys were dressed like, you know, cocaine cowboys, but they weren't right, somehow, all their clothes were brand-new and they couldn't walk in cowboy boots for shit. They looked like a bunch of *mojados* fresh over the borderline. Hell, one guy couldn't figure out how to get the safety off on his Uzi."

Wynona sighed so hard that Lester's head lifted like a deep ocean swell on her chest, then continued. "And like I said, my Spanish ain't all that terrific, but when they were looking for me and Baby Lester, they were standing out on the deck right by the hot tub and talking, and I could tell they didn't know what it was. One of the guys thought the cover was a short table, so these dudes ain't exactly your sophisticated world travelers."

Then Wynona sighed again. "We hung out under there for hours, 'til we didn't hear nothing. There were fucking bodies everywhere. So me and Baby Lester split to the other house because we didn't know what the fuck to do. Then I called Mel— we been friends since Telluride, you know—'cause she was always smarter and tougher than I was and now she's . . ."

We waited until she composed herself, then I said, "I don't mean to push you, love, but you told me that you knew where Sarita was."

Wynona brightened in that pretty way only young girls can, then said, "Oh, sure. I heard 'em talking. Whoever those guys were, they thought it was funny to carry her someplace nobody would ever think of looking."

"Where's that?" Solly asked.

"Oh, a hunting lodge on her own ranch down in Coahuila, up in the Encantadas, you know, south and west of Big Bend," Wynona said. "You cross at Boquillas del Carmen, on a rowboat. Lenny and I came back that way one time. He fucked up a little drug deal in Musquiz, you know, and we were running from the

Mexican law. Stupid asshole tried to stiff a *Rurale* captain for chicken-shit money . . . So one of Sarita's cousins who had the hots for me up here once, hid us out until we could get back across the borderline."

"How do you get there?" Norman asked.

"I can't tell you," Wynona said, "but I can show you." She let that gem of information rattle around the table, then added, "In person, I mean. Not on some pissant map."

Lester kept sleeping while Wynona and I lounged in the sauna. She couldn't seem to get enough of the hot dry air. While sweat poured, glistening, off her lovely body, I kept checking on the napping Lester just to get enough of a lungful of cool air to keep breathing. Finally, I had enough and quit even though she laughed at me. I showered, dried, then flopped on the bed beside Lester. Then I unwrapped my duck and set it on the night table.

After a bit, she joined me on the bed. We made a couple of cursory attempts at pre-foreplay, but we were both too tired, so we just lay there holding each other as our skin cooled.

Then she saw the duck, sat up, and elbowed me happily in the ribs. "All right, Sughrue," she chortled, "you found it." Then she threw her arms around me.

"And all the firepower, too," I said. "Why did you take the duck?"

"Oh, hell, I don't know," she said sharply. "I just wanted to hurt the son of a bitch. That's why I stole Lenny's twenty-two, too. He fancies himself a hired killer, you know, but he's just a little twit . . ."

"A tough little twit," I interrupted.

A comment with which she agreed, then continued, "And I took the Glock, too, thinking Joe Don's metal detectors would catch the twenty-two and miss the Glock, and then I could shoot the bastard dead . . ."

"What happened?"

"He laughed at me, and I couldn't pull the trigger," she admitted sadly. Then brightened. "So I just picked up his lousy old duck and walked out with it. Joe Don's such an idiot about those old things. He's just thrilled down to his dingleberries that nobody knows what they are or where they came from. And the fact that that black, sticky shit is blood . . . well, that makes his pecker dance for joy. He's not just a turd, Sonny, he's an asshole, too. And kinda stupid. I guess he thought I'd bring the goddamned thing back."

"Well, it's mine now," I said. "He'd have to kill me to get it."

Wynona suddenly looked worried. "Is there some kinda curse on the fucking ducks? Jesus, don't you go crazy on me, too, Sughrue. I couldn't stand that." Then she hugged me so hard it seemed to make her yawn. She lay back across the bedcover.

I stared at her for a moment where she lay, as nakedly natural as the waxing and waning of the moon, the turn of seasons, life and death, one wrist propped against her forehead, her rib cage rising and falling in soft, slow rhythms.

"How come you're a-starin' at me, Mr. Sughrue?"

"Wynona, baby, you are lovely," I said.

"Time will take care of that," she said quietly. Then she rolled over to stare at me. "Except it didn't happen with Sarita," she said incredulously. "She's different somehow. She'll be beautiful until the day she dies, absolutely beautiful."

"Well, some of her children have come a little short of true beauty," I suggested.

"You mean that scut Norman?" Wynona scoffed. "He ain't no more kin to her than I am." Then she paused. "I don't know what's going on . . ."

"Neither do I."

". . . but I'm comin' along 'cause I'm the only one who knows where we're going and I promise you, Sonny, ain't nobody looking for their mama . . ."

But as if to simply prove us wrong in all our philosophies, Baby Lester whimpered in his small sleep, squirming out of the darkness of his dreams toward Wynona's waiting arms.

"Would you get me a towel, please, Sonny," she said, "I'm leaking . . ."

I grabbed a towel, then, when they were asleep, draped them in a cotton blanket and carefully repacked the Mexican Tree Duck. Then quietly strapped on my Browning, covered it with a loose sweatshirt, slipped into jeans and a pair of running shoes, chopped a small line of crank, and went about my dirty business.

Even though the desert sun was as warm as a cooling brick, the air was still cut with the edge of the desert night, but Frank and Jimmy, dressed in trunks and thongs, acted as if it were still full-blown summer. As a concession to the Agent Orange acne on his back, Jimmy had thrown on a tee-shirt, but the pustules still burned like unbanked coals through the thin fabric. Jimmy had his piece wrapped in a towel; Frank had stashed his in a belt pack. We were ready for anything. Except for the ease with which we came up with the answer.

The chili processing and packing plant sat atop a large daylight basement. Barnstone and the phantom road guard supervised the cleanup as a small group of men attacked the walls, floor, and ceiling with steam hoses and scrub brushes. A refrigerated semi and tractor sat idling outside the basement. We assumed that the bales had been transferred and were waiting to move.

The road guard nudged Barnstone as we stepped up behind him. Barnstone turned, smiled, and shook his head. He introduced us to the road guard, then said, "Yeah, shit, he recognized the van, so I knew you guys would be poking around. Too much of a coincidence, right?"

"Right," Frank said flatly.

"Smell's almost gone," Barnstone said placidly.

"*Mota* smell's almost gone," Jimmy said, "but the bullshit still stinks."

"Sorry," Barnstone said as if he meant it, turned away.

One group of men began to scrub the floor with piles of crushed chilies, which would surely kill the last remnants of the odor of the marijuana bales, while another group began to unload the semi. It was full of washing machines, televisions, microwave ovens, VCRs, and other electronic gear.

"You got a fucking appliance store?" Jimmy said.

"Sort of," Barnstone said, then blushed and turned to look me in the eye, adding, "Look, man, when I got out of the drug business—and I have been out all these years; that last shipment, a buddy of mine, when the plane went down, his ass was hanging out, and I owed him, so we took it out—but I still had all the contacts, all the routes, and all the equipment. So I go the other way now, hauling freight, you know, so rich Mexicans can avoid the import taxes . . ." Then he blushed so hard he had to turn away.

Jesus, he was embarrassed. It was hard to get your mind around it, given Barnstone's two tours in Vietnam, one as a riverboat commander, the other as a SEAL, and given his twenty years as a drug kingpin, hard to realize that he didn't want his friends to see him acting like a child. Perhaps somebody should learn how to smuggle common sense into the human psyche.

It took Jimmy and Frank a moment to get it, then they laughed wildly, but I didn't know what to say, then I did.

Thirty-six hours later, just before moonrise and just outside Boquillas del Carmen, Coahuila, Mexico, we loaded into the closed bed of an American Army surplus three-quarter-ton truck. Barnstone and Jimmy had flown in with our side arms and the crate the Dahlgren twins had shipped to El Paso; Solly and Norman had crossed legally, flown from Ciudad Juárez to Monterrey then Monclova, where they joined our Mexican cohorts and checked out the road north; then Frank, Wynona, and I, playing drunk *gringos*, had crossed the Rio Grande by rowboat at dusk, just in case Joe Don had the border crossings watched.

Wynona had resisted all our efforts to leave her behind, as had a series of Mexican maps and officials who wouldn't or couldn't tell us where to find Sarita's family hunting camp. For a while after Wynona first bowed her neck, it looked as if Wynona was not just going *along*, but going *alone* and also taking Baby Lester with her. Finally, she wore us down, then agreed quickly to leave Baby Lester with Dottie and Mary, then went to work with the breast pump to store up goodies for the little guy.

Barnstone claimed that the two guys driving the three-quarter were Mexican military officers, but they looked like *banditos* to me. At least until they opened their mouths. They spoke better English than most of us, especially the one who looked like Dagoberto's brother. We drove until just before dawn, bouncing like marbles in a sink in the back of the unsprung truck as it fought the unimproved dirt track, then bivouacked in a *huisache* grove. We set up camp and camouflaged the truck as the officers wiped out our trail where it left the road. Nobody knew what we were getting into, but everybody remembered Wynona's line: "Them that didn't run, fucking died."

After a breakfast of cold beans and stale tortillas, we spread out the officers' military maps and even some high-altitude shots that must have come from the DEA. The two officers had no trouble locating the runway on the map and in the photos, but neither had any idea where the lodge might be.

"I remember," Wynona said, "that we came past the runway, then up a narrow, dry wash to a really steep grade. We had to back and fill at all the switchbacks, and Flavio's Jeep nearly didn't make it . . . But when we topped the rise, man, it was like something in the movies, a little blind canyon and a hidden valley. Waterfalls and creeks and deer and the whole fucking ball of wax.

"No, it was better than the movies. It looked like Montana . . ."

Wynona mined that vein for a few minutes, then came back to the serious part.

"It's a huge log house, you know, perched below an outcrop, and you probably can't see the house or the road from the air because of the pines. They looked like ponderosas, but down here, I just don't know."

"And the house looks out over the valley," I said, "and one guy can cover the whole thing with a BB pistol . . ."

"Well, it's not my fault," Wynona said, then flounced off behind a rock to pee.

We all tried not to look at each other as we listened to the splash of urine, tried not to look at the dark trail that circled the other side of the rock and lost itself in the sharp gravel.

Finally, one of the Mexicans said, "Goddamned *ricos*, they hide their shit even when they aren't doing anything illegal . . ."

Then his partner said something in Spanish, and the first one replied in Spanish. They chatted until Wynona came back around the rock. My command of the language was even more minimal than hers, but I could tell they were talking politics. It's all the Latin cognates. Later, I thought, I would ask her again about the conversations in Sun Valley. But first we had to sleep. And in spite of the hard ground, sharp rocks, and thin bedrolls, sleep we did.

When I woke at dusk from a dreamless sleep, I eased Wynona's leg off mine, then rolled off the bedroll. Beyond the three-quarter, Frank and Jimmy and the two officers hunkered around a small, smokeless fire boiling coffee, chattering softly. I took my toilet and joined them.

"How goes it, *compañeros?*" I said, pouring coffee the consistency of old motor oil.

"We were telling these gentlemen what a bad-ass and a fearless leader you were," Jimmy said.

"Why's that, Mr. Gorman?" I asked, waiting for the joke.

Frank took a deep breath, then spoke with great seriousness: "Because neither one of us has had a nightmare since we hooked up with you, Sughrue."

"Neither has he, I'll bet," Solly said as he hopped on one foot around the latrine rock. "And he's been considerably sweeter over the telephone," Solly added, "when he bothers to telephone at all."

"You guys pick on somebody your own age," I growled. Since I had served some time playing Army football, I was an old guy of twenty-seven by the time I got to Vietnam.

"Or a cripple," Solly said, perching on a rock to reattach his prosthesis. Then he looked up to stare into the fire. "I figured out how to fox the nightmares years ago."

Only Jimmy bothered to bite. "How's that, Captain?"

Solly fixed him with a stare that looked right through him. "I gave up sleep, soldier," he said so softly we had to lean toward him to hear and believe. "I quit fucking sleeping." Then he laughed hollowly. "That's the secret of my success, right, Sughrue?" he said, then laughed again.

By then, the rest of the bunch was awake, so we feasted on another guerrilla marching meal of beans and tortillas, broke camp, and headed for the happy valley of Wynona's Montana dreams and the elusive Sarita Pines.

"Well, they're sure as hell there," Barnstone said as he handed me the bulky German binoculars. "I counted ten," he added. "Except for their weapons they looked as much like hard-hat NVA as anything I've seen since the real thing."

I scanned the front porch as quickly as I could before the morning sun topped the ridge above the lodge, then passed the glasses to Frank. "Quick," I said, "watch the sun, but see if those guys don't look familiar."

It only took Frank a second to look and agree. The last time we'd seen two of these guys, they had been heading south into the mountains of Colorado. Four of the others we had left afoot in the New Mexican desert. Two we didn't know, and two more were women with submachine guns slung across their chests. Changing the guard and cooking breakfast over a tiny fire built on the top of a steel drum. Two brand-new four-wheel-drive Japanese vans were parked just below the porch. And above it all, standing tall and slim on a second-story balcony, Sarita Pines stood wrapped in a wool *sarape*, her pale Spanish face glowing in the morning air. Sarita looked more like the commander in chief than the prisoner.

Then the sun broke the crest, and we had to whistle Jimmy in from flank security and belly down the reverse slope toward the temporary safety of our dry, cold camp.

The night before, the Mexican officers had taken us as far as a gulch just off the canyon mouth beyond the runway, unloaded our gear, then hiked back over the rocky ridge to the main road. Barnstone took his cellular telephone and climbed a nearby rise to arrange for a plane to wait at a strip outside Musquiz in case we needed to be extracted faster than the ancient three-quarter could run. Then we made a slow and easy scout up to happy valley. We had to threaten to bind and gag Wynona to make her stay behind.

Now back at midmorning we knew what we faced. Without

coffee or cigarettes, we sucked on coffee beans and gathered to consider our plight. Except everybody looked at me as if it were my plight alone.

"Looks like it's up to you, Sughrue," Solly said, smiling. "Go. No go."

"Nope. It's up to Norman," I answered, "it's his mom."

Norman looked at the rocky ground. "I can't ask you guys to take on something like that," he said slowly. "You're the only person here I know, Sughrue, and I can't even ask you to go up against those kinda odds. But I'm going to at least go up and see if those guys will let me talk to her, see if she is my mom . . ."

Wynona spit on a flat rock between them, then said, "Well, fuck Norman. He doesn't even know if Sarita's really his mom. But I know she's my friend and she's in trouble. And I'll bet the son of a bitch who killed Mel is up there laughing about it. So I'm going no matter what you guys do." Then she stared at me as if I were a shit-weasel trying to squirm out of my bound duty.

"Fuck it," I said, "I never had any choice."

"If you're waiting on me, you're walking backward," Jimmy said.

"I don't know what that means," Frank said in a fake country accent, "but I'm bound to dance with the one that brung me."

Barnstone nodded slowly, then smiled. Solly just looked at me.

"You guys," Norman said, then stopped. "I guess all this bullshit started with me, but I know that woman's my mom." Then he turned to Wynona. "And don't you be spitting on the ground again, little girl."

"Fuck you, you walleyed son of a bitch," Wynona said, but didn't spit this time.

Then they all looked at me again. So I had no choice. I stepped over to crack the lid off the Dahlgren boys' crate of arms.

"Let's hit them just at sunset," I said. "They'll think we're coming out of the sun. Frank and Jimmy and I have all day to get above and behind the lodge." I started loading weapons, a grease gun first. "Norman," I said as I pitched it to him, "your legs are too fucked for the climb . . ." Then I pulled the BAR out of the crate. "But the first thing they'll do is send a couple of guys to take out the BAR, so you can cover the position . . ."

"And I'm the fucking cripple who has to cover the retreat," Solly said before I could toss him the automatic rifle.

"Right," I said. "There's a little draw that angles off just below the ridgeline where you have at least three positions with a clear field of fire at the lodge. It's at least eight hundred yards, and you'll want to stay way high and to the left until we come out, but that shouldn't be a problem . . ." Then I dug up Barnstone's German glasses and handed them to Wynona. "Because this young lady is going to shut up, follow orders, and spot and load for you." For once I thought Wynona was going to do what somebody said for a change. But I was wrong.

"What about a weapon for me?" she demanded. It took the Glock and one of the carbines to placate her. I made sure it was switched to semiautomatic so she didn't spray Solly and Norman.

Then I dug in the crate again. "God love those fat boys," I said when I found an assortment of grenades—two smoke, two fragmentation, and two of the new flash-bang concussion-and-confusion babies hostage teams used—then I looked at Norman. "You know," I said, "if you weren't such a jealous asshole, they might have shipped their Sherman tank down here." But Norman didn't laugh. So I continued, "So, Barnstone, you're going to have to be my tank. And my diversion."

"Okay."

"What the hell is your first name, anyway?" I said.

"Roland."

"Okay, Barnstone. You drive the three-quarter up the road and stay low until they fire at you, then get the fuck out of it and behind one of those big-ass pine trees until we come out of the lodge and you can cover us."

"If you come out," Solly said.

"That's the kinda pissant officer attitude that cost us the fucking war," Jimmy said. And nobody argued with him.

"*When* we come out," I repeated, then picked up an M-1 Garand from the crate. When I held it up, it felt like a rock—warm, steady, and heavy—and I knew I could shoot the nuts off a gnat at five hundred yards.

"It'll work," I said to nobody in particular, as I lifted three Kevlar vests from the crate, another blessed gift from the twins. "It'll fucking work."

And it damn near did.

After six hours of rock and thorn, slim concealment and thin mountain air, and a belated appreciation of our misspent youths, Jimmy and Frank and I huddled at the edge of the small patch of scree below the outcropping of rotten stone, some twenty yards above the rear of the lodge. We had made the last rush an hour before when the guard had changed.

I had to have a heart-stopping hit of speed just to get my breath back. Frank joined me reluctantly, because the climb had seemed to age him twenty years, the dark lines of his face as deep as knife scars. But Jimmy declined, already bursting with excitement. So we watched the sun touch the rim of the valley below and listened to the whine of the transfer case of the three-quarter as it growled slowly up the slope below the lodge, its noise overwhelming the soft grumble of an undergound generator and the muted murmurs of a televised Mexican soap opera that drifted out of the back windows of the lodge.

The guard patrolling the back door stopped and turned at the sound of the truck. As I covered him with the M-1, Jimmy steadied the suppressor of the .22 on the back of his wrist, which rested on a waist-high rock, then shot the guard three times in the side of the head. We ducked, waited for somebody to notice; when nobody did we scrambled down the slope, the small sounds of our rush hidden by the sound of the truck.

Frank boosted Jimmy to the small gable over the back door, where he paused a minute, crouched below the window, trading his .22 for a grease gun, then he smiled down at us, grinning like a bad, bad leprechaun—the one who knows the pot of gold is a thunder jug full of old, watery crap—then he rolled silently over the windowsill as I held the back door open for Frank to slip inside.

The four guys gathered around the kitchen table watching television couldn't have been more surprised if we had been mountain gorillas or ghosts; they confronted us with open mouths and empty hands. Frank covered them with the shotgun as I covered the long hallway leading toward the front door, where I could see other people watching the truck grind up the road. The guys at the table stayed still long enough for Frank to whisper something in Spanish to the effect that they could raise their hands and live.

But some poor bastard stepped out of the hall toilet, whooped when he saw me in the kitchen, and dug madly for the stainless-steel automatic strapped under his coat. Like an asshole I pulled the trigger of the M-1 until I heard the *ping* of the clip flying out.

Mostly, I think, I missed his vital parts. At that range it didn't much matter. The muzzle blast tore his forearm in half, set fire to his blanket coat, and sent him reeling down the narrow hallway toward the front door where a not-so-innocent bystander fell forward through the shattered glass, a victim of unaimed fire.

With the ping of my empty clip, the guy nearest me at the table rushed me while the others scrabbled for their weapons, the cheap Chi-Com version of the Soviet AK. I butt-stroked mine into eternity while Frank piled the others like bloody rags into a corner by the stove with buckshot rounds. Then he calmly re-loaded while I checked the bodies and unloaded their weapons, except for one, then I shoved another clip into the M-1.

Upstairs the grease gun stuttered, answered by the clatter of an assault rifle, distant sounds to our ringing ears, and the BAR began taking the shingles off the roof and the glass out of the far side of the house.

"She's up here!" Jimmy screamed between bursts.

With Sarita upstairs, Frank and I could escalate. I jerked a fragmentation grenade off my vest and pulled the pin as Frank fired five rounds around the corner of the hallway. While he reloaded, I tossed the grenade atop the two bodies in the doorway, jerked as many rounds as I could through the fake Kalashnikov before it jammed, then scuttled back behind the refrigerator.

Some screams and curses and running footsteps followed the explosion, and the BAR rounds stopped chewing at the side of the lodge. Frank and I cleared the downstairs rooms carefully, checked the porch, from which we could see four guys making tracks across the small valley, the BAR kicking up dust at their feet whenever they paused. I emptied the M-1 again, knocking one down with a ricochet or a rock, but he bounced up like a ball and chugged across the valley floor.

"Great weapon," I huffed to Frank.

"Different war," he sighed, so I unholstered the Browning for the rest of the close work.

Then there was a distant rattle of small-arms fire from down the hillside, and the BAR stopped. The running guys paused, then Barnstone threw a magazine of hunt-and-hope rounds at them from the carbine, and they trudged on without another hesitation. A few moments later, the BAR kicked in again, its deep booming crack filling the valley. But the rounds weren't coming our way.

"What the fuck?" Frank said, then we went back inside to clear the second floor, which had been silent since the grenade.

"Hurry," I whispered to Frank as I jerked one of the flash-bangs out of my vest, then shouted, "Jimmy! Ears!" and tossed it up to the second story, and Frank and I ducked beneath the stairs. Even under cover and at that distance, the little grenade still cut through the ringing in our ears and the flash seeped through our hands pressed hard over eyes squeezed shut. As Frank and I charged up the stairs, I could only hope that Jimmy had sense enough to get down.

Frank went to the right, I went to the left.

My bedroom was empty. A jammed AK lay on the bed. "Jimmy!" I shouted. "Here!" Frank answered, so I put a couple of rounds into the bed, then a couple more into a mirrored antique wardrobe.

One of the women tumbled out, bleeding from the thigh and the abdomen, a suppressed .22 clutched in her hand. She got off one wild round, by which I mean she hit me in the vest right over the heart instead of the eye, and I put two jacketed hollow points into her chest as I hit the wall behind me hard enough to splinter the oak panels.

The Kevlar had stopped the .22 round, but I had absorbed it. If she had hit me over the liver or the spleen, I might have been sorely fucked. As it was, I was just sore.

"Sarge," Frank shouted.

"Here," I answered, trying not to groan, trying to stand up without leaning on the wall. "Where's the woman?"

"Right here, gentlemen," came a soft voice from the landing between the bedrooms. "And she's got a gun to my head . . ."

When I peeked quickly around the door frame, Sarita stood in front of the bedroom at the end of the wide hall, the other woman guard behind her holding a small automatic at the base of Sarita's skull and chattering in terrifically rapid Spanish.

"And she will kill me in five seconds if you don't throw your weapons out . . ."

"Sughrue?" Frank said softly.

"Let's do it," I said.

Frank slid his service .38 across the floor toward the guard. "It doesn't work that way, honey," he said.

When she glanced down, I put a round through her elbow, then the next one through her ear. The woman guard hit the floor dead; Sarita hit it in a dead faint, covered with brains, bone splinters, and blood.

We looked at each other and smiled. I hope I looked better than he did. Our blood still boiled, but this part was done. Whatever waited at the bottom of the hill hadn't begun yet.

Sarita had to be carried; Jimmy led. She wouldn't come around, and Jimmy still couldn't see or hear from the grenade. But we got them down the stairs and out to the porch, where Barnstone waited at the top of the steps.

"You heard?" was all he said at first as he heaved Sarita over his shoulder. "I don't know what we're going to find down the hill. But I got a call as I was driving up."

"A call?" The modern world of cellular telephones and satellite communications had ended for me in the kitchen.

"Dottie called, man, and said that the baby was bugged," Barnstone huffed as we stumbled down the steps.

"The baby was bugged?" Frank said.

"And everything else Wynona carried," he explained.

Just then another rattling burst of automatic gunfire echoed up the hill.

"Joe Don," I said. "And that's the only way out, right?"

Barnstone nodded grimly.

"I wouldn't have it any other way," Frank said softly, pumping up.

"Let's take these rides," Barnstone said, nodding toward the Japanese vans. "And let's hurry. The plane can't land after dark."

Barnstone dumped Sarita in a backseat, strapped her in with the belt, then went to work on the keyless ignitions. Frank and I put Jimmy beside her before we ran back into the lodge to search for the keys and gather and reload whatever weapons we could find as the tiny firefight moved up the hillside toward us.

Some shit never ends.

In spite of Norman's legs, smashed in a dozen motorcycle wrecks, and Solly's fake foot, they had done a good job of holding off Joe Don's minions as they moved up the hill, so they weren't ready for us when we came through. We picked up our gimpy fire team about halfway down the road, then sent the first van down the hill with a grenade strapped to the gas tank.

When it exploded among them, we charged through the fire with Sarita, still unconscious, wrapped in our flak vests, and the windows of the van bristling with firepower. Nobody could tell if it was the curtain of fire we laid across Joe Don's hoods—nobody had a confirmed kill—or the forest fire we started, though a crazed but semi-lucid Jimmy claimed a dozen hits, but we made it through them and to the runway just before dark, and took off into the roiling clouds of smoke black in the final rays of dusk.

Sarita was awake by then, staring out the window of the small South American prop jet at the flaming remains of her hunting lodge. I wanted to ask her something, but her face seemed so painfully resigned, tears spilling silently down her tight high pale cheekbones glowing pearlescent rose in the failing light, that I turned away before asking.

Then Solly limped down the stripped interior of the plane to me, his right side sodden with blood. Either a series of flattened ricochets or flying gravel had chewed up his side from the trapezius to the hip. And he had taken a round through his artificial articulated ankle.

"Guess you need a new foot," I said.

"I've needed a new foot ever since that day I wasn't quick enough," he said. Solly had been humping down a paddy dike when his foot caught the trip wire that jerked the unpinned grenade out of the Coca-Cola can. He had nearly caught the handle, but even as he missed it, he dove into the paddy water before the grenade exploded. If it hadn't been an old pineapple, circa WWII, he would have been either dead or even more badly fucked. "I'm really sorry, man," he said, "but she stepped off to pee behind a bush, and they got between us."

"At least she's not dead," Norman said as he joined us. "I saw this blond guy with his hand in a cast dragging her away."

Fucking Lenny. Not a good sibling. Now I regretted not hitting him harder.

"Goddammit," I said, "what's Baby Lester going to do without his mom?"

"I'll provide," Sarita said softly, staring out her window into the star-studded darkness of the eastern sky.

"Have you talked to her?" I whispered to Norman. But he shook his head and retreated. I patted Solly on his unwounded shoulder, then hobbled like an old man to the front of the plane, where Frank and Jimmy leaned against the bulkhead, flanking Barnstone. The two Mexican officers sat across the airplane from them.

"Where we headed?" I said to Barnstone.

"Durango," he said, "to divest ourselves of the weapons and get legal again so we can cross the border."

I leaned against the bulkhead and slipped out the Browning, replaced the half-empty clip, then charged it, leaving the hammer cocked, and stuck the barrel into the face of the tall one who looked like Dagoberto. "Who were those guys?" I asked them. "And who are you guys?"

Barnstone reached for my pistol, but I slapped his knuckles hard enough to draw blood with the barrel, then put it back on the Mexican officers. Who, quite frankly, didn't seem impressed.

"I believe we're pressurized," the short one said, "and decompression might put us down."

"Tell somebody who gives a shit," I said. "Fucking answer me."

"Peruvians, maybe," he said quietly. "*Sendero Luminoso*, probably, Shining Path hard-core Maoists."

"What the fuck are they doing in Mexico?" I said.

"Too much cocaine and money on the deal from them to stay out of it," the other one said angrily. "*Gringo* money for *gringo* noses."

"And you assholes?"

"Mexican military intelligence," Barnstone said tiredly. "Anyway that's my guess." Then he paused to sigh. "Shit, I'm sorry, Sughrue. How the hell was I supposed to know I was supporting these assholes with washing machines?" he said.

"Antiterrorist command, actually," the tall one corrected him.

"You let us go up against those bastards," Jimmy said to the Mexicans, "those hard-core motherfuckers, you let us go up against that kind of shit without a fucking word. Thanks for letting us do your dirty work."

"We've done yours often enough," the short angry one said. "Usually with hoes and cotton sacks."

"What do I know from cotton?" Jimmy said. "Fucking cotton comes in shirts and shorts, not sacks."

"Excuse the fuck out of us, sir," Frank said, suddenly in the conversation. "What's your plan now? How about a couple of rounds with a Cuban parachute brigade?"

"After you turn in your weapons and we debrief you in Durango, you will understand . . ." the tall one started to say.

But his voice trailed off when Jimmy placed the suppressor of his .22 against his nose. "You're gonna debrief shit, man. Talk to us now or fucking die. This pissant little round won't make this fucker decompress, but it's bound to run around inside your head like a fucking rabid mouse!"

"Easy," I said, acting calmer than I felt. "I ain't exactly happy about any of this. I find it hard to believe that Wynona is alive after all this, and I feel mightily shit upon, so I'm with Jimmy . . ." I had to grab a sob. "It might be Mexico where you are, motherfucker, but where I stand it's fucking America—not the government, man, but a horde of redneck motherfuckers, and I'm in front . . . So like they say in my part of the world, you'll get my weapon when you pry it from my cold, dead fingers . . ."

Suddenly, Sarita was standing between us, tall and lovely in the dim light as she pulled the pins from her dirty hair and let it hang in shining strings around her oval face. "Please, gentlemen," she said softly. "I believe I can shed some light on this before we suffer more gunfire . . ."

She tried.

However tough, fucked up, and dirty we were, Sarita was still an imposingly lovely and composed middle-aged woman, even in stiffly stained jeans and a *sarape* that looked as if it had survived the revolution, and we made room for her, found her a place to sit, gathered at her feet as if she were *La Lengua Materna Verdad*, the mother tongue of truth. Sarita smiled once, sadly and briefly, amused at our efforts to please, and for a moment I caught a glimmer of what Wynona admired, that breeding and social ease that rednecks so often secretly admire and so terribly mistake for integrity. Sarita clasped her hands together, swung them between her slim legs, and talked.

"My husband, it is no secret, has suffered losses recently," she began, her voice barely audible above the prop wash, "losses of a political, personal, and financial nature. As a result, he has not been himself in some time now. Not for a very long time. And quite frankly, my family did not help.

"Not that they did not offer financial assistance. They did. They offered it in embarrassingly large amounts, amounts so large they robbed him of that dignity without which a man cannot live." Then she paused, glanced around the rapt group, smiled self-effacingly, and continued. "I must confess that occasionally we Mexicans, who treasure dignity with pride, are guilty of failing to remember that you Americans are capable of that same dignity and pride.

"My husband was such a man," she said, her tones as somber as a state funeral. "As often happens, he made a foolish mistake trying to regain what he considered his rightful place in society . . ." Then she paused again.

"Joe Don went into the cocaine business," I said into her silence.

Sarita stared at me as if she had never seen me before, then smiled indulgently, as if I were a particularly pretty but stupid child.

"Just this once," she finally said, "and at such a level that he would never have to do it again . . ."

"And with the wrong people," I suggested.

"How very true," she said. "Suddenly, there was so much money involved . . ."

"How much?" Frank wanted to know.

"During my captivity, I heard the figure fifty million in street value mentioned several times, but fifty million what, I am not sure," she said. "Quite frankly, gentlemen, my captors did not have an impressive command of the language. Their grammar was as confused as their politics," she said, then lifted a long slim finger as if to lecture. "They kill their own people, you understand. As far as I am concerned, that is revolting, rather than revolution. And completely untenable, untoward, and unforgivable . . ."

"Lady," Frank said, "your fucking husband wants to smuggle tons of cocaine into the country, and you think you have the right to judge some *peones* who at least have the courage of their convictions?"

"Your people," Sarita said stiffly, staring at Frank's dark face, which to her eyes could have been Indian or Negro, some *mestizo* mongrel mix. "Your people," she repeated so we would know what she meant, "have a particular greed for drugs that passes understanding among decent people of the world."

"And you *ricos* simply have a particular greed?" Frank said.

"I am certain that my husband meant no harm," she said. "Now if you gentlemen will excuse me, I am tired." Then Sarita stood as if to exit to a royal bedroom just offstage.

"No, excuse me, please," I said, "but I'd like to know why you went to Sun Valley with Wynona."

Sarita answered from her great height without pause. "I had just discovered my husband's plans to . . . to recover his losses and I needed some time to myself to consider these new developments. Also, Wynona is a sweet child, a good friend, and the mother of my husband's son."

"Oh," I said. "Then who were the Mexicans waiting for you in Sun Valley?"

"Friends," she said simply, then swiftly turned and vanished toward the darkness at the rear of the cabin.

"What a piece of work," Frank said.

One of the Mexican officers started to say something, but I couldn't tell which one in the dark. "You fucking guys shut up," I said to them. "I still ain't happy about you letting us walk into that shit without a single word, and I ain't happy about your facial features, Short Round, so unless you want me to turn the dwarf loose on you, just shut up . . ."

"Who you calling a dwarf?" Jimmy wanted to know, but we ignored him.

"And we ain't going to Durango," I said to Barnstone. "Fix it." He nodded and stuffed his bulk into the cockpit to talk to the pilot.

"Frank," I said, "you and Jimmy tie these guys up. Tight. If they complain, gag the fuckers with their own socks."

Solly, Norman, and I gathered at the middle of the cabin, crouched as if over a small fire. "You got any whiskey?" I asked Solly.

"In the cargo pocket," he answered, "but my side's too stiff to reach it."

I could, so we all had a good hard taste out of Solly's flask full of ancient Scotch. "That's better," I said, then turned to Norman. "What do you think, man? Is that her?" I asked.

"Just like I remember, C.W.," Norman said quietly, "but she used to be nicer."

"That wouldn't be hard," I admitted, then turned to Solly. "You're a professional," I said, "so I won't try this at home, but what do you think, counselor?"

"I think I'm tired, old, shot to shit without glory waiting in the wings," he said, then tried to sit down on a duffel full of weapons. I helped, and we shared the flask again. "What sort of Purple Heart do you think they give if you're shot in a prosthesis?"

"Artificial?" I said.

"Perfect," he said. "You should have been a lawyer, Sughrue."

"No, thanks," I said, waiting for the rest.

"Jesus, man, I'm just guessing but my best guess is that the lady is scared to fucking death," he said. "I don't think she has the vaguest idea what's going on, and I think her family is involved in this shit up to their *cojones*."

"At least we agree on something," I said.

"Get me some more codeine, Sughrue," he said, "and I'll always agree with you. But I'd sure like to know what made Mrs. Pines run to Sun Valley . . ."

As I dug into Barnstone's first-aid kit for the painkillers, Norman moved over to kneel next to me.

"What should I do?" he whispered.

"What do you want to do?"

"I guess I want to talk to Mary, man."

"Jesus, Norman, you are in fucking love," I said, still amazed.

"I guess I am," he answered, a goofy grin shining in the dark. "And, man, I'm really sorry about Wynona. She's one tough little number. But it wasn't Solly's fault. Really."

"Right," I said. "We'll get her back. We've got a body to trade. You always need a body to trade."

And a place from which to trade it.

Since Barnstone's pilots had some experience crossing the border at brush-top levels, we decided to return to America low-level and low-profile. Also, since Joe Don had proved less worthy of trust and smarter than any of us expected, we decided to get to the heart of the matter.

After we landed on a dirt strip south of Palomas to clean up, release our Mexican nationals with a cover story that matched ours and a promise to make public their ownership of a restaurant in fucking Aspen if they didn't cover our asses, we let Barnstone make his arrangements by cellular telephone, then executed a brief hop across the border right to the airstrip at Joe Don's ranch. Sarita stayed apart from us, silent and distant, almost bored. A stance, I was now convinced, she held out of fear.

On the other hand, Joe Don's mom wasn't afraid. She was at the ranch, unguarded except for two ancient Mexican retainers, who probably would have died for her, given the chance, but

they had no chance. They were still struggling with their specta-
cles and boots by the time we had rushed down the road into the
Hole. The elder Mrs. Pines was snug abed, thankfully; if she'd
been awake, I suspect we would have had to shoot her to settle
her down and get her outside. After fifteen minutes enduring her
prickly pear of a tongue, I was more than willing. But Sarita
managed to stuff her with bourbon and Valium, a mix with
which the old lady seemed quite familiar.

Then it was business.

Although Barnstone, Norman, and I tried to talk them out of
it, Dottie and Mary arrived with Lester and the extra gunhands
from Stone Wash Springs. Lately, it seemed I had had a remarkable string of bad luck trying to get women to do anything I
ordered, asked, or begged. We nearly lost Mrs. Pines the elder
as we swept the ranch house for the dozen bugs we eventually
found.

At first, Mrs. Pines had a screaming fit about the DEA interfer-
ing in the private life of her son. When we pointed out that all
the electronics were German or Polish, which probably meant
that her son had bugged her, she had another more inchoate
episode, during which she claimed that Joe Don wouldn't make
a pimple on his father's ass. Sarita gave her another dose of
Valium, minus the excitement of bourbon this time. So, except
for Sarita and Mrs. Pines, we were finally able to settle around
the kitchen table for several cups of cowboy coffee while we
watched the sunrise shatter the dark rim of the Hole.

First we did information. Barnstone suggested that between
his own contacts and Dottie's they could spin the buzz on the
firefight to make it sound like a rip-off or an internecine war
between partners, and he believed that since he owed them a load
of VCRs the Mexican Army might hold up their end.

Then we did blame.

After finding the directional bug in the briefcase, I should
have realized that Joe Don was committed to the modern world
of electronic marvels. It was all my fault. But Solly came to my
defense. I didn't think of it, he suggested, because I didn't quite
recognize the modern world. Which wasn't the same thing as
being my fault.

I agreed for the sake of brevity, always a blessing during conversations with lawyers.

Then Solly wanted to blame himself for not being able to talk Wynona out of her modesty, but Norman verified his efforts and all of us could vouch for Wynona's stubbornness.

Then Mary started her blame rap about Norman's mom and all that, but Jimmy shut up everybody, saying, "Yeah, well, I started the fucking Vietnam War! So don't fucking argue with me!"

So we gave up blame. Even me, who could feel the loss of Wynona again like the terrible jungle cramps that came in huge empty waves when you had to hold the watery shit inside your guts on a night ambush.

But nothing got me off the hook. I was still in charge. So, at last, we did *plan*. I've always done better at *do* than *plan*, but what the hell, we all have to suffer sometime.

So that's how I found myself sitting on the sunny patio above the first tee at the Santa Teresa golf course having a drink with Joe Don.

"How many guns do you have on me?" he wanted to know.

"Nice body armor," I said, "but no good against a high-powered rifle round, say a .300 Weatherby."

"Yeah," he said. "I got tired of those bulky Kevlar things. As you know, they're just too fucking hot."

"So, let's deal," I said, trying to ignore the sweat pouring off me.

"What have you got that I could possibly want?"

"Your mother, your son, your wife," I suggested, "your money, and your fucking duck. The mortal nuts on your drug deal."

"And what have I got that you could possibly want?"

"Wynona Jones."

"I know a great deal more about you now than I did last time we talked," he said calmly. "You're not as dangerous as you seem. Except to yourself. What if I simply said 'Fuck you'? You're not going to harm any of those people. I can always get more money. The Peruvian deal may have already gone south.

And I've got two ducks. Wouldn't it make sense for me to say 'Fuck you'?"

"Well, jerkoff," I said, "I know a great deal more about you, too. You're a shit-sucking dung beetle of a man, and a dead yellow coward."

Joe Don tried to act as if that didn't bother him. He stared down the sloping ridge past the overdressed golfers toward the highway east of the country club as he unwrapped a cigar. Two telephone cable diggers, one from each side of the international border, approached the newly built border crossing. Joe Don's drilling rigs labored away at the earth, seeking pockets in the Overthrust Belt.

"Drill stem doesn't seem to be spinning too fast," I suggested. "How deep are the holes?"

"Deep enough," Joe Don answered, "to have found a hard rock strata that's chewing up drill bits like peanuts . . . You familiar with drilling rigs?"

"Third-generation oil field trash on both sides," I said.

"Oh," Joe Don said with that sort of turned lip and cocked eyebrow I had seen too much of as the child of a wandering derrick-hand and the local Avon lady.

"And I spent my time in the weevil corner," I added, but Joe Don had already stopped listening. I felt my hands torque into fists.

When Joe Don had his cigar firmly emplaced in his teeth and smoking in the pale, cool air, I reached over and broke it in half, stubbing the lighted half against the back of his hand.

"Hey, man," I said to his green face, "I'm trying to quit." Then I pressed the cigar harder into his hand. "Think about this. You won't be saying 'Fuck you' to some tired middle-aged drunk, Joey, you'll be saying 'Fuck you' to two Colombians, who will, in order to collect their—or should I say, your?—hundred grand, be more than happy to kill everybody you've ever known. At least, that's the way I put it to them." Then I tossed the cigar into the ashtray. "Understand, Joey?"

"You son of a bitch," he hissed, holding his hand like a broken animal to his chest. "You just bought a one-way ticket to hell."

"Remember, you weekend warrior piece of officer shit," I

whispered, "I've done been there and back. I might have shit my pants, but I didn't run away. I was in the war, asshole, and you were on television."

"Call my office," he said, trying for military crispness, but failing. "Work out the details with Lenny."

"Not Lenny," I said, "you. And on my terms."

Joe Don hesitated, then nodded and fled to the men's room. From the front he might have looked like a hero, but from behind he looked like a pear-assed wimp waddling toward the toilet before he wet his pants. Again.

Back in the rented car, Frank and Jimmy wanted to know what was wrong. But I drove all the way to the Upper Valley Bar and had two drinks before I could talk.

"Frank?" I said. "Can you stretch two more favors out of your computer buddy in Denver?"

Frank sipped his beer, then looked at me, grinning like a Chinaman. "Sure," he said, "Joe Don Pines and . . . Lawyer Rainbolt."

"Good guess," I said, waving for another drink.

"Wasn't a guess," Jimmy growled from the pool table. "What are you going to do?"

"See what the weather is doing this time of year," I said, "up in Montana."

"Never been to Montana," Jimmy said, "but I remember red skies over Montana."

"Bloodthirsty little bastard," Frank said.

"Just thirsty," Jimmy said, "and it's a movie. With Richard Widmark and the guy with the nose bigger than his hat."

"Richard Boone?" Frank asked.

"Karl Malden," Jimmy said. "Spigger hick."

When we stopped laughing, I called Barnstone at the ranch house in the Hole, suggested a brief rest for us. He encouraged it. With that blessing, Jimmy, Frank, and I sat down to slake our thirst.

Thanks to the vested unfairness of the Selective Service Act, a lot of guys who shouldn't have been there ended up in Vietnam.

But not all of them in the bush. It usually takes six to ten troopers in support to keep one on the front lines. Of course, in a war where the enemy gerrymanders the front line every night, the combat zone can be anywhere.

And because the American military and political establishments used the war for their own benefit, then manifestly displayed all the meretricious mendacity of a Mafia don or a Hollywood whore, a huge number of kids ended up in the bush who should never have been allowed to leave their hometowns.

Some couldn't learn and didn't make it; some could and did. But even in a slightly better world, none of them would have been there.

William Curtiss Williams, Jr., was one of those.

Willie had the lanky frame, hip-hop walk, and narrow feral head of a bad-ass street nigger, plus a pair of the meanest light green eyes anybody in the company had ever encountered. But Willie was of such a fine disposition and had one of those high soft sweet voices that made you realize that his eyes were shining with intelligence rather than malice and that his walk was simply an expression of his basically good-natured resilience—he seemed to have come from another world. Of course, he had.

His parents were both doctors who practiced in the middle-class black environs of Minneapolis. Willie was an only child, asthmatic and sickly for most of his childhood, then suddenly blessed with health for the first time in his youth just in time to run into a white radical antiwar activist psychology professor at Carlton College, who convinced him that the war was being directed by the white devils to exterminate the brown and black races.

Well, like a lot of radicals, the professor was half-right: there were a bunch of white devils in charge, evil because they were too often blessed with equal parts of greed for "career advancement" and simple stupidity. They were all right until they came in country, where they quickly learned that a field command could be worth their lives. If Charlie didn't kill them, their own grunts would.

Half-wrong, the professor didn't understand that in the bush we were all the same, the mud people, much hated in recent days

by the idiots of the Aryan Nation. And completely lacking in
any basic knowledge of individual personality, a terrible but all
too frequent failing in his profession, the son of a bitch killed
William Curtiss Williams, Jr., and broke his folks' hearts.

Willie volunteered. And volunteered again. In spite of the fact
that the first real physical activity of Willie's short life came in
basic training at Fort Leonard Wood, he signed up for jump
school. Then for the 1st Air Cav. Then for Vietnam. Then for a
second tour.

Willie, who flinched obviously when his black brothers called
him "nigger" in high laughing tones, refused to go home as long
as he could help one brother adjust to the war. Because Willie,
who wouldn't have the vaguest idea how to survive on the mean
streets of Hough or Bed-Sty or Cabrini Green, who showed up
in country carrying a fucking briefcase full of books and wearing
gold wire-rim reading glasses, was a pro in the bush.

Willie lost the briefcase, the glasses, and all the reading material the first day when a mortar barrage racked Headquarters
Company. After being blown ass over earlobes, maybe Willie
understood that he was lucky to be alive and intended to stay
that way. Nobody ever took luck out of the equation, but smart
and careful was always luckier than stupid and lazy.

So when I met him, eight months into his second tour, Willie
was about the best jungle fighter around. But the most tired,
too. He lived on amphetamines, slept on black hash and heroin-
soaked Kools, and snacked on his liver and lights.

Then he died.

We were humping out of the bush from picking up Solly. We
were wet and wrinkled like the big toes of the dead, so tired we
slept walking, hungry because we hadn't been resupplied for six
days, and after a night ambush and another at the river crossing
our nerves itched like pumpkin vines.

Then Willie hooked a boot lace on a trip wire. And froze.
Thank Buddha.

I didn't care anymore. I ran everybody out of range of the little
bouncing beauty, ran them off at gunpoint, then got on my belly
to dig out the mine.

Bellied in the muck, listening to the cool chatter of Willie, smelling the rank bite of hash, watching Willie's knee tremble ever so slightly, I fell in love with life, fell at least as much as it was possible for me. And I got him fucking out. About the sweetest moment of my life.

Then the next night in his tent, I pulled an overloaded spike out of his arm, an American-made disposable syringe filled with our heroin. The CIA had bought the opium, flown it to labs on Taiwan, then flown it back to Vietnam just to kill William Curtiss Williams, Jr.

My brief love affair with life ended.

At the end of the afternoon in the Upper Valley Bar, without telling a single war story, Frank and Jimmy and I lifted our glasses to Willie. As we always would.

Barnstone had asked me to stop by to check on Carney because he wouldn't answer the telephone. We found him sitting at the backyard table, his meager goods in a feed sack. He was in the van before we could stop him, saying simply, "No sense in you guys having all the fun," then he fell into the black hole of silence wherein he dwelt.

PART SIX

PART SIX

It took some money, which we took out of the funds Joe Don put up to keep me from finding his wife, and ten days to set up the exchange, but finally we were ready, standing on a deeply snowdrifted ridge above the abandoned mining town of Pride & Joy a full two days before Joe Don and his boys were due to arrive. Frank, Jimmy, and I had helped Solly snowshoe into his firing position, built a BB bag rest—sand would have frozen—for his .300 Weatherby, and set up his expedition gear. Then Frank wrapped a chain around the nearest ponderosa pine, locked it to a set of leg restraints, then slapped one on Solly's good ankle.

Solly just stared at me without complaint, then asked, "So what now?"

Jimmy answered. "You fuck up, Captain, you'll have to shoot off your good foot and crawl home. In fact, I'll be more than happy to help you."

"What did I ever do to you, kid?"

"If you don't know, asshole, I can't tell you," Jimmy said, then trudged away as if he couldn't stand our presence another second. Frank shrugged and followed him through the light, drifting flakes.

"So it comes to this, Sughrue?"

"I didn't start this shit," I said, "but I intend to finish it."

"You want to hear my side?"

"Not particularly," I said, "and particularly not now."

"What gave me away?" he asked, then answered himself when I wouldn't. "I told those idiot fucks at the DEA to at least fake a file, that somebody would check someday. I'm just sorry it had to be you, man."

"Look," I said, unable to restrain my anger any longer, "just shut the fuck up. Shut up now. Put your fucking headset on and do what I say, when I say it, and we'll all walk away from this. Sort of."

"You're in charge . . ." he started to say, but I had already headed my snowshoes down the long slope toward the empty shacks of Pride & Joy, ghostly in the fading light.

On the long drive back to Montana, all of the guys jammed in the van, Frank had forced a detour on our caravan, out of Taos and over to Eagle Nest, where a father had built a memorial to his son dead in Vietnam, a shell-like building surmounted by a split column. Simple but effective. We all left in tears, except for Carney. Only Solly bothered to speak. Once again he asked about Willie Williams. Once again we lied.

Once in the van, though, just about the time we cracked beers and bad jokes, Carney started. When we stopped for the night in Pueblo, Colorado, Carney didn't. We had to do something. Like a bunch of Sunday School liberals we sat around in one room trying to talk Carney out of his fucking tears.

Finally, he whispered, "I don't deserve to be with you guys. I was a fucking coward over there."

The ever-sensitive Jimmy told him to tell somebody who gave a shit, then opened a round of beers. But Carney maintained his guilt. Then he burst into story as well as new tears.

"I did dogs," Carney said, then fell silent.

After a moment Jimmy pointed out that he hadn't exactly fucked beauty queens. Until he went over to advise the ARVN Rangers.

"Scout dogs," Carney explained. "I lost so many dogs, man, I just couldn't do it anymore. Had three or four blown to fucking pieces. Then I got scared."

Frank leaned forward so that his deep sorrowful tones might

penetrate this foolishness and said, "Hey, man. You ain't talking to a soul who gives a shit about that."

"Fuck, man, I'd go on patrol with these beautiful Dobermans and watch them sniff out a mine, then fuck up," he said.

"We all fucked up, kid," Solly said. Frank and I looked at each other, nodded without smiling.

"No. The dogs would fuck up. Dust and blood, man. I couldn't do it anymore," Carney said. "So I started stepping on their feet, breaking their toes so they could go home and I didn't have to be scared any fucking more."

"Makes sense to me," Norman said. "I got so tired of looking at guys all fucked up, I still . . . Well, fuck it, you know the rest."

"Then he found out the fucking Army was killing the dogs," Barnstone said.

"The green shitty machine," somebody said.

"So what the fuck did you do after that?" Jimmy wanted to know.

Carney mumbled something. Frank asked him what he had said. Then Carney whispered louder: "I did another tour. As a LRRP."

"Well, no fucking wonder you were scared," Jimmy said, relieved. "You guys were crazy."

We'll never know who laughed first. But we were all guilty. Before the laughter was over, Carney was laughing, too, and crying, and it was over.

We still had some problems, but this part was over.

During the ten days and nights of hiding and planning the slippery preparations, we had crashed out at Solly's ranch, except for Mary and Norman, who felt safe enough in the confines of their biker bastion up Clatterbuck Creek. Dottie still had her bundle of comp-time so she could take care of Baby Lester. And now that they had made friends with Millard Fillmore, Carney and Barnstone refused to even talk about going back to El Paso. Although it seemed clear by this time that Sarita had no notion of escape, we kept her locked up down in the mother-in-law apartment in the daylight basement of Solly's place.

Frank and Jimmy didn't have much trouble talking me into staying out of sight, hanging out at the house with Dottie and Sarita. Barnstone, Frank, and Jimmy took care of most of the preparations, buying weapons and electronic gear from the Dahl-gren boys and expedition winter clothes and camping equipment all over town. Leaving me in the devil's most dangerous position: with nothing to do.

Baby Lester missed his mom in a thousand ways. We could see the loneliness and fear on his small, stained face, could hear it in his cries, which sounded hopelessly lost. So Dottie spent all her time trying to make it better for him. And none of it on me.

One afternoon early on, though, she let Barnstone take care of the baby while I took her for a brief bar tour of the Hardrock Valley.

The November snow reflected a winter sky as thin and gray and ugly as slug tracks. A sharp, unforgiving wind scraped our faces to the bone. The weather acted as if it were already February. So did we. The cocaine froze in our noses, the marijuana smoke drifted darkly in the van, and even the Buffalo Springfield tape sounded tired. We wrestled briefly and ineffectively on the crib in the back of the van. Dottie said she didn't care about coming while she was worried about the baby. And I just said I didn't care.

On the way back to the ranch, our tour aborted, we stopped at a small, cold roadside bar. A couple of Benniwah breeds and their women played pool like ghosts, occasionally dozing over their shots.

Dottie and I began to argue about Baby Lester and Wynona before the bartender delivered our first drinks. We endured the trip back, but no more, then drifted apart at Solly's, neither drunk nor high, without even the energy to argue, complain, or mourn. That was the end of something.

And, of course, the beginning of something worse. Days of daytime television, cocaine, and beer; nights sweating. At some point Sarita joined me on my day watches, her elegant neck arched over a lacy line of cocaine, lines chased with red-wine winter cool sparkling on her dark red lips.

That's how it started, as I remember, my tongue licking a

drop of Bordeaux off her upper lip. Then from the hollow of her neck, the hollows beside her hipbones, the smooth edges of her thighs. Sarita became the drug; I, the addict.

A most generously sensual woman. I could hug her fully dressed and feel my body sink into the peace and comfort of her creamy dark flesh. When she lifted her legs to accept me, or mounted me, or raised her buttocks toward me, or took me in her mouth, it was like fucking the sun, the fire, or the wine-dark sea, the wave, or the darkness beyond death, the heated wind. And the few times she stopped giving and started taking, her orgasms were as impressive as natural disasters, earthquakes or prairie fires or human plagues, leaving her spent and weeping, forlorn and empty.

Wynona, gone, occupied my mind endlessly. The easy grace of her body, her laughter, her child. Even gone, she still had her hand on the remains of my heart. But Sarita took something else from me: the waking fear; the gutshot dreams. Beside her body, you could not dream.

Once in that timeless afterward time as I licked the tears from her face and held her long, smooth quaking body, Sarita whispered, "Thank you. I never knew any love but duty."

"I hate like hell to trade you, lady," I said, "but I have to do it."

"I understand," she murmured against my arm, "*la familia* is love, also. Wynona is tied to you by the blood of friends. You two are family."

"What are we, you and me?"

"A lovely accident," she said.

"And your husband?"

"My husband," she said, "no more. But no less, either."

"You know I'm going to kill him," I said. "After the exchange."

"I think not. I hope not. I pray that you are the man who makes love to me," she said, "and not the man like your friend Rainbolt. He can only hate." Then she turned back to face me.

Her dark eyes possessed a knowledge that I could only imagine.

Her family had existed for three hundred years, had occupied the same hacienda for two hundred of those years. My people had just stopped sleeping with the barnyard animals shortly before WWII. And I was the last of them. "I cannot beg, Sughrue," she said, "but I can ask: please don't kill him." And then she said something so startling that at first I didn't understand it. "He needs me."

"What?"

"Like you, my friend, my love, he cries in the night."

"He never did shit over there, lady," I said. "He has no fucking right."

"Just the right of those who have never known any part of life but the fear," she said softly, then her voice went flat with promise. "If you kill him, I cannot love you."

I thought about it, did a line, poured her a glass of wine, opened a beer, then did the only thing possible: I lied.

"I guess it's time to tell me what you know," I said. "That might change my mind."

"I told you about the cocaine . . ." she began, suddenly stoned and frightened.

"You told me," I said, "but I don't believe it. This is not about fifty million dollars' worth of coke."

"Without the money, my husband will lose the drilling rigs," she babbled, "and without the rigs, he will be nothing again . . ."

And there it was: the big truth in the little lie.

"If everybody's looking for drugs," I guessed, standing up, watching in my mind Joe Don watch the ditchdiggers toiling toward the new border crossing, "nobody's paying attention to the Mexican crude in the Pemex pipeline. The son of a bitch is smarter than I thought. He's going to run crude across the border to salt his dry holes." Sarita stared at me, her eyes gleaming with anger. I remembered that Rose Rosenbloom had said that Sarita was the real money, Joe Don just the front. "Or maybe it wasn't Joe Don's idea at all. You and Dagoberto—shit, I'd bet money he's your cousin . . ."

"Nephew," she said flatly.

"Fucking rich-bitch dilettante revolutionaries financing your cause with stolen oil instead of your own money," I said, then laughed. "You gotta love it," I added. Sarita didn't; she wasn't even faintly amused. "That's the best kind of revolution," I added, "the bourgeoisie take up the call. Usually, it takes the real guys, like those bandits from *Sendero Luminoso*, guys with the theory and the training, about twenty minutes to fix your wagon."

"Fix your wagon? I don't understand," she said, even more angry than before. She stood up, proud and lovely and naked as the day she had crawled out from under a flat rock. "Don't mistake us for dilettantes," she hissed, then took a swing at me. I took a fairly good right cross, then turned away, laughing.

"Right," I said, chopping lines. "Let's have one for the road, honey, or two, and a cocktail. Then maybe we'll open our asphalt hides, let the real people out for a fuck."

"*Chingadero!*" she screamed, then hit me again, this time in the back, spilling cocaine across the night table. "I have!" Then she threw herself into me.

I wouldn't call it love. We fucked as if trying to scour the skin from our flesh, the flesh from our bones, as if we could get deep enough to find some remaining heart gristle. Sarita tore at my short ribs and back like a rapacious cat; I tasted the cords of her neck, the muscled flesh of her thighs. Even our sweat seemed bloody, our secretions a precious fluid. It was either the best or the worst twenty-four hours of my life. Whichever, I wasn't unhappy when Jimmy came to bring me the news.

"You guys have a fistfight?" he asked when I closed the bedroom door.

"Something like that," I said. "But it's over now."

"Just beginning," he said, then told me we were ready. We had transportation, three days of snow and ice predicted, perhaps twelve inches. I raised an eyebrow. He told me the rest. Solomon Rainbolt's name did not appear even in the deepest recesses of the DEA's computer files; nor did that of Joe Don Pines.

Back in the bedroom as I dressed, Sarita stretched like a sated jaguar, the weak winter sun mottled across her dark flesh. Then she smiled. "Your friend the lawyer, you won't let him kill my husband, will you?"

"Not on your life," I promised, kissed her bruised lips one last time, then I left, climbed the stairs back to the main floor.

Pride & Joy had suffered boom and bust three different times. The last time during the War to Make the World Safe for Democracy. Three thousand souls had riven their hearts for greed, lust, and glory in the single-wall shacks and badly supported shafts and drifts at that time, but the ore was so poor and the thirty-five miles of mountain trail often too tough for even mule-drawn wagons, so the town died. The miners, gamblers, bootleggers, soiled doves, and decent god-fearing citizens just walked away. In the early sixties, the state tried to restore the town for tourists, but the road was too much a chore for even four-wheel-drive rigs. But it was perfect for us.

Joe Don had to come in by snowmobile with Wynona, come into our waiting while Dottie held Baby Lester at Solly's place. It seemed like a clean exchange—deep snow, winter silence, and we held the high ground—but Joe Don showed up a day early, lazy and thinking we must be stupid, because he left Wynona with three of his men and the Cuban woman at the bottom of the slope, where I had left Barnstone and Norman in insulated tents with a pair of the Dahlgren twins' air-cooled fifties and Carney with a knife.

Joe Don came in flanked by his two Cuban bodyguards, bulky boys in snowsuits driving the snowmobiles as if they were tiny tractors, with another riding point and Leonard riding drag. Joe Don dismounted his machine, slapping the snow off his suit, then looked around as if he was making plans. But we had been in place for twenty-four hours. I hoped for a chance at civilized conversation, a chance to get Wynona out of his hands before the gunfire started. He couldn't let me live any more than I could let him.

When I stepped out of the remains of the community church, my hands spread wide and empty, Sarita stolid beside me, Joe Don would have jumped a foot if he could have gotten his feet out of the snow. The Cubans scrambled for their suppressed MAC-10s hanging from slings, but their mittens got in the way. Leonard, though, had bought some shooting mittens, so he straddled his snowmobile with a large fancy automatic pistol in his bare fingers.

"Hey, Lenny," I said, "you fire, man, everybody dies."

Either he didn't believe me, or he didn't care. I don't know how he missed me as I shoved Sarita one way and dove the other, shouting into the mike, "Kill somebody, Solly!" rolling in the snow. So much for civilized conversation. "Kill one of the Cubans!"

The point bodyguard dove left and exploded just as I got behind a large stump in front of the church, digging for the Browning in my parka pocket. The bodyguard's vest was useless against the heavy-caliber round. The hydrostatic shock blew his eyeballs out of his head and jets of blood out of his ears and mouth.

Then the sound of the .300 Weatherby followed like a single round of howitzer fire. I thought we must all drown in avalanches.

Then a second rifle round knocked over a snowmobile and gave me time to put three rounds into the hip of another one of the Cubans who flew through the side of the old saloon, his arms flapping like a man who had to fly or die.

Joe Don fell to his knees, crawling toward Lenny and his snowmobile. But his other bodyguard got his MAC-10 out just as Jimmy burst through the sidewalk boards across the street. The Cuban got one burst at Jimmy before I put two 9mm rounds into his chest, which knocked him down long enough for Frank to step around the corner of the old mercantile store and put a load of buckshot into his helmeted head. The Cuban flew sideways into a deep drift.

But by that time I had dashed to Jimmy, who was filling the snowy air with goose down and blood. Most of the subsonic rounds had lodged in his vest, but one had cut a deep furrow into the meat of his right shoulder. And pissed him off. If he could have gotten his breath, he would have cursed the sky. With Frank's help, I got the little fart under control and sitting down, cut away the parka sleeve, packed the flesh with cocaine and snow, then wrapped it in torn nylon.

By then, though, Joe Don and Lenny had fled down the hill,

leaving his wife to me. Sarita hadn't moved since she hit the bare frozen ground behind the church, and when I rolled her over, I saw why. One of Lenny's rounds had punched through her thigh. The leg of her down expedition suit lay heavy with blood. But by the time I cut it open the dark bloody seep had already slowed. The jacketed round had missed the bone and the artery. I tore off my mittens, stuffed one over each wound, then bound them with her belt. Just before she fainted, Sarita smiled, grasped my hand, and whispered, "Remember. You promised . . ."

Then the deep-throated chug of the .50-calibers echoed up the mountainside. Snow streamed from the pine branches and the roofs in the echoes. I turned to Frank, my face frozen.

"Hey, man, get Solly loose," I said, "then you guys bring Jimmy and Sarita down."

"No," Frank said.

"Over my dead body," Jimmy groaned, propped against the raw boards of the abandoned saloon.

Then the voice in my ear: "Sughrue, too bad the deal got fucked," Solly said over the communicator, "but it wasn't my fault, so get me off this fucking mountain before I freeze my butt off."

Frank and Jimmy stared at me. They had heard, too. Small-arms fire rattled downslope, then the .50s fired again.

"Fuck you, Rainbolt," I said. "I'll be back."

"I made the shot once," Solly said, "and I've got a lot more time now. If anybody moves but you coming up the hill with the key, I'll take Gorman's head off. And that's a promise."

"I told you we should have killed him," Frank said softly.

Solly said, "Sughrue doesn't like to kill people he knows."

"That's never been *your* problem," Frank said. "Has it?"

"You don't know everything," Solly said. "Get up here, Sughrue. Or I promise . . ."

"Keep your fucking promise," I said, then walked to Frank without a word. He handed me the key, then I headed up the ridge.

"Let them go," I said into the mike. "Put me in your cross hairs, Rainbolt."

"Not a chance, Sughrue," he replied. "You never gave much of a shit about dying. They stay where they are."

When I made it to Solly's position, he held the rifle on me as I unlocked the leg cuff. "You know, Sughrue," he said, "you think you could kill me with your bare hands, right?" I nodded slowly, staring into his blue eyes, dark with laughter and pain. "Look at my foot," he said.

When I got the insulated snow pack off, I took off his heavy sock. Parts of his small toes came with the sock, and the others were as black as a dead man's face.

"The cuff was too tight, I think," Solly said. "Aren't you going to laugh?"

"Sarita's shot," I said, "and Wynona's down there. I ain't laughing."

"Let me have the Browning," he said. "You'll have to carry me."

"No shit," I said, handing him the pistol. "My people have been carrying your people for generations."

"What the hell's that mean?"

"Like Jimmy said, if you don't fucking know, I can't tell you."

With my own pistol held to my head, with my snowshoes sinking deeply into the snow, I piggybacked the son of a bitch down to the ghost town and the snow machines.

Frank strapped Jimmy behind him and draped Sarita across his lap on Joe Don's snow machine, while I carried Solly to one of the bodyguard's machines, then we eased down the old road toward the occasional sound of gunfire, down toward disaster.

Barnstone and Norman had let Joe Don, Lenny, and the remaining help make it to a rocky depression just down the hill from their positions, then pinned them there. The Cuban woman held an automatic at Wynona's head. As we watched from the switchback just above, Carney in a camo snowsuit slithered toward the depression, bounded over a boulder and a dead bodyguard, and faster than I could see, sliced the Cuban woman's throat, then shoved her body away and grabbed Joe Don's head and pulled it back and lay the blade against his exposed throat.

But Lenny leveled his pistol at Wynona's prone blue-suited and helmeted figure.

"He hurts my daddy, Sughrue, I'll blow her head off!" Lenny screamed in a high, frightened voice.

"She's your fucking sister!" I shouted.

His laughter sounded like pond ice cracking. "Half sister," he giggled, "and bad half at that."

"What's wrong with her?"

"Drugged," he answered.

"Just walk away," I shouted. "But leave Wynona there."

"No fucking way!"

Barnstone picked up his .50 and the tripod and stepped out of the tent. The surviving bodyguard threw his M-16 into a snowbank. You could almost hear the knuckles turn white on the triggers.

Suddenly, Carney started talking in one of those soft, slow Texas accents, confident and almost happy, like a broker who advises you to invest in research rats. The coming thing. And you're writing the check even before he stops talking.

Carney said, "You, sir, please, the brother. Why don't you take your piece off the girl and put it against the back of my head. Please. Do it easy and nobody will get hurt . . ."

"Wait!" Solly screamed. Everybody did. "Take me down there," Solly whispered into my ear. "I want to look the fucker in the eye." So I did. Then we climbed off the machine, and like some odd beast, I carried him into the depression, filled with spent brass and rock chips where the .50s had torn a ragged edge.

"I've got a bead on him," Frank said, "but watch him, Sarge."

"Back off," Solly said over my shoulder to Carney as he leveled the Browning in Joe Don's face. Carney took the knife away and stepped back. "Joe Don Pines," Solly said, "you dirty rotten son of a bitch."

"Who the fuck is this?" Joe Don asked, desperately confused. "I never did anything to him. Hell, I've never seen him before in my life."

"Solomon Rainbolt," I said, "Captain, U.S. Army."

"Oh," Joe Don said, "you're the guy with the offshore list . . ."

Now it was my turn for confusion.

"Bank accounts" was all the explanation Solly bothered to offer me.

"Drug money?" I asked, and Solly nodded. "You guys were stealing drug money from the CIA? Jesus. How much?"

"You can't count it in dollars," Solly said. "Let's just say that they sold out a dozen American troops, twenty Chinese mercenaries, and two hundred Meo civilians . . ."

"Then sent us in to dig up the list," Frank said. "What did we lose, Sarge? Nine KIAs and fifteen wounded . . ."

"I don't know what this shit is about," Lenny growled, "but me and my daddy are walking out of here, or Wynona dies."

"Frank," I said, "give him Sarita." Joe Don humped his wife over his shoulder like a sack of shit without even checking to see if she was alive.

"Back off, Carney," I said, "and check Wynona." And like a good soldier, he did. Immediately. He dug open the collar of her snowsuit, felt for a pulse, then said, "It's weak, Sarge, but it's there."

"If she's hurt," I screamed at Joe Don, "you fucking die!"

Joe Don turned to walk away, and Solly shifted his weight on my back as if raising the pistol, whispering, "You fucking die." So I just let his weight pull us over, and the round he fired went into the white-clotted sky. He got another one off before I rolled over and started pounding him in the face until Frank pulled me off, saying, "It's not polite to hit a cripple."

"Kick him," Jimmy suggested.

"What about Joe Don?" Barnstone said from his position above us, the long-barreled machine gun aimed toward the motor home in the parking area at the bottom of the trail.

"Put a burst over their heads," I said, "to hurry them along."

"Right, Sarge," he said, then let the forest ring and rattle with the huge rounds. It could have been shouts of joy. Or the clatter of death laughing.

I carried her out of the depression and propped her in a clear space against the trunk of a bull pine. Somewhere beyond the cloud cover and the falling snow, the sun managed enough light to force the snowbanks to glow with a soft white shimmer almost like a flame, a glow that the deep golden highlights of her skin reflected. I found myself digging under her collar for the pulse, laughing and crying, then I felt the thin, thready tick of her blood under my fingers, then I eased the helmet off to expose the already blank stare of her eyes.

It seemed to take forever to find the wound: a needle-sized puncture in the corner of her right eye. At first I suspected chicanery from Joe Don, but Frank reached over my shoulder and opened the wound to expose the end of a long, thin stone sliver. I gave her my breath until her heart stopped forcing blood to the brain, then held her until the heat left her body, held her until Frank took her away from me.

"You have to let it go," he said softly. "You have to let it go, Sarge."

I stood up, spinning, looking for somebody to kill, but all I could find were my friends and a sad ugly biker and a crippled lawyer. And the remains of my love. We fell as deeply silent as the trees. Until somebody said: "Will this shit never end?"

Mopping up took place as if in a dreamy fog. I spent most of it snorting and drinking at Slumgullion's while my old partner took care of me, occasionally pouring a bowl of soup down my throat and making sure that I had a safe place to pass out.

Solly handled most of the cleaning chores from his hospital bed, using his Washington contacts to dispose of the bodies and cover up the gunfire. He got out of the hospital just about the time I checked in.

Norman had come into the bar, probably to apologize, but I tried to kill him. He didn't resist, but Beater Bob and the rest of the boys put the boots to me. I checked myself out as soon as I was mobile and made it to Norman and Mary's wedding. In spite of the lies, I guess the love made it all right, even if his mother wasn't there. Like most of us, when Norman ran out of choices, he lied for Solly. I couldn't forgive him, exactly, but when Norman handed me the keys to his VW van as a peace offering, I accepted it. I kept his money, too.

Then I went back to the bar, where I stayed so long and solidly that one by one my buddies gave up on me.

Barnstone and Dottie rented a house and a lawyer, who managed to get them temporary custody of Lester. Even Carney rented a cabin up the Hardrock to settle in for the rest of winter, stole Solly's goose for fowl company, and came to his senses so well, or so badly, that he enrolled in law school at Mountain States, and he was so busy with briefs that he had no time for self-destruction. Frank went home to spend Christmas with his kids, then checked into the hospital and checked out courtesy of a young doctor with a handful of sleeping pills.

After Jimmy and I buried him during a winter sandstorm in a small cemetery outside El Paso, after an explosive and blazing borderline wake, I came home, but Jimmy stayed at Barnstone's to house-sit and take over the appliance business.

So I was alone at the bar when Solly rolled his wheelchair through the front door. I glanced at him, then turned back to my Scotch. "Sughrue," my old partner said from behind the bar, "cool it. You hit a guy in a wheelchair and you won't be able to come in here even if I buy the bar."

"Fuck it," I said, "there's always another bar just down the street."

But Solly followed me there, and to the next one, and the next, until I finally gave up and sat down at a table with him in the plush foolishness of the Riverside Lounge.

"I heard about Frank," he said. "I'm sorry."

"Fuck you," I said. "Let me see your arms."

Solly took off his jacket and rolled up his sleeves. I couldn't tell how old the tracks were, but none of them were new.

"I've been clean a long time," he said.

"You'll never be clean."

"You'd be surprised how easy it is to be a junkie when you can afford it," he said. "But revenge is a dish better eaten cold."

"Fucking idiot," I said. "You wanted to kill the son of a bitch, you should have killed him there. Christ, he didn't even know who you were."

"Yeah, that kinda hurt," he said. "I hear Joe Don had one hell of an oil fire down on the border."

"You're still connected pretty good," I said. "The papers said it was the first shot in a border drug war."

"Connected is not exactly the right term," he said. "Did he know it was you?"

"I didn't bother to send him a telegram," I said.

"How much do you know?" he asked suddenly.

"How much do you want to know?" I said. He seemed to want to hear me say it. "Let's see, Lawyer Rainbolt, you were up to your ass in the drug trade out of the Golden Triangle, and after your wife and kid fled from you in San Francisco, you freaked and fled and got popped with a pound of blow, somewhere . . ."

"Santa Barbara."

"Rich territory," I suggested, "then got your old buddies in the government to find you an out. That's when you became a drug lawyer. You won all those cases because the bureaucrats with guns let you. What better informant can you find than one who beat the fuckers at their own game? In court."

"I did some other good cases," he said weakly, suddenly so old and tired that I knew I couldn't kill him. "Good case work."

"You shit," I said. "You squeezed Norman until he lied to me, and Norman never lied before in his life."

"Not much of a loss."

"And back in the bush you shot up and played dead . . ."

"But Joe Don pushed the orders that sent you guys into the bush."

". . . and you fuck, you walked out on the nod and Willie saw it, then the two of you hit it, and you left him there with a spike hanging out of his arm. Don't tell me you did good work, you son of a bitch. He'd never put a fucking needle in his arm before. He just smoked the shit."

"Just a matter of time," Solly said lamely. "And I saved your life at the river crossing."

"I'd rather be dead," I said.

"So would I," he said, "but it would be better if Joe Don was the one to die."

"Why didn't he?"

"I had him in the cross hairs a dozen times but I just couldn't fucking pull the trigger anymore."

"But the Cuban?" I asked.

"He just got in the way. Bad luck."

"Boy, you were always officer material," I said. "When you get back to the office, Lawyer Rainbolt, you make damn fucking sure that Joe Don never gets his hands on Lester. Ever."

"I'll do my best," he said helplessly.

"Do it," I said, then left him there at the table, watching the cold water tremble beneath the river ice.

As far as I know, he's still there.

But if I had known that just talking to him would get me out of my slough of self-pity and bring me back to life, I would have talked to him sooner. Joe Don wasn't going to stop coming after Lester through the courts, and Solly couldn't stop him, so for the first time in years, it seemed, I knew what to do next.

It didn't take long for me to discover that I couldn't pull the trigger, either. I told myself that a bullet was too good for Joe Don, but I had to eat the truth every time I had him in the cross hairs of my scope.

It took a new plan, the rest of the winter, and enormous help from the Dahlgren boys, but I finally was set. So one lovely spring desert day, dressed in a stolen UPS uniform and hidden behind sunglasses and a new beard, I delivered my Mexican Tree Duck directly into the hands of Joe Don Pines in his almost bare office. Hard times in the oil business, I thought. Then I walked back to the elevators.

This is how it must have happened. Joe Don read the note I had taped over the hole in the duck's back: "I understand that this fake belongs to you. It was constructed by my brother-in-law, a high school art teacher in Gadsen, New Mexico. What he told you was a river-clam pearl is just a rock-hard dog turd." Then Joe Don had to lift the ceramic beauty out of the Styrofoam peanuts, admire it briefly, then hold it to his ear and shake it to hear the sound of the dog shit rattle.

Perhaps he saw the slim green form of the viper slip out of the duck's back. Perhaps not. But once the snake struck him in the face, he knew what had happened—he was one of the hard guys across the clearing when the major got his—and maybe he knew who had made it happen. Maybe.

Whatever, Joe Don beat me to the ground. His body was embedded in the roof of a taxi outside the front door of the building. I didn't give it a second glance as I climbed into the UPS truck Jimmy had stolen to go with my uniform.

I think it was Francis Bacon who suggested something along the lines that revenge was a wild justice. I'm not sure about that. I don't even think about it very much. All I know is that when I heard Joe Don's screams echo down the marbled hallway, I felt good, and when I sat in Barnstone's backyard in Meriwether the next afternoon, holding Baby Lester laughing in my arms, I felt better. It was almost as if the little fart understood that I had served his purposes.

"I hope you guys get along okay," Barnstone said.

"We get on fine," I said.

"And you take as good care of yourself, Sughrue," Dottie said, "as you do of Lester."

"What?"

"Wynona would want you to raise the little guy," Barnstone said. "We're going home."

And they did.

After a couple of months, Sarita, old and querulous now, stopped bothering me about the baby. I heard that she moved back to Mexico where she lives like a queen in exile alone in a desert hacienda.

So it's mostly diapers and day-care and tending bar again these days, and I don't have much time to think about the theories of revenge or justice. Or even time to talk about them. Except for the occasional afternoons when Carney drops by for a drink when I'm behind the stick at the Slumgullion and wants to talk about how he will be able to manipulate the legal system. "It's like the war," he said. "You must become the enemy to kill him."

That's what we were doing the beautiful spring day on my old partner's fifty-second birthday when he came into Slumgullion's sporting a brand-new suit and announced he was off to the bank to pick up his inheritance, which had been locked up all these years by his crazy mother's will.

I poured us all a single malt Scotch. Carney and I drank ours, smiling. My old partner left his standing on the bar, saying he might drink it when he came back, then he hiked toward the bank.

Carney and I had another, slow and grinning. Which made it hard to remember the times when he had been death incarnate in black pajamas and I had simply been dead.

After half an hour or so, my old partner came back to the bar, an odd smile on his face. He gunned the shot of Scotch, grimaced, then said, "I'll be goddamned."

"Why's that?" Carney wanted to know.

"I was going to buy the bar today," he said, "but I was a year early."

"How the fuck?" I said.

"I get the money at fifty-three, not fifty-two," he said. "How the fuck could I forget something like that?"

"Drugs, sex, rock and roll," Carney suggested, already thinking like a lawyer.

We laughed. Life is a joke. You just have to hope it's funny. Instead of bad.

I whipped out my checkbook, wrote one to him for thirty thousand, which was about half the ill-gotten gains I had left, and said, "Will this do for a down payment?" Then I headed for the door.

"Thanks," my old partner said. "Where the hell are you going?"

"I don't know," I said, "but me and Lester, we're Texas boys. I think we'll go home. See if it's still there."

We all shook hands, and he let me get to the door before he hollered: "How am I going to explain to the government where this money came from?"

"Fucking lie about it," I said. "They don't mind lying to you."